Little Bookshop of Murder

Little Bookshop

of

Murder

A BEACH READS MYSTERY

Maggie Blackburn

NEW YORK

Published in the United States by Crooked Lane Books, an imprint of The Quick Brown Fox & Company LLC.

Crooked Lane Books and its logo are trademarks of The Quick Brown Fox & Company LLC.

Library of Congress Catalog-in-Publication data available upon request.

ISBN (hardcover): 978-1-64385-438-0
ISBN (ePub): 978-1-64385-439-7

Cover design by Teresa Fasolino

Printed in the United States.

www.crookedlanebooks.com

Crooked Lane Books
34 West 27th St., 10th Floor
New York, NY 10001

First Edition: July 2020

10 9 8 7 6 5 4 3 2 1

For my daughters, Emma and Tess,
and for my other "daughters"—the other
Tess, Lucie & Nora, Margo, Gracie,
Rebecca, Destiny, Violet, Vali,
Ella & Lydia.

Also dedicated to Paige Edwards, who
stole me away for a few days to a magical
beach and helped to inspire this book
and my fantasy bookstore —Beach Reads.

Chapter One

S ummer Merriweather slipped off her flip-flops, allowing the
sand's warmth to comfort the bottom of her feet like it had thou-
sands of times before. She looked out over the waves, the water shim-
mering in the soft pink morning light. She walked toward the water
and gazed over the horizon—the line between the sky and sea barely
visible. A seagull cried in the distance. Another one flew in front of
her and landed on the wet, shiny sand. "Sorry, I have nothing for you
today." As if understanding, the gull flew off across the water.

Behind her, down a short, sandy, rocky path cut between brown
sea grasses, was her childhood home. She felt its presence although
she didn't even take a glimpse. She couldn't look at it. Not yet.

She and her mom would walk out here almost every day, look
at the ocean together, walk, talk, fight, cry, yell. But it all seemed so
small next to the ocean. Next to now. Now, when she had to place
one bare foot in front of the other and walk to her mother's funeral.

She'd almost missed it. Her own mother's funeral.

In a jet-lagged, sleepy haze, she took a step toward town and
another. She walked past what was left of her old neighborhood,
little brightly colored shot-gun houses and cottages, one right next
to another. Five of them remained out of the original twenty. She

moved past the neighborhood of expensive brick condos lining the beach. Condos for the tourists. Or for the summer people, those who came to bask in the joy of summer on Brigid's Island.

She'd been away from home for years, yet when she remembered the summer people, her stomach soured still. How the locals loved and hated them at the same time. They needed the summer people's money but hated their city, self-involved ways.

She stopped moving as the famous Brigid's Island breeze circled her, cooled her. As she drew in air, the scent of Wanda's Hog Dogs hinted in the air. *Best hot dogs on the planet.* Wanda's cart must be nearby. She didn't have time for a hot dog. She was late.

Summer hurried past the condos and a park-like town square. At the far end were the town offices and the square, lined with little shops, mostly geared to the tourists, like the ones on the boardwalk up ahead, including her mother's shop, Beach Reads.

At the corner of this square sat Beach Chapel, a non-denominational church, and this was where Summer's bare feet led her. If only she'd been here, if only they'd known how to reach her sooner, her beach-loving, free-spirited mom's life would not be celebrated in a church, a place that Summer didn't even think her mom had ever set foot in. Summer had nothing against churches—in fact, she belonged to one in Staunton, Virginia, where she lived. But her mother didn't like churches.

Who'd decided on this service for her mom? Shouldn't they remember her the way she would have wanted it? Why wasn't there some earth-mother-goddess woman standing at the shore, offering words of wisdom?

Okay, Summer had been out of the country, in England, researching and writing, hoping to save her job, but why not wait until they'd reached her?

She'd always admired the white clapboard church she walked toward, but today it looked more like a prison than a church. How was she going to sit through this, knowing her mom would've disapproved? Summer stepped onto the concrete sidewalk, slipped on her flip-flops, and opened the door.

*   *   *

The service was a blur for Summer, and soon enough her silver-haired Aunt Agatha was at her side, leading her to the lunch the church held for them. "I'd like to go lie down," Summer said.

"They've gone to a lot of trouble. You should come along." Aunt Agatha wore a red dress with a mermaid print. Red was the favorite color of Summer's mom, and everybody knew how she felt about mermaids. Summer's heart fluttered—her hand touched the silver mermaid pendant she wore almost every day. Hildy, her mom, had given her the necklace for her sixteenth birthday.

"I don't want to be rude, but I don't think so, Aunt Agatha. I couldn't eat a thing. I don't understand why we're here. And I need answers about Mom's death. None of this makes any sense to me."

"You're in shock. Of course it makes little sense."

Was that it? She didn't know, and she didn't care. An impulse or longing moved through her. What was it she needed? What was calling to her?

Beach Reads. She needed to visit the bookstore her mom had owned and loved. She needed to feel her mom. This place? These people? This didn't feel right.

Summer started to leave, but Aunt Agatha held her back. "Where are you going?"

Summer paused. Would her aunt even believe her? That she wanted to go to Beach Reads, the bookstore she had always hated?

That suddenly it was the one place she wanted to be? "I'm going to the bookstore."

Her aunt's face softened. "Oh, Summer." Her chin quivered. "Let me get my things. I'll come with you."

"Don't feel like you have to."

"You ought to know me better than that. I'm at the age where I do what I want. Who needs more bloody green bean casseroles and scalloped potatoes, anyway?"

Summer grinned. There was the Aunt Hildy she knew and loved. Her mom's only sister, Agatha garnered no foolishness. Never had. In fact, it was one quality Summer loved about her. She was quite the opposite from Hildy. Summer's mother was all sparkles, peace, and free love. Aunt Agatha scoffed at such notions, but her love and respect for Hildy was deep and abiding.

It was good and right that Aunt Agatha come along to the bookstore. And if anybody knew what was going on with Hildy and her death, it would be her. Summer wanted answers. And she wanted them now. Why would a healthy sixty-four-year-old woman just drop dead?

Chapter Two

Beach Reads sat on the far corner of the four-block-long boardwalk. Summer, her aunt, cousin, and cousin's daughter walked down it, even though the boardwalk was closed because it was a Monday and the summer season hadn't fully begun. The scents of the previous days' treats hung in the air—buttered popcorn, funnel cakes, and soured milkshakes, probably coming from a nearby trash can.

One seagull landed in front of them and stood, sizing them up. Agatha eyed Piper, her daughter, and Summer. "Have you been feeding them again?"

Long, lean, fair-haired Piper wrapped her arms around Summer and laughed. Physically, Piper resembled the Merriweathers, who were blonde, blue-eyed, and lean, where Summer was olive skinned, black haired, brown eyed, and curvy. They'd gotten in trouble more than once for feeding the wild birds. She smiled back at Piper as she recalled the two of them sneaking food to what others called the "pesky seagulls."

"Shoo." Agatha waved at the bird, and it finally flew off, allowing them to continue their walk.

"She wasn't hurting anybody, Gram," Mia, Piper's daughter, said.

"Mind your tone," Aunt Agatha said as she walked up to the Beach Reads front door, where a lopsided sign hung announcing the store would reopen soon. Summer picked up an unmarked, large, brown envelope, leaning on the side of the door, and tucked it beneath her arm.

The carved mermaid arch above the doorway had weathered and appeared as if it had emerged from the bow of an old shipwrecked vessel. Agatha slipped the key in the lock. As the four of them stepped into the shop, the wood floor creaked, just like always, and the scent of fresh books, with a hint of patchouli, hit Summer with a whoosh. She dizzied and clutched her chest, searching for a chair.

She found the pillowed window seat, facing the boardwalk and beach. Small stacks of books sat near the blue starfish-patterned pillows, as if someone had just been there reading. She took in the view—the waves rolling in beyond the rickety boardwalk and gray sand. Some beach visitors dotted the landscape, with their colorful chairs, umbrellas, coolers, and—yes—books in their hands. A few brave souls walked along the surf's still-cold edge.

"Are you okay?" Piper asked.

"I just need a minute." Summer swallowed a burning sensation creeping into her throat. "That damned patchouli," she muttered. But in some strange way it comforted her.

She breathed in the scent again—it brought her mother to her. It was almost as if she was sitting right next to her. This was what Hildy always called her center of power. Summer closed her eyes, drew in the scent, and remembered the day the bookstore opened the second floor. It had taken years for Hildy to save for expansion.

Summer had been eleven years old during the grand opening of the second-floor room. Walking upstairs had been like entering straight into her mother's imagination. Neat rows of books. Nooks

6

with comfortable spaces to read. The new room offered more wall space, which Hildy decorated with colorful mermaid art, mostly by local artists. But it was the view that made the place, with floor to ceiling windows and a wrap-around balcony with comfortable furniture where you could sit, read, drink, chat with your friends. The room felt open, but Hildy used every space in the room for books or useful book gadgets, like bags, lights, and bookmarks.

Growing up, Summer had loved to sit on the balcony underneath the seashell-patterned blue and white umbrellas, looking out at the beach or with her nose stuck in one Shakespeare play or another. It was the only thing she liked about the store. But as a small girl, before she'd discovered Shakespeare, she'd sit among the books, not quite allowed to read the adult books, and imagine the stories. Imagining the words, the language, coming to life on the pages, whispering stories to her.

Agatha walked over to Summer and handed her a bottle of water. Summer took a drink.

"I need to ask you something," Summer said after a few moments.

"Yes?"

"What happened to my mother? And why was her service in a church?"

"There was a mix-up at the hospital, and I'm afraid it was my fault. I just wasn't thinking and signed the wrong papers," Hildy said. She sat next to Summer. "The autopsy results on Hildy aren't back yet. We've no idea what happened to her."

Maybe Summer was imagining it, but it seemed Aunt Agatha was avoiding eye contact. "How long will it take?"

Agatha shrugged. "A few more days, I should think. Remember, we don't have such services on the island. All the labs, or whatever, had to go to Wilmington."

7

"Mom was one of the healthiest people I know. Other than her cat allergies, I can only remember her being sick maybe twice." Summer sat the brown envelope down on the other side of her.

Agatha started to say something, when Piper and Mia ambled over to them.

Summer looked up at them and caught a category title on the bookcase behind Agatha's head. "Werewolf Romances."

"Werewolf romances?" Piper said.

"What?" Agatha looked around.

"Behind Piper. The sign says 'Werewolf Romances.' What the heck?" Summer would much rather feel indignant than sad.

"Oh, heavens yes. It's a huge market. Takes up those three long shelves. Do you see?" Agatha pointed toward the books.

"Seriously? I need more water." Summer took another drink.

"You should look around. The romance genre has grown since when you and I worked summers here." Piper gently nudged her.

Maybe the romance genre had changed, but Beach Reads was still the same. Full of "easy" reads and brimming with books, comfortable chairs in reading nooks, and a never-ending pot of free coffee.

"I remember the vampire romances, but not werewolves."

"Back then, I think the only vampire romances were by Anne Rice. Now there is a whole section." Piper grinned. "Okay, it's not your thing. But I love a sexy vampire or werewolf."

She wriggled her eyebrows comically, forcing Summer to laugh.

Summer stood, needing to stretch her legs. She walked down the aisle, chock full of romances of every strange variety. Werewolf. Shifter. Vampire. Paranormal.

Summer ran her fingers along the spines of the books until she reached the end of the row. An overstuffed cobalt velveteen chair sat there with a throw flung over it, and a floor lamp was strategically placed for good, well-lit reading. Anne Rice's signature was on the wall above the chair. All the authors who'd visited had signed the walls throughout the store. Other bookstores sometimes had one wall where authors signed. But Hildy allowed the authors to sign wherever they wanted—and it had become a game with readers to try to find all the names. As you walked along, you read autographs on a wall, on a shelf, or even on the wood floor. Painted handwritten quotes from Hildy's favorite novels also donned the floors.

Summer spotted one from Jane Austen: *"It is a truth universally acknowledged, that a single man in possession of a good fortune, must be in want of a wife."*

Hildy would laugh every time she read it. "Well, let the men of the world know, I'm nobody's wife."

Still, Hildy loved the line, considered it brilliant. And even though Summer was no fan of the romance genre, like her mom, she liked the line well enough and appreciated Austen. Thinking of the line and her mom's reaction always made her smile.

"Hey, you forgot this." Piper handed Summer the brown envelope.

"What is it anyway? I picked it up outside." Summer walked over to her mom's display case of first editions. *Pride and Prejudice* was one of her treasures, along with *Wuthering Heights*, and *Gone with the Wind*.

Piper fidgeted with her sandal strap, which had worked loose. "Open it and find out."

Agatha flicked on the light, and it was almost as if it had awakened the place. A tingle moved through Summer, calming and centering her. She was glad she'd come to the store before going to the house.

She opened the envelope and slipped out the blank piece of black construction paper. "What is this? There's nothing on it."

"Turn it over." Piper gestured with her hand. "There's something on the other side—an ad maybe."

Summer wanted to blink, but she couldn't. She froze with fear as she read the note: *"Sell the bookstore or die."*

Piper gasped. "What the hell?"

Mia took a sudden interest. "Let me see." The three of them stood reading over the note, which was fashioned from words clipped out of magazines and newspapers. All three were speechless—until Agatha came around the corner.

Summer held up the paper for her to see, and she snatched it, flustered. "Hooligans. That's all. Nothing serious, I assure you."

Mia's eyes widened. "Looks pretty serious to me."

Summer's thoughts exactly.

"Prankster kids. That's all." Agatha waved them off.

"Aunt Agatha, has this happened before?"

"Not this exact thing, no. Now let's go home, shall we? You must be exhausted. We can talk about this later." She was flustered, her cheeks red and jaw clenched.

Summer was too tired to argue, but she wouldn't let Aunt Agatha off the hook that easily. "What do you mean by 'not this kind of thing exactly'?"

Agatha motioned toward Mia. "This isn't the time, Summer. Please. Let's talk later."

Summer's eyes met with Mia's, who rolled her eyes and folded her arms. "I'm not a baby," she said.

What was going on here? Something wasn't right about her mother's death. What kind of secret was Agatha keeping? Had someone threatened her mom?

"Let's go, shall we?" Agatha opened the door, and three other women entered the store as if they belonged there.

"Summer!" Glads, said as she circled Summer in her arms. She rubbed Summer's back as she held her in a long, drawn-out hug. One of her mom's Mermaid Pie Book Club members, Glads was tall and thin, with a pointy nose and chin, and dressed in black jeans and a red T-shirt draped with beads. Her name was Gladys, but everyone just called her Glads. A memory poked at Summer: the last time she'd seen her, Glads was dancing naked on the beach with a group of women, including Hildy, much to Summer's embarrassment.

After their embrace, tears streamed down Glads's face. She reached into her pocket, pulled out a crumpled tissue, and blew her nose.

Another woman stepped forward. "Hi, Summer. I'm not sure you remember me. I'm Marilyn, and this is the newest member of the book group, Doris." She gestured in Doris's direction. "We just stopped by to see when the store would be open again."

Summer remembered Marilyn, the sixty-something-year-old, spike-haired town librarian with floral tattoos. She wanted her skin to look like a field of wildflowers. She'd partnered with Summer's mom on book events. The book group, her mother's pride and joy, had been thriving for twenty years.

"I'm not sure, but maybe tomorrow," Summer said. The bookstore was usually open Tuesdays, but things were off kilter.

Pink-haired and dressed in a dark suit, Doris smiled politely and held out her hand, with long, manicured pink nails matching her hair. "I'm so pleased to meet you, Summer." Her voice had a soft, lilting, nasal Charleston accent. "So sorry about the circumstances."

"We're hoping to continue the book group." Marilyn pressed her purple glasses back on her nose.

"You should. It would please Mom."

"Are you planning to keep the bookstore, then?" Doris asked.

Summer's heart thudded in her chest. Was she? Was the store even hers to keep? If it was, she'd get rid of it as soon as possible. Yes, she would. It went against everything she stood for. She was a professor of literature. The real stuff. Her Ph.D. was in Shakespearean Lit. She had no use for a bookstore whose claim to fame was that it sold "beach reads" only.

She needed the money from selling it. But who would buy it?

Piper to the rescue. "Doris, I think Summer needs time to process. She's only just gotten back from—"

The women leaned closer as Summer held her breath. Was she going to spill the beans about England and the underlying reason she was there? "I mean," Piper said, correcting herself, "she's just gotten here. She must be exhausted."

True, Summer hadn't slept in over twenty-four hours—but exhaustion wasn't the only thing she felt. Confusion. Fear. Anger. Why would someone leave a note like that for her mom? Why was Aunt Agatha so hushed about it? Was it only because young Mia was there? Or was something more serious going on here?

Chapter Three

Walking into her childhood home filled Summer with a wild mix of nostalgia, dread, and longing. She half-expected her mother to greet her with a cup of peppermint tea and a plate of vegan cupcakes. But those days were gone. Long gone.

If only Summer had a chance to explain how horrible she felt at a job she'd imagined perfect for her. How she felt that if she didn't focus on the research and writing during summer break, she could totally kiss the job goodbye. *I'd have called you more, Mom.*

She started upstairs with her bag and stopped. Where was she going to sleep? In her old bedroom, full of things of her youth—tantalizing her with unachieved dreams? Or in her mother's bedroom, which had always been mostly off limits? *"Everybody needs a private space. My bedroom is my sanctuary,"* her mother had said. Summer remembered fondly the times she'd been invited into her mom's room.

She took in the living room from her perch on the stairs—her mom's altar to Selena, the moon goddess, was in the left corner of the living room, and in the right corner was a photo display of Summer and all of her accomplishments. National Spelling Bee Champion. Shakespeare Scholar of the Year. National Forensics First Place Award. Three graduation pictures—high school, college, and grad school. Every school picture—first grade through twelfth—stared back at her. Mom still had the "shrine," as Summer used to call it and tease her about. Now what used to seem like overkill seemed genuine and charming.

Her gaze fell on the living room couch in the center of the room. Next to it was Mr. Darcy, her mom's African grey parrot asleep in his cage. He was getting old and wouldn't be a bother.

Okay, the couch would suffice for now. She padded her way back down the steps and plopped her bag onto the La-Z-Boy. She flipped on the TV, accustomed to its sound in the background. Sometimes it was better than silence.

Weariness tugged at her, but she needed to wind down before she slept. What time was it in England? She couldn't even figure that out right now.

A stack of magazines, bills, and papers was scattered across the coffee table. Craft magazines. How-to. Herbs. Gardening. Her mom had a magazine problem.

"Ever heard of Pinterest, Ma?" *Great, now I'm talking to myself—or rather, to my dead mother.*

Mr. Darcy stirred, lifted his head from beneath his wing, shuddered, and tucked it back in.

Summer continued sorting through the papers. Among the white papers, the corner of a thick black paper caught her eye. She slipped it out from the messy stack.

Summer blinked. What was this? Some kind of sick joke? Hooligans, again?

Pasted on the page were the words *"Sell the bookstore or DIE!"*

Again? What the hell? Did her mother make this? Was this some kind of strange dream board thing Mom was working on? Or was this another actual threat?

Crazy. That was just a crazy thought.

Okay, get a grip. I'll sort through these magazines, and I'm sure I'll find the pages where she's cut out these letters and words.

Twenty minutes later, she shoved the magazines aside. They were all in perfect shape.

Now what?

She stood and paced between the couch and the La-Z-Boy, with the statue of Kali, the mother goddess, looking down at her from a shelf.

Summer should go to the police. But Ben's face flashed in her mind, and humiliation and anger swept through her. The chief of police in their little town didn't like her. She'd left his son at the altar.

No, she wasn't ready to face Chief Ben Singer.

What to do?

She was being silly, right? This was the fantasy stuff of mystery novels. People didn't kill people because they wanted them to sell a bookstore to them.

She caught herself. *People killed each other every day for less reason.* She'd only to look at the headlines.

She dialed Aunt Agatha.

"Yes, dear," her aunt answered the phone. "Piper is on her way over."

"Good, but that's not what I'm calling about."

"What is it?"

How to spit out the words "I think someone murdered my mother"?

"I found another threatening note telling Mom to sell the bookstore or die. It's the same thing we found at the bookstore. Do you understand what's going on?"

Silence.

"Aunt Agatha?"

"Yes," she said after a moment. "Your mother wouldn't pay attention. She'd received several of those and a few calls. She laughed it off."

"'Laughed it off'?" Summer repeated her aunt's words, trying to believe them. "My mom was a healthy sixty-four-year-old woman, and she just dropped dead? Did nobody consider this?" Rage burned in Summer's chest.

"Summer, people die every day. Even young people. It's not that unusual." Agatha paused. "But I have to admit, I've had similar thoughts. I talked myself out of them. They're too far-fetched. People loved your mother."

"There's at least one person who wanted the bookstore so much they threatened her."

After another silence, Agatha cleared her throat. "Now, do nothing rash. But Rudy made your mother several offers, and he creeped Hildy out."

"Rudy Irons? The owner of the arcade next to Beach Reads?" Summer's mind raced. Old coot. She remembered him, though he hadn't been at her mother's funeral. Had he?

"Yes. He wanted to expand. But you can't go around accusing people of murder."

"If he killed Mom, he needs to go to jail—after I'm through with him, that is."

"Now, Summer, you're overwrought. Please don't do anything foolish."

Overwrought? Overwrought? Why, yes. Yes, I am. She had no proof but the note in her hand, and the sudden, sharp, intuitive impulse that someone had murdered her mom.

"Summer?"

"Yes, Aunt Agatha."

"Let's talk about this in the morning, okay? Let's talk after a good night's sleep."

Summer heard the words but had no idea how she'd sleep soon. She continued to pace, stopped and glanced up at the Kali statue, then continued moving.

"Please promise me not to do anything until you and I talk this through more. Summer? Promise me."

"Okay," she replied. "We'll talk in the morning."

And morning could not come fast enough.

She stood in front of the picture window facing the beach. The moon lit the now deep purple-black water, sparkling silver where the light hit the surface. How many times had Summer taken in this view—the waves; the rocky sand; the small dune with craggy grass, hard to see in the moonlight. It was there, along with seaweed, driftwood, and sometimes nuggets of treasured sea glass and seashells. She loved this view. It grabbed her by the guts. She envisioned it at night when she was too stressed to sleep. It calmed her.

Mia and Piper arrived a few minutes later, loaded down with their bags. Piper announced she'd sleep in Hildy's bedroom. "I've got no problem with that. Her bed is fantastic." She traipsed upstairs, dragging her bags with her.

A sweet memory of lying next to her mother in her bed plucked at Summer. She had been sick. Maybe it was strep throat? Or maybe it was the chicken pox? Lying next to her mom in her big, soft bed—feeling her warm smooth skin, hearing her heartbeat, and smelling her lilac perfume—was such a treat, even if she was sick. She felt protected tucked next to her mother. Summer swallowed a sob and lay down on the couch, pulling an old quilt over her. She spread her anti-insect blanket, which she never left home without, on top of the quilt. Maybe she was losing her mind, but she could swear the quilt still smelled of lilacs. Next, she yanked her nylon mask over her face. *No spider will enter any of my facial orifices.* She drifted off into a dream world filled with lilacs, porch swings, and Lady Macbeth.

It seemed as if Summer had just closed her eyes when a loud knocking left her clutching at the couch as if it would tip over. She sat up. *Where am I?*

Pound. Pound. Pound.

"Jesus! Would someone answer the door?" Piper's voice rang out, snapping Summer back to reality.

The door? Yes. Okay.

Summer untangled herself from her blanket, lifted herself from the couch, pulled the mask from her face, and padded to the door. She peeked out. A group of women with casserole dishes and paper bags in their arms stood on the porch.

She cracked open the door, a spray of sunlight entering the dimmed room. She winced.

"Good morning, Summer." Glads peeked through the cracked-open door. "We've brought breakfast—and maybe enough food for two days."

She opened the door further and walked in.

"How are you, dear?" Doris followed behind Glads. Today, Doris looked more relaxed in shorts and a T-shirt.

"I'm, ah—"

"Who is it?" Piper said from the top of the stairs. "It's early. Is the sun even up yet?"

She trampled her way down the stairs.

"Sorry, is it too early? We assumed since Hildy was such an early bird, you all would be too." Glads talked as she worked, placing food on the counters or in the refrigerator.

Summer followed the women into the kitchen, with the strong scent of cinnamon wafting. "No, this is lovely. Thank you so much. What smells so good?" She'd forgotten about these good women and their ways. When there was a death, birth, hospital stay, the Mermaid Pie Book Club were there with food. So gracious and supportive.

"It's my homemade cinnamon rolls," Doris said with pride. "I hope you like them."

"Smells delicious," Summer said.

Glads agreed with her, nodding her head. "Oh, they are divine. But she won't give the recipe to anybody."

"A girl has to have some secrets," Doris said, a little too girlishly for Summer, who hated when women referred to themselves as girls. Or when men did. The cinnamon rolls were perfect round swirls of spiraled cinnamon with white icing drizzled on them. Her stomach growled. Summer wouldn't bring up the "girl" thing. Not today. Pink-haired Doris, creator of the cinnamon rolls, was easily forgiven.

The women fussed about fixing a buffet of a sort with the rolls and quiche and fruit and heaps of scrambled eggs. Summer's eyes met Piper's. Still dressed in a T-shirt nightshirt with a lopsided pink fuzzy robe hanging from her, Piper stood, yawning.

"I've put two casseroles in the fridge," Marilyn said, shutting the fridge door and revealing a daisy tattoo as her sleeve moved upward. "It should hold you—for a couple of days anyway."

"Thank you."

"Coffee's on. And there's juice in the fridge. Do you need anything else, dear?" Glads turned to Summer.

Summer blinked. These women were a tour de force. "I can't think of a thing."

"We'll leave you to it. If you need anything, holler." Marilyn opened the door.

"Thanks so much, ladies. For everything."

After the women took off, the place felt empty and quiet. They left behind a delight of scents. Coffee. Cinnamon. Quiche.

"I texted Mom. She's coming right over."

"What about Mia?"

Piper waved her hand. "She won't be up for hours. Remember what that was like? Sleeping until noon, without having to get up to pee? Or worrying about your back?"

"I almost remember it," Summer said and laughed as she made her way to the cupboard for a cup. She needed coffee. That was all she wanted right now.

She poured herself a cup. "Do you want some?"

"Sure," Piper said.

Summer poured her cousin a cup, adding cream.

"Well, I see you waited on me." Agatha entered the room from the back kitchen door.

"Sorry, I—"

"I'm just kidding, Summer." Agatha examined the food. "Nice."

"Help yourself," Piper said.

Summer held up the coffeepot. "Can I get you some?"

"Never touch the stuff." Agatha reached into the cupboard for a plate and filled it with food.

The three of them sat down at the kitchen table together. The same kitchen table her mother had had for years, where Summer had sat every day as a child. She ran her fingers along a gray swirl on the 1950s chrome table, the way she'd done countless times.

Summer swallowed the lump forming in her throat. "So, Aunt Agatha, tell me about this Rudy character and what happened between him and Mom."

Piper sat her coffee cup down with a thud. "Not this nonsense again."

Agatha held her hand up as if to stop Piper. "I'm aware of how you feel about this. But I say Brigid's Island is still Brigid's Island. We do business like people, like friends."

"The man has every right to expand," Piper pointed out.

"He does." Agatha slipped out a slice of quiche. "But he had no right to speak to Hildy like he did. And he wouldn't quit."

Summer sipped her coffee, then shoveled in the cinnamon roll—warm, gooey, sweet, and spicy. She hoped she wasn't drooling.

"She told him in no uncertain terms she was not interested in selling," Agatha continued. "He said he'd take her to court and then called her a crazy old witch." Her round cheeks flared pink.

"He couldn't have taken Mom to court for that reason. What's his problem?"

"He had a thing for your mother. Unrequited. And it drove him bonkers."

"Mom, you see romances everywhere." Piper rolled her eyes. "Geez."

"It is what makes the world go around, dear."

Summer spooned fruit onto her plate. The healthy fruit would offset the effect of the rolls. Or so she told herself. "Okay so if you're right, unrequited romance or not—what makes you figure it went any further?"

Agatha swallowed her bite of quiche. "He bothered her almost every day about it. Then about the time she told me about it, she got those threatening phone calls and notes. We both thought it was him."

"Did you go to the police?"

"No police. As if he'd pay attention."

"Do you have proof of his threats?" Piper asked.

"Proof? I don't know . . ." She gazed into the distance as if trying to remember something.

"I have at least one letter." Summer walked off into the living room to fetch the note. "And the one at the store."

She handed the paper to Piper. "Another one. What do you think of that?"

Piper's eyes widened. "Call the police."

Calling the police wasn't as simple for Summer as it might be for her cousin Piper.

"I'm not sure that's a good idea." Dread filled Summer as she remembered chief of police of Brigid's Island, Ben Singer, the worst smug, small-town cop on the planet. Never cut her a break as a kid. Once, he'd caught her swiping candy from Sal's Sweets on the boardwalk, and you'd have thought it was the Hope Diamond.

"That girl of yours will come to no good," she'd overheard him say to her mother. "She runs around this island unattended, steals, and God knows what else. Hildy, something has to be done about her."

"Thanks for your concern," Hildy had said, tight-lipped. "She's just bored. Bright girl like Summer. She needs more to keep her mind occupied."

"What she needs is a father. A stern hand."

Summer's face heated with a rush of embarrassment even now. Everybody had always said that when she'd gotten in trouble. It was a cruel thing to say. But Hildy always handled it.

"Thanks, Ben. I'm not sure what you expect me to do about that. Are you on the market?"

He huffed off that time.

* * *

Her most recent sin against the Singer family was not showing up for her wedding, the groom being his son. She hadn't spoken to any of them since—but then again, she didn't need to. She knew how they felt about her. And they had every right to.

"Ben Singer hates me. I doubt he'd listen."

"Well, that's just crazy. Ben Singer doesn't hate you." Piper glanced at her mom, who was shaking her head.

Agatha winced. "Yeah, he kind of does. Not Summer's biggest fan."

"But even so," Piper persisted, "Summer's an adult now. A college professor. She's made something of her life. What she did or didn't do as a kid should have no bearing. What happened between her and Cash was so long ago."

Summer turned back to her fruit. She picked out the pineapple, which she didn't care for, and stabbed the watermelon with her fork.

"Well, who cares?" Piper's nostrils flared slightly. "I mean, if you think someone killed your mother, I say buck up and deal with this jerk, jilted son or not."

Summer set her fork down and studied Piper. Steady, kind, and stronger than what Summer had ever given her credit for, Piper was right. What was wrong with her? Who cared about Ben Singer's opinion of her?

Chapter Four

The police station was nothing like Summer remembered. Funny, what time does to memories. The big scary station had somehow morphed into a tiny, shoddy office with the scent of stale coffee permeating.

The receptionist behind the desk chewed gum, cracking it, and eyed the three Merriweather women. "Can I help you?

Summer's mouth felt as dry as cotton, but she spoke up anyway. "We'd like to see Ben Singer."

"The chief is busy. Do you have an appointment?" She drew out the word *appointment*. Strange accent. *Not from around here.*

Agatha stepped forward. "No, we figured we'd stop by and chat. When will he be available?"

She checked over her computer screen. "Looks like he's not available until about two."

Summer's heart pounded in her chest. "We're not waiting until two to see him."

"Tell him I'm here, please. Agatha Merriweather St. Clair.

"Uh. Okay." She groaned and lifted herself out of her chair as if it were torture.

Piper wrapped her arm around Summer's shoulders and whispered to her, "He's not doing anything back there. Probably just eating donuts and drinking coffee. Trying to act like he's big time, shoot the dime."

Donuts? Such a cliché. Even for Ben.

The strange fluorescent lights snapped Summer's attention to the past—memories of running from this place. One of many things Ben hated about her. She wouldn't sit still. He'd bring her here, turn around, and she'd have vanished.

"Squirrely," he'd called her.

She may have been squirrely then, but she was here on business today. Besides, the good Piper and the even better Aunt Agatha flanked her. Three against one; Summer liked those odds.

The young woman entered the room. "He'll see you ladies. Right through there." She pointed in the direction.

They marched down the corridor to his office. Ben Singer stood behind his desk, looking like, well, a lot older, a lot smaller, and a little unhealthy. Sort of green at the gills. Was he hung over? Sick?

"Ladies, please take a seat."

They sat down almost in unison. Three brown chairs. Leather-ish, perhaps pleather. Squeaky.

"I'm very sorry for your loss. I'll miss Hildy." He sat down, placed his elbows on the desk next to a half-eaten donut. Summer refrained from pointing it out to Piper as she bit the inside of her cheek so she wouldn't laugh.

"Thank you," Summer said. His attention shifted toward her.

"Good to see you. How are you?"

"I'm upset, as you can imagine. Mom's death was unexpected."

He nodded, frowning.

Summer deemed it best to just put it all out there. "That's why we're here. We suspect someone murdered her."

He sat up. His eyebrows gathered. "What?"

Summer handed him the black paper. "I found this."

He read it. "This is troubling, but it doesn't prove Hildy was murdered."

Agatha cleared her throat. "No, but this wasn't the first note she'd gotten and there were phone calls." Summer was glad for her company.

"Why didn't she come forward?"

"Well, you knew her. She shrugged it off. Believed no one would harm her." Agatha's jaw clenched. "If she were still alive, I'd throttle her for that."

He smiled, deep creases forming around his eyes. "I get that. But you can't go around accusing people of murder."

"We're not accusing anyone," Summer spoke up. "We're saying it's a strong possibility, and we'd like it if you'd look into it."

His chin tilted in interest. "I don't have the resources to launch a murder investigation based on a note or two. I need more proof."

"Mom was only sixty-four years old and dropped dead. That seems odd enough in itself."

"Not really. And we just got in the initial autopsy report, which said it was a heart attack, I believe."

"Heart attack? Hildy had no heart problems. She was my sister, and I'd know it if she did."

"Look, grief is an odd thing." He paused, as if he was searching for the right words to say. "Many people who lose loved ones to suicide think it's murder. People who lose someone like Hildy, who was healthy and vivacious, try to make sense of it. Claiming it was murder is one. It's a defense mechanism sometimes. You ladies need to go home and get some rest."

"Rest? How patronizing can you get?" Summer blurted out.

He lurched back as if someone had slapped him, and Agatha and Piper's attention shifted to Summer.

"Please look into this for Mom."

Agatha frowned. "She was your friend."

Friend? Since when?

He folded his hands on his desk. "I loved her, like everybody else in this town. I can't imagine why anybody would want to kill her."

"For her property," Piper explained. "She was fielding offers. People wanted her property. Both Beach Reads and her house."

"What? The house? What?" Summer's voice lifted in surprise.

The image of the house she grew up in sprang to her mind. A small pink beach cottage with sea foam—colored shutters and the front porch with a swing. Memories of that swing tugged at her. Days of lying there, listening to the waves, gulls, and sometimes wind, reading Macbeth for the third time, or Romeo and Juliet for the umpteenth, made up her core. She fell in love with Shakespeare on that porch and wanted nothing more than to study and learn all about him and his plays and to spread her passion through teaching, igniting young people's minds.

But who would want to buy it? There was not much to it.

"Killing her wouldn't solve that problem." Ben ignored her outburst.

Agatha stiffened and sat straighter. "Yes, it would. They'd understand it would go to Summer, and nine chances out of ten, she'd sell it."

Silence permeated the room.

Is that why Agatha and Piper hadn't told Summer about the offers? Summer's mind raced as they all looked at her. "I've not considered selling the house at all."

"But what about the bookstore?" he asked.

"Yes. I've always despised the place." She said it without thinking.

Maybe *despised* was a harsh word. Even though they were romances, they were still books. Summer didn't understand why people would fill their brains with such nonsense when there were good books—better books—everywhere.

But it was more than that. It was that her mom refused to carry any of the better books. She'd not even give them a shelf when Summer pleaded with her from time to time.

"Who wants to read Shakespeare at the beach?" she'd say and wave her off.

Who, indeed?

* * *

"With everything you told me, I see no cause to launch a murder investigation. I'm sorry. Sometimes people just die."

Agatha sat even further forward, as if she might hop on the desk at any moment. "But what about Rudy?"

One wiry gray eyebrow cocked. "What about him?"

"He threatened her all the time."

"He did?"

"He wants to expand the arcade and said he'd take her to court."

Ben grinned. "That old coot. Well, okay, ladies, I'll talk to him. But that's all I will do. I'll tell him to cool his jets. You understand? This is not a murder investigation."

He smirked, then laughed as he eyeballed Summer. "You breaking any hearts these days?"

Sweat prickled Summer's forehead. Her pulse raced as she felt flushed. She grabbed the armrests of her chair, standing. "Every chance I get, Ben. But we're here for my mom. Could you focus on that?"

Piper stifled a nervous giggle.

Ben's jaw tightened as he gestured for them to exit his office.

If only Summer felt as strong as she sounded. So angry that she felt like she might combust at one moment, and the next moment wanting to curl up in a fetal position of shame about her past. How dare he bring that up when they were there on official business? When her mom had just died?

She brooded on the way back to her mother's place, telling herself she needed to get over this. People made mistakes every day. Had she made a mistake by leaving Cash at the altar? Most of the time she was certain she'd done the right thing. But she was ashamed she'd never talked with him. Instead, she'd just left him, never facing him.

Summer, Agatha, and Piper ambled into her mother's house. Overgrown plants hung from hooks in the walls, and bookcases brimmed with romances. Hildy's African grey, Mr. Darcy, wide awake, jumped back and forth in his rattling cage, hungry.

"Are you hungry, Mr. Darcy?"

The normally talkative bird didn't reply.

As Summer scooped the bird food into the tray, a wave of regret came over her. She had to leave. It was that simple. She wasn't ready for any of this. She'd come back in a few weeks, maybe a few months, to deal with her mother's things. The rest of the estate, such as it was, she'd deal with over the phone, online—whatever. She didn't need her past thrown in her face constantly, especially when she was trying to deal with her mother's death. Obviously, the local authorities weren't taking her suspicions seriously. And she wasn't certain about Aunt Agatha and Piper.

Summer lifted her suitcase onto the couch. She folded her sweatpants and T-shirt and shoved them in the bag, zipped up the case, and set it on the floor.

Agatha padded into the room. "Do you want to eat with us?" She then noticed the packed suitcase. "What are you doing?"

"I'm leaving, Aunt Agatha."

"What? You just got here."

"I'm just not sure about being here." Summer swallowed hard, willing away the burning in her throat. "I want answers about Mom's death. People are hiding things from me. I wasn't aware she was getting offers for Beach Reads. I'm in the dark about the house and about her death threats. I want to know what's going on. You two need to be honest with me. Otherwise, what's the point?"

Agatha moved toward Summer and placed her hands on her shoulders, leading her to sit on the couch. "I see. Please sit down. You shouldn't leave. Not yet. We need to talk."

Agatha took a seat next to Summer as Piper strolled into the room. "What do you want to know?"

"What kind of offers were made on the store and who made them?"

Aunt Agatha shrugged. "I wish I knew the details, but your mother kept them to herself. She never considered selling. That bookstore meant the world to her."

Summer kept her own counsel. It might have meant the world to her mother, but selling it would help out. Mired in debt, uncertain of her job, selling Beach Reads sounded like the exact thing to do.

"Your mother had the house appraised not too long ago," Piper said, sitting on the La-Z-Boy, crossing her long legs. "It's worth well over a million dollars."

"What?" Summer said, her heart racing, picturing the ramshackle cottage. Two bedrooms. One bathroom. Small eat-in kitchen. A million?

"It's beachfront property." Agatha folded her hands on her lap.

"But it's always been beachfront property."

"Things on the island are changing," Agatha said in a wistful tone.

Summer's mind raced with all the new information. She tried to piece everything together to make sense of it. Her mother's death, threatening notes, the offers on the store—and the house. "And then there's Rudy."

"I'm sure he's got something to do with her threatening calls. And maybe something to do with her death." Agatha squinted her eyes, calculating.

"Really, Mom?" Piper said, incredulous, voice raised. "Murder? Rudy?"

Agatha's eyes lit, hand on her chin. "Yes, but how to prove it?"

The word *prove* rambled around in Summer's brain. Why hadn't she thought of this before? Hildy had been a wonderful mom. Odd. But wonderful. They fought like any mother and daughter, and Summer was a handful. Admittedly.

Her mother deserved answers. If the local police wouldn't take her seriously, she'd have to investigate it herself. It couldn't be that difficult, could it? After all she was smarter than the average person, wasn't she? Visions of a female version of Sherlock Holmes played in her mind. "I'll make it right. I'll find justice for Mom's death."

Those words formed a heartfelt resolution in the center of her. Summer Merriweather wasn't leaving this island until she found her mother's killer.

Chapter Five

First things first. Summer needed to investigate the details of her mother's death. "Where did Mom die?"

"I'm sorry. I've got to run," Agatha said. "I've got a doctor's appointment."

"Everything okay?" Summer asked.

Agatha finished loading the dishwasher and closed the door. "Just my yearly physical."

"Well, look who's still alive," Piper said when Mia came stumbling into the kitchen.

She grinned back at Piper. "What's for breakfast?"

"Breakfast? Don't you mean lunch?" Agatha said and kissed her granddaughter.

"Whatever, Gram," Mia said, her words muffled with her face being smothered by a huge hug.

"I'm off. Catch you all later," Agatha said. And just like that she vanished.

She didn't answer the question.

Piper turned to her daughter. "There's a lot of food in the fridge. Help yourself. "

She opened the door and shuffled stuff around, then pulled out a few containers and set them on the counter.

"I'm glad you decided to stay," Piper said, focusing back on Summer.

Summer lifted her chin.

"I've missed you," she said. "I've always considered you more a sister than a cousin."

Both only children, cousins, born days apart. Because of that, there was always a lot of comparison in the family and the community. As children, they used to laugh over what the adults said about them. Oddly enough, they were pretty much right. Piper was the beauty queen, a good athlete, and all-around girl next door, and Summer was intelligent, creative, and a handful. Funny how those observations clung to them and perhaps formed their adult selves, like some incantation. Summer often wondered if she was what she was because of those statements. Children are like sponges.

Piper, gifted with long legs and golden blonde hair, had been Miss North Carolina and progressed to the national pageant, where she came in second place to Miss Texas. But she didn't make it through school because she'd fallen in love and gotten pregnant. Almost simultaneously.

Summer was short, slight, and so envious of her cousin's golden hair that she'd tried to color her own a few times. But it was no match for the real thing and became a pain in the ass to maintain. So she returned to brown.

"Do you have to work today?" Summer asked.

"Nah. Bereavement leave," Piper said. "Same with Mia. She goes back to school Monday. It's her last week."

"Thank Goddess!" Mia said. "I like school, but I can't wait for summer break."

"I know the feeling," Summer said, then turned to Piper. "What should we do first? I mean, I've never been a sleuth before. My instincts tell me there's something in this house that may point us in the right direction. But where to look?"

Piper shrugged, her arm gesturing outward. "I think we take it one room at a time. But in the meantime, we should go and talk with Rudy."

Summer's heart thud against her rib cage. "Rudy."

"He's one nasty piece of work."

"I remember him, but only vaguely. Like I don't think he ever hung out much around Mom when I was here." She tried to remember him—all she managed was a misty memory of him grumbling at her as she ran through the arcade, yelling at her to "slow down, kid."

"No. He keeps to himself," Piper said.

"You know what they say . . ." Summer said.

"It's always the quiet ones!" Piper said.

"What are you talking about?" Mia said and then stuffed a cinnamon roll in the microwave and turned it on.

"We think Aunt Hildy's death was suspicious," Piper said.

"Suspicious? You mean someone killed her?" Her eyes widened. "Do you think those letters had anything to do with it?"

"We don't know," Piper said. "So calm down."

"But she had a heart attack. She was old," Mia said, sliding the cinnamon roll out of the microwave. She opened the refrigerator and pulled out a soda.

"Well, from your point of view, she was old, but sixty-four is not old these days," Piper said.

Darcy interrupted with a loud squawk. The three of them walked into the living room.

"Darcy hungry," he said, his bird head tilted. "Hungry!"

"Darcy just ate!" Summer said. "Poor bird, don't you remember?"

The bird blinked and calmed down. *Darcy must be getting old—how old is he anyway? Eighteen? Nineteen?*

"Poor old bird," she said to him.

He ignored her and turned toward his water.

Story of my life. She watched as he nibbled at his food, crunching loudly.

"Oh my goodness," Piper said, coming up beside Summer. "Your mom loved that bird."

The bird stopped eating and looked at them, spread his wings. "Love. Love. Love. Hildy love Darcy. Darcy love Hildy." He returned to his food.

In a flash, hot tears burned in Summer's eyes, then streamed down her cheeks. She remembered the day her mom brought the bird home. A rescue bird. Someone had left him behind in an apartment and she heard about it and immediately adopted him. It was love at first sight for both of them.

"Summer," Piper said, sliding her arm around her. "Are you okay?"

She nodded. "I'll be fine." But she wished she believed that. She relied so much on her mom's constant reassurance. Being able to pick the phone up and ask her advice. Her mom knew of the situation at school, Summer's dreadful love life, and her fear of spiders, and of course, she loved her, anyway.

"What are you going to do with Darcy?" Mia said and flopped down on the couch.

"What do you mean?" Summer said, disentangling herself from Piper and sitting next to Mia on the sofa.

"I mean are you taking him back to Staunton? Giving him away?"

"Mia!"

"It's okay, Piper," Summer said. "I hadn't thought about it. So much to think about. To take care of. But Darcy should be a priority. I think I'll keep him."

Being responsible for another creature had always scared her. But now in this moment, she felt content, as if the responsibility was nothing compared to the joy of companionship. She couldn't guess what her therapist would think about this. But things happened. People died leaving animals behind. Summer hadn't had time to prepare herself. Sometimes that's just the way it is.

"In the meantime, we have an old man to visit," Piper said. "So get dressed. You're coming with us."

"I am dressed," Mia said, still in her PJs.

"I know it's the cool thing," Piper said. "But no kid of mine is going out in her pajamas. At least not with me. Get dressed, girl."

Mia huffed off.

The two cousins sat in silence for a few minutes.

Summer cleared her throat. "You are such an old fuddy-dud."

Piper eyed her cousin and laughed. "Takes one to know one."

Chapter Six

A fter talking it over, Summer and Piper decided to stay home
for the remainder of the day. But the next morning, Wednesday. Summer girded her loins and joined Piper on a visit to the
Seaside Arcade.

Summer always hated the Seaside Arcade, even as a child and
a teenager, when all the rest wanted to hang out and play pinball and Skeeball and all the computerized games. Between the
pinball machines and their music and bells, and the Skeeball rattling around, and the starship noises from whatever space game
was popular, it was just too bloody noisy for her. She preferred
quiet.

So because she never hung out there, she never got to know
Rudy. From what she was hearing about him, she was glad. But
now as she, Piper, and Mia stood outside the arcade, what loomed
in the right-next-door distance was Beach Reads with a closed sign
in the window.

Summer blinked. She'd deal with that later.

"Are we ready?" Piper said.

"I suppose."

The three of them walked in the entrance to the usual cacophony of sounds and the scent of cotton candy, candy apples, and sticky sweet sodas.

"Can I play some pinball?" Mia asked, holding out her hand to Piper.

"No, you're with us," Piper said. "I need your powers of observation, remember?"

Mia crossed her arms and cracked her gum. "Okay. Whatever."

"My kid is psychic, I swear," Piper muttered. "She takes after your mom."

Oh boy. Summer's mom had skilled powers of observation that even she had to admit bordered psychic ability. But she was uncertain that her mom was a true psychic.

An old man sat behind the counter and looked up at Summer, startled.

"You look just like your mother," he said. "You must be Summer."

"I am," I said. *I don't look a thing like my mom.*

"It's been a few years since I've seen you," he said, with his eyes darting to Piper, then Mia.

"I live in Virginia," Summer said.

"Oh? Yes, I think I remembered Hildy mentioning that," he said, bushy gray eyebrow lifting.

What was she going to say? Did you kill my mother?

His hands reached over and hit a buzzer. A teenager came over to the counter.

"Can you take over here?"

The tow-headed boy nodded, then took in Mia, who shot him a look of overwhelming boredom, which made Summer want to chuckle.

"I'd like to take these ladies into my office and chat," he looked over at us. "How does that sound?"

"Fine," Summer said. Well, this would be easier than she imagined.

They followed him through a snaking path through machines and games into a quiet sanctuary of a room. *Must be soundproof.* Summer strained to hear anything from the arcade. Nothing. Soundproof was nice, but also kind of creepy, considering.

"Please ladies, take a seat," he said. "I assume you're here because you know I want to buy the bookstore."

Summer nodded. "So I'm told."

Piper sat forward in her chair. "But it's early. We still have no idea who's inherited the store. The funeral was just two days ago. It was lovely. Did you attend? I don't think I saw you."

"No," he said. "I've got a business to run and Hildy and I didn't see eye to eye."

"She didn't want you to buy her store," Summer said.

"That's right," he said nodding, turkey neck jiggling. He picked up a pen from his desk and started to tap it. Beady blue eyes.

"Why is that?" Summer said.

Mia cracked her gum loudly, prompting Piper to turn her face and rolled her eyes at her daughter.

"Well, she was stubborn, that's why," he replied. Those beady eyes slanted. "Couldn't get her to see things right. Things change. The market shifts. People are interested in games, not books. Hell, now most readers use Kindles."

"You can't read most kindles at the beach," Mia said with disdain in her voice.

He ignored her. "I told her I'd give her a fair price, enough money that she could retire. She was so unreasonable."

Summer bit her lip. She couldn't imagine her mom ever retiring. Her mother planned to work into her eighties or nineties.

"She loved the store. Her whole life revolved around it. She was healthy and happy. Why would she want to retire?" Piper said.

"Everybody knows indie bookstores are struggling," he said. "She should have cut her losses, taken my money, and run."

The tone in his voice irritated Summer. Patronizing. She recognized it. She had a PhD in Shakespearean literature, and yet several of the men on the faculty at Staunton College often gave her that same tone. It was maddening. And now she'd given them more reason, with her public debacle. Once again, the video of her jumping on to the chair, screaming, ran through her mind.

"I don't think Beach Reads was struggling at all. My mother's business acumen was incredible. She built that bookstore from nothing, based on a hunch that people would buy books at a store right at the beach. And they do. Remarkable, when you consider she had neither a degree nor a husband to help her out," Summer said.

His jaw angled out. "I heard you didn't like the bookstore."

How did he know that? Obviously he'd been digging around.

"How badly do you want the bookstore?" Piper spoke up.

"I'm willing to make a fair offer," he said.

"Someone had been sending my mother notes. Someone is very interested in the bookstore," Summer said.

His chin tilted out. "Notes?"

"And phone calls," Piper said. "Someone wants the bookstore badly."

"Would that person be you?" Summer said.

He shifted around in his seat. "I'm not sure what you're accusing me of. But I don't need to send notes. I've made offers, fair and square."

"But my mother ignored them. Didn't that anger you?"

"Yes, of course," he said, his voice raising a decibel. "But I don't have time to write notes and make phone calls to chase after her. In fact, I need to ask you to leave. I need to get back to it."

"Fine," Piper said, as she stood. Summer and Mia followed her lead.

"Before you go, Summer, I just want you to know I'm sorry about your mother. And if you decide to sell, come and see me."

Over my dead body.

Chapter Seven

Piper and Mia had some errands to run, and Summer was weary, so she slipped off to home for a nap. It had been years since she had taken naps—but she'd developed the habit in England, where she'd read and write herself into weariness, drift into a nap, and get back up to work. Besides, she was still dealing with jet lag.

She curled up on the couch, with Mr. Darcy watching. It was unnerving the way he watched her. But not so much that it prevented her from sleeping. Hunger pangs woke her about twenty minutes later.

Summer made her way into the kitchen and pulled a pan of quiche out of the refrigerator. As she stood there, waiting for it to warm up in the microwave, she examined her mom's refrigerator door. Several photos of Summer hung, clipped to magnets. One when she must have been in about sixth grade, gangly, and barely smiling. There was also the high school graduation photo, which made Summer want to gag. Surprisingly enough, her mom had also clipped out an article about Summer's first book, published soon after she'd gotten her master's degree: *Everyday Shakespeare*.

Something bloomed in her chest. *Hildy had been proud of her.*

But there were some things her mother never understood about Summer, including Summer's fear of spiders. Hell, Summer still didn't understand it. How could she have expected her mom to understand? If only she were still alive, they could talk about it, tear it apart, and analyze it. She'd tell her mom everything she'd learned about arachnophobia during her forced therapy.

If only.

If only those spiders hadn't escaped from the lab at school. If only they hadn't come wandering into her classroom, where several students caught her on their Smartphone making a complete fool of herself as she jumped up on the chairs, screaming and flailing her arms around. To her humiliation, one of the videos went viral on a website called "Vine."

After, she'd tried to laugh it off. It was funny—not when it was happening, but later even she considered the video funny. But the dean didn't. He was a humorless buffoon, but he was her boss. They pressed her to get an actual diagnosis of arachnophobia, just to make her case. Then she'd slinked off to England until it all died down.

Summer took her plate back into the living room and sat on the couch, shoving aside the blanket.

She loved quiet. She planned her life around quiet. Why did this quiet disturb her? Gone were the noises of her mom singing and dancing, the stereo blasting, and kitchen sounds. Happy sounds.

The place was empty without Hildy's presence.

Even as empty as the place was, how could she sell it?

She sighed. Summer needed the money. Why keep this house if she lived and worked in Staunton, as usual? If.

She twisted her hands together, wishing for a decision about the job. Not knowing was torture.

A pounding at the door interrupted her meditative stance.

She opened the door to a red-faced Rudy.

"What the hell are you doing sending the cops to my place?"

"Uh, I—"

"I'm not telling you again. I didn't hurt your mother. I didn't threaten her, and I have no idea who was. But back off, lady," he said, stepping forward and pointing his finger in her face.

Well!

Her heart jumped against her rib cage. *How dare he!* She stepped forward and stared him down. He finally stormed off.

She watched him walk off as Aunt Agatha came up the walkway, with a pan of food in her arms, and passed him, not even looking his way as she made her way into the house.

"What did that rat want with you?"

"Our chief of police visited him, and he's not too happy with me," Summer said.

"Ben! Why would he tell him you were asking about him? What an idiot!" Agatha said.

"Ben never was very bright. I've always wondered how he even became a cop. Most cops are sharp," Summer said.

"It's about time for him to retire. We need some young blood in there," Agatha said, moving toward the kitchen. "He has an assistant, but he's only part-time. Ben needs to step aside."

"What do you have there?" Summer said.

"Lasagna, sent over by Marilyn," Agatha said. "Wasn't that nice? It smells divine. Her mother-in-law came over from Italy, and she taught Marilyn all about Italian cooking."

She set the full pan down on the counter.

"I can't believe Rudy had the balls to come over here," Agatha said. "I've a mind to call Ben. Maybe I will. He's got no business threatening you."

"He pointed his shriveled, bony, finger in my face. I didn't appreciate it. If he hurt Mom . . ."

"Now, Summer, vigilante justice is not our cup of tea. We let the authorities deal with people like that," she said. "Besides, you've got enough on your plate with your job and the spider thing."

Hearing her say "spider thing" struck Summer as funny, and she laughed. It was true. It was ridiculous, yet true. She wasn't sure about selling Beach Reads, or this house and all of her mom's things, but one thing she knew was she needed money. And she still hated spiders.

"Yes, I do," Summer said, "but you don't."

Agatha grinned. "Now don't get any funny ideas. Despite it all, I'm a law-abiding citizen."

"Who's talking about breaking the law? Look, we just need to prove that Rudy killed her. We don't need to break the law to do it."

She turned the teakettle on. "I need some tea," she said and turned to face Summer. "I have no idea how we'd do that. That's why we need to leave it to the police."

"Well, we just got a little glimpse of how our local cop is handling things. I've been thinking about this. We already have a clue that someone wanted the shop enough to threaten her. What if there're more notes and other things around here? If there are, we'd take them to Ben. That'd be a start."

Agatha clapped her hands together in excitement. "If we could somehow link those notes to Rudy before we go to Ben, he'd have to do something."

"First things first," Summer said. "We take it room by room and see what we find."

"Sounds like a plan," Agatha said, and then the teakettle whistled, which set Summer's nerves on edge. Just a little.

45

Chapter Eight

Aunt Agatha searched through kitchen drawers and cupboards, and the creaks and sighs from the old kitchen comforted Summer in an indescribable manner as she took on the living room, gathered and stacked magazines in one pile, mail in the other. Then Summer investigated the desk drawers, brimming with papers, cars, bills. *Oh, Mom.*

Summer moved on to the bedrooms, sorting through drawers and closets, relieved to find no stacks of papers or magazines, just old clothes, linens, and jewelry. She headed back to the living room just as Aunt Agatha entered it.

"I found something," she said as Summer toppled one of the desk drawers, its contents splaying out over the desk.

"What's that?" Summer stood from the desk chair.

"Another note." She handed it to Summer. "A note on black construction paper."

"Okay," Summer said, examining it. "It's the same as the others."

Agatha nodded.

"Why didn't Mom get someone involved?" Summer asked. "I just don't understand it."

Agatha sighed. "There's a lot about Hildy I never understood. She was her own person. She did things her own way. She refused to believe anybody on this island would harm her."

"She loved this island." A twinge of a sick feeling came over her. How sad would it be if they did prove that someone—Rudy or anybody—killed this woman who loved her community so much that she didn't pay any attention to weird creepy notes.

"She also loved the bookstore," Agatha said. "She grew that place into a tourist attraction itself. Romance and mystery writers made special trips to come here and sign books. Sometimes several of them would get together and sign. It was so exciting to meet these writers."

Summer twisted her lips. She didn't like romance novels. At all. Her mom used to say it was because she had no romance in her life. God knows it wasn't because Summer didn't try. But nobody's life was a romance novel—even Hildy would have to admit that. As would Agatha.

"You don't like romance books," Agatha said, "but they're not what they used to be. I firmly believe that some of the best authors these days are romance writers.'

"Really? That's interesting." Summer sorted through the junk on the desk. "I've not read a contemporary novel of any kind in a long time."

"You should give it a go. Hey, the book club is reading one of the best books . . . I love that writer. What's her name . . .? Hannah Jacobs. Her book has been number one on the *New York Times* list for a long time," Agatha said.

Summer kept her opinion to herself—about the *New York Times* bestseller list. "Speaking of books," Summer said, sorting through business cards and stacking them in piles, "summer is upon us. I suppose we need to make some decisions."

"I think we should open the bookstore on Friday," Agatha said.

"We?"

"Well, it has been a family affair for quite some time. Piper and I work part time. There's one other full-time employee. I'm not sure you ever met Poppy. She moved here last year."

"I don't think I have," Summer said. "But between all of us, I think we can manage to open. It's a week before the big weekend."

"It's settled then," Agatha said. "We'll open. It'll be good to keep busy. It's just that . . ." Her face fell, reddened, and then she let out a huge sob.

"Oh, Aunt Agatha," Summer said, running to her and wrapping her arms around her. She'd been so self-indulgent with her own emotions. How did she not see what her mom's death was doing to her sister?

"I just-just—"

"Shh, Aunt Agatha. You don't need to talk." Agatha felt warm and bony. Had she lost weight?

After a moment of sobbing, she pulled away from Summer's arms.

"It's just that I don't know how I'll face digging through that space without your mother. This?" she gestured to the house. "This is easy. She was never here. But that bookstore . . ." She didn't finish her sentence. She didn't have to. Summer had been dreading sorting through it for very same reason.

"Beach Reads Bookstore," Mr. Darcy said with a tone as if he'd just answered the phone. "Beach Reads Bookstore."

Agatha blew her nose and giggled. "That bird."

"Bookstore whore," the bird said in another tone. "Bookstore whore."

"Did he just say—"

"Whore!" The bird said. "Hildy is a bookstore whore!"

The tone was sickening. Menacing. This bird had heard those words enough that he was repeating them. Summer's stomach squeezed.

"Aunt Hildy, maybe the person who hurt Mom was right here," Summer said with her voice quivering.

"Who would have called her a whore?" Agatha asked. Angry red face. Indignant.

"Not just any whore. A *bookstore* whore."

Summer's emotions tangled. What had been going on in her mother's life? Why hadn't she reached out for help? Then it hit her with a stone-cold thud. *If this person was in the house, it was definitely someone in my mother's circle. Someone stood in this house and called her that name. Which would be kind of funny, if I weren't so certain the same person must have killed my mother.*

Chapter Nine

Agatha left to return some casserole dishes, and Summer was alone in the house, mulling over the "proof" they had found so far. Not much. Three notes and the bird's statement. Summer was no lawyer, but she figured none of that was enough for a murder case. They needed more.

She sat on the couch and glanced over at the coffee table, where she'd stacked the magazines. There was a book sitting there—out of habit she picked it up and thumbed through it. It was filled with handwritten notes. Her mother's handwriting. This must be a book club book. A romance?

Summer's heart skipped a beat or two. Her mom's handwriting was so similar to hers. And Summer wrote in books in a very similar way. Funny. She hadn't realized where she'd picked that habit up until now.

She circled a line where her mother had written: "What a lovely metaphor. Want to point this out."

Summer smiled.

The book's title was *Nights in Bellamy Harbor*. Hmm. A beach book? She grinned. She read the blurb on the back and surmised there was an evil developer who had his mind set on a beautiful beach village—and on the daughter of his arch enemy. Interesting. In a sort of Romeo and Juliet–ish way. She recalled the stanza, forever blazed into her brain:

Two households, both alike in dignity,
In fair Verona, where we lay our scene,
From ancient grudge break to new mutiny,
Where civil blood makes civil hands unclean.
From forth the fatal loins of these two foes
A pair of star-cross'd lovers take their life;
Whose misadventured piteous overthrows
Doth with their death bury their parents' strife.

Nothing like a beach developer character to get a beach community wound up. There'd been several deals that Summer remembered. Failed deals. The community of St. Brigid wasn't going down the development road without a fight. It helped that the community was a thriving one with very little in the way of unemployment. In some other communities Summer read about, it was a challenge to keep the developers out because people needed work. That wasn't the case for St. Brigid, a thriving fishing community, as it had been from the start. The island's community suffered bad years along with the good years, but even the "bad" years were not bad enough to even consider selling out to some developer.

The geography of the island was its blessing. Fisherman never had to travel far out to sea for a decent fish; the island was famous for its shrimp and always had been since its first settlement in 1796.

And the tourist season was an extra boon to the community—as much as some members despised it. Of course the tourists didn't discover the little island off the coast of southern North Carolina full force until the 1970s. They were all about the Outer Banks and Myrtle Beach, South Carolina.

Summer cradled the book in her hand; the weight of it gave it agency. It was a good-sized paperback, Summer's favorite kind. She'd always preferred hardback books, but she grew accustomed to soft covers. And now preferred them.

She curled her feet up under her and cracked the book open. *This is probably the last book my mother ever read.* Summer drew in air, and her lip quivered.

Oh, Mom, what happened to you?

A crushing sensation filled her chest, and she wailed a sob of anger. *If I had been there for my mom. If I hadn't been in England.*

The book paper felt good on her skin. She turned the page. The sound of the page turning, at once familiar and also a direct line to memories of reading with her mom. Now, here was a book once cradled in her mother's hands, and here were the words she'd been reading and thinking about.

Chapter One.

Summer stopped. These were the very words her mom had been reading. She may have thought about these characters, this story in her last moments. Who knew?

Summer read the first paragraph, then the next.

She awoke with a start to her phone ringing, sitting up as the book dropped to the floor.

"Uh, hello," she said.

"Hi, Summer—this is Marilyn. How are you doing, dear?"

Marilyn. Marilyn. Oh yes. In her mom's book group. "I'm fine," she said. "I've just been lying down." *After searching through Mom's house for clues,* she didn't say—because murder felt like a family matter.

"I just wanted to call to see how you're doing, and we also want to invite you to the next book club meeting if you're planning to be in town. It's next Wednesday," she said.

"I've not read the book." It was a good excuse.

"That's fine. There's plenty of time to read it between then and now," she said. "But if you can't do it, we'd still like to have you. We're doing a little something special for your mother."

Something in her chest fluttered. That felt more like an honor for her mom than that ridiculous church service, which she still didn't understand. Her mom was a happy, goddess-worshipping pagan and hippy. She didn't do church.

"Oh," Summer said with a funny little sigh she didn't recognize as coming from her. "That's so lovely."

"We can count on you being there, then?"

"Absolutely."

"Hildy gave so much to us and this community. We want to honor her. Something a little more private."

"It's very thoughtful of you," Summer said, her voice cracking slightly. People thought so highly of her mother. Why couldn't the two of them have gotten their acts together?

Because you are a mess, Summer Merriweather. Correction: Were a mess. No longer. You will get over this fear of spiders. You will keep your job. And, you will find the person who killed your mother. If only she knew.

"While I have you, Marilyn, do you mind if I ask you a question?"

"Anything," she said.

"Did you know about the offers Mom was getting for the bookstore?"

"Offers? No, I don't think she mentioned anything recent. I also don't think she'd have sold her beloved store. Do you?"

"That's what I'm trying to figure out. I found some . . . things . . . offers," Summer said.

Summer pictured Marilyn in her small Victorian home a few blocks from the beachfront. Plum, with mocha shutters and trim.

"Well, if I were you, dear, I'd trash them. That's where they belong. Beach Reads is more than a bookstore. It's a second home for so many of us. We're hoping you don't sell, of course. We're hoping you'll stay. Hildy would have loved you managing her store," Marilyn said.

"I'm not so sure about that," Summer said and tried to laugh, even though jabs of regret poked at her. "But thanks for saying it."

After they hung up, Summer picked the book up off the floor, and a slip of paper fell out of it. "This character must be based on Rudy!" the note said. *Rudy? The owner of the arcade? It had to be!*

Why would the writer of this book base any character on people in St. Brigid? She flipped the pages to the acknowledgments and scanned them. There, in black and white, was the name Hildy Merriweather. The author was thanking her for inspiration and for providing a safe, comforting space for readers from all walks of life. Safe, comforting space? An unnamable emotion plucked at Summer's chest.

Her face fell into her hands as she unraveled, sobbing.

Chapter Ten

"Summer? Are you here?" The words awakened her.

Who was that?

"Summer?" The voice came again. She sat up; she had cried herself into a nap. She blinked.

"There you are!" The voice said, coming up behind her. Summer turned her head and saw one of the women from her mother's books group. *What was her name again?*

"I'm sorry. Were you sleeping?" she said.

Doris. Yes. Doris. Pink-haired. Cinnamon rolls.

"Yes," Summer managed to say.

"I'm sorry to just walk in, but the door was open, and I wanted to drop off a basket of food. I left it on the counter for you," she said. "It's a basket from the church ladies."

"Church ladies?"

"Yes, your mother had struck up a friendship with several of the women from the churches. That's why the service was held there," she replied.

Oh, makes more sense now.

"I'm sorry," Summer said. "I've completely forgotten my manners. Please sit down. Can I get you something?"

"Oh no, dear. I can't stay," she said, but she sat down anyway. "My husband is rather ill, and today is not a good day for him. So I need to get back. But a little breather is nice." She sighed.

"I'm so sorry to hear about your husband," Summer said.

"Thanks. Hey, is that the book we're reading for the book club?"

Summer nodded. "It has my mom's notes in it. She must have read it already."

"She's probably read it several times," Doris said with a wave of her hand. "Are you reading it?"

"Yes, I just started to read it. It seems Mom knew the author."

"She knew a lot of authors. Several of them would make certain Beach Reads was on their tour. I've met a lot of writers. They just blows me away, you know? How do they think of all those plots and words and everything?"

"I agree," Summer said. "It's admirable. I'm not sure I could do it. Of course, I do have to write for my job. But that kind of writing takes very little imagination."

A pang of fear shot through Summer. She'd been trying not to think of her job—or the fact that she'd not heard from her boss. What if they let her go?

What then? Would another school hire her?

"Hildy had a great imagination. I used to tell her to sell the bookstore and write books," Doris said.

Summer sat forward. "Sell the store? What did she say?"

Doris shrugged. "You know your mother. She didn't want to sell. But I think she wanted to write a book. The only way she could do it was to get rid of the store. It was like a deadweight to her."

Deadweight? Hildy loved the store. "Many offers have been made," Summer said. "Do you know anything about them?"

Doris's fleshy face fell, stiffened. "I don't know what you're talking about. But I've got to run. My husband must be wondering where I've gone off to."

Summer stood to walk her to the front door.

"No need, dear," she said, holding up her hand. "Just don't forget about the food on the counter. Some of it needs refrigeration."

Summer walked her to the door, anyway, trying to get a sense of why she was leaving so quickly. Why did the conversation about the bookstore make her nervous? Was she worried that Summer would sell?

She turned and looked at Summer before opening the door. "Summer, I hope if you sell, you'll come to the book group. There may be one or two members who'd like to buy it."

"I'll take that under consideration," Summer said. Maybe that was Doris's hesitation moments ago.

As they opened the door, Mia and Piper walked in, smiled at Doris, and kept walking toward the kitchen.

"Look at all the food," Mia squealed from the kitchen.

"Mia's a live wire," Doris said, grinning. "She was very close to Hildy," she said, lowering her voice. "Is she okay?"

Summer was aware of their closeness. But she wondered why Doris felt like she wasn't. She shrugged it off. People did and said the oddest things when in the shock of mourning.

Summer said goodbye to Doris and made her way into the kitchen, where an astonishing array of food filled the counter. Casserole dishes brimming with food. Baskets filled with bread and muffins. Tupperware containers filled with soup, chili, and god knows what else.

Well, if nothing else, they'd not go hungry.

"I ran into Rudy again today," Piper said.

"And?"

"I told him to stay the hell away from this place and you," Piper said. "Mom said he'd been over here threatening you. I told him if he came over here again, we'd get an injunction."

Summer cracked a smile. "Do you think that will stop him? I mean if the man killed my mother, what makes you think an injunction will prevent him from doing anything?"

"I tried to tell her that," Mia said. "Killers don't care about the law."

Out of the mouths of babes. A shiver traveled through her. If he had killed her mom, would Rudy be coming after Summer next?

Chapter Eleven

Summer's therapist insisted on a phone appointment. Summer wasn't sure how well it would work given that she was used to in-person therapy with eye contact and other subtle signals.

"How are you doing?" Dr. Gildea asked.

Summer didn't quite know how to answer that. Her mom had just died, and she strongly suspected she'd been murdered, plus she was uncertain about her job. She felt like everything was spinning out of control.

Dr. Gildea didn't give Summer a chance to answer. "The death of a parent is one of the most earth-shattering losses. You must be feeling a variety of emotions. I'm concerned that you won't allow yourself to feel them. Are you?"

"Yes." Summer glimpsed at Mr. Darcy, who was completely ignoring her—just like most males of any species. "Of course I am."

"You have a tendency to intellectualize everything." Summer didn't respond. *What was wrong with intellectualizing, anyway?*

"Are you doing okay? Have you seen any spiders?"

"No, and so I've not been challenged."

"I'll increase the dosage on your meds, and we'll go from there. How does that sound?"

"Fine. do you think that will do the trick if I see one?"

"Look, there're no guarantees, and you're in such a stressful situation. It may not completely diminish your fear, but it may. We've talked about this before, but we need to get at the root of this fear to resolve it. But in the meantime, I think the medicine will help."

"Thanks, Doc." Still, she'd steer clear of basements, attics, or camping out any time soon—tempting the hand of spider fate.

* * *

Aunt Agatha was making noise in the kitchen, humming softly as she did so. Happy kitchen noises and a delicious scent drew Summer into the room. Agatha stood at the stove, stirring.

"What's that?"

"Vegetable soup," Agatha replied. "Smells wonderful."

Summer looked around at the counters, brimming with food. "It just keeps coming, doesn't it?"

"This community loved your mother, and it loves you too. Food is one of the great comforts and healers in life." She continued to stir. She blinked and suddenly she looked older. Summer wrapped her arm around her.

"I love you, Aunt Agatha,"

She looked over at Summer. "I love you too, dear."

"What's in the oven?"

"I'm heating up the biscuits Doris brought over."

"Store bought?" Summer asked and grinned.

"Who knows?" Agatha waved her hand. "The woman has a very sick husband. I've no idea how she does anything else but take care of him. I keep telling her she should get a nurse. But she won't have it."

Summer opened the oven door. "The biscuits look ready." She reached for an oven mitt and slid the pan out of the oven, placing it on the counter.

"Wow, it smells so good here," Piper said as she walked into the kitchen.

"Where's Mia?" Agatha asked.

"There's a slumber party tonight. I almost insisted that she go. I know she's upset about Hildy, but it's important that she continues to do things she enjoys. Life goes on."

"It certainly does," Agatha said, spooning soup into bowls.

The scent filled Summer with comfort. She'd never given grief much attention. But Agatha was right: food was one of life's great comforts. People bringing in so much good food soothed Summer. She'd not be eating this well otherwise. She just wanted to sleep, cry, and dwell.

"I didn't think people brought food in anymore," Summer said as she took her bowl to the kitchen table. "At least that's what someone said in Staunton."

"Well, we do it here," Agatha said. "I hope we always do. Grieving is exhausting. Who wants to cook? Heating up food is about all I can manage."

Once again, Aunt Agatha looked her age, and a pang of sadness moved through Summer. *Agatha has lost her sister.* They'd been together their whole lives.

They ate the soup and biscuits in quiet. Summer couldn't get Rudy's rudeness out of her mind.

Could he have killed her mother? Just to expand his arcade business? Summer hated the bloody arcade, but it did bring a lot of people to the boardwalk. Sometimes mothers brought their kids to the arcade and then wandered over to Beach Reads to browse.

"I see you've been reading *Nights at Bellamy Harbor.* What do you think?" Agatha said with a glimmer in her eyes.

That was a loaded question. Summer had never read a commercial romance in her life. She was a classics person all the way around and had been vocal about people filling their brains with trashy books. She drew in a breath. "It's not as bad as I imagined it would be." Truth was, she found it entertaining, but Summer wasn't ready, quite, to admit that yet.

Piper laughed. "Told you the romance genre isn't quite what it used to be. The female characters are strong, feminist types a lot of the time. I relate to them. The romances from when we were kids? Not so much."

"All those heaving bosoms," Agatha said and laughed.

"Not to mention the consent issues. Men just helped themselves apparently."

Summer rolled her eyes. Men. She'd not had a man in her life for at least a year. It just never seemed to work out for her. According to Doc Gildea, it was unusual for a woman who grew up without a father to not feel an immense need for men in her life. Summer filled that void in herself with education and independence.

But men? No, she'd not been able to manage a relationship for longer than six months.

Maybe she'd take after her mother. Just have lovers, no real commitment. But even that didn't happen for her. She didn't have the time to manage any kind of relationship.

"What next?" Agatha said. "Have we found any more clues to who may have killed Hildy?"

"Nothing."

"It has to be Rudy, right?" Piper said. "Who else?"

Summer shivered. "I just don't know where else to look."

"Tomorrow, we need to look in the bookstore. Her office," Piper said.

That was the best idea Summer had heard in a long time.

Chapter Twelve

B each Reads was still closed after Hildy's death. She'd be turning over in her grave if she had one. Summer had said she'd help Agatha and Piper out, but none of them had taken any steps forward to open the store.

The three of them entered the shop, keeping the lights off so no confused customers would come traipsing in. They moved through the front end of the store into the back end, where unopened boxes of books were piled in haphazard stacks.

"Someone has been letting shipments in," Piper said.

"Maybe Poppy."

"Yeah, I'll call her. We need help to get this organized."

Summer drew in the scent of cardboard and books. A scent of full of memory. One task she loved to help her mom with was opening the boxes—it was almost as good as Christmas. Even though she didn't like the books, she adored the spectacle of the covers.

"There's magic in those boxes," Hildy would say. "There's nothing better than a good book."

As a child, Summer imagined fairy dust, mermaids, unicorns, and sparkles every time her mom said those words. As an adult, she imagined words, pages, and beautifully fashioned leather-bound books. *Okay, maybe some fairy dust sprinkled within.* She smiled to herself.

The three of them made their way to Hildy's office, in between the full cardboard boxes.

Summer opened the door, expecting to find what Hildy had always called her "happy mess." Instead, it was tidy and smelled as if it had just been cleaned.

"What is this?" Summer asked.

Agatha shrugged. "She'd been trying to be more organized, but I didn't know it had gotten this far."

"It's freaky," Piper said. "I don't like it."

Summer turned around. Three hundred and sixty degrees. "It's almost as if it's not her office."

"Where are the stacks of files?" Piper asked.

"In the filing cabinet?" Agatha shrugged and banged on the thing. She opened a drawer. The three of them peered inside at the neatly labeled and vertically stacked files. "I don't understand it."

"Right?" Summer said. "Mom didn't do this. Come on. I love her. But she was . . ."

"Organized in her own way. But nobody else could make sense of it," Agatha finished the statement.

"It must be Poppy. She's been working here awhile."

"Well, I suppose it doesn't matter," Summer said. "Should we just divide the files?"

"What are we looking for again?" Piper cocked an eyebrow. "Another one of those notes?"

"Yes, and anything odd, like . . . I don't know . . . offers on the bookstore."

"Or uncashed checks. Wouldn't that be nice?" Agatha said and grinned.

"You're dreaming now," Summer said. Her mom went through money as quickly as she could get her hands on it. "It's for spending. That's what is for!"

Agatha reached in and grabbed a handful of folders, handed it to Summer, then did it again for Piper and herself. The three of them sat at Hildy's old desk. Piper flipped on the radio. They sorted through the files to the sound of Billy Joel, Madonna, and Elton John.

"I'm not finding anything. Just boring stuff. Receipts from publishers, bills for website design—that kind of thing," Piper said.

Summer glanced up at her and a photo caught her eye. "Look at that, would ya?" She reached for it. A photo of her and her mom walking on the beach. Summer wished she remembered the day this photo was snapped, or the circumstances, or who snapped it. But she didn't. Her mom looked happy and peaceful, and Summer grinned up at the photo. "Did you take this picture?" She showed it to Agatha.

"I doubt it. How am I supposed to remember something that specific?"

Piper examined it. "Doesn't look like our beach. Maybe this is on the other side of the island." She set the photo down and kept sorting through files.

"I don't remember ever going over there. But that doesn't mean we never did."

"Here's something interesting," Agatha interrupted. "An offer for the bookstore. But it was made five years ago. This probably has no bearing on anything today."

"Maybe they came back. What's their name?" Summer took down all the contact information. She'd definitely follow up.

"Marilyn and Glads are coming over to help with the stock," Piper said, holding up her phone, which had just gotten a text messages from them.

"Fabulous. There's just too much of it for us," Agatha said. "This exercise doesn't appear to be getting us anywhere." she dropped a folder.

"We need to keep looking," Summer said, opening the next file, which had a few letters from someone named Rita Mae Elison. As she read the letters over, she figured that Rita was a romance author who had visited the bookstore. "Letter from Rita Mae Elison."

"Oh, she was such a wonderful author and person. She died a few years back."

"Why would Mom be saving her notes?"

"She was just so nostalgic," Agatha said. "She saved everything from every author she'd ever met."

They continued sorting. When they reached the end of their piles, Summer stood and gathered all of the folders. "Nothing interesting, not even any more notes from authors."

Piper opened the drawer for her. "I think it's suspicious. Like someone came in here and cleaned up after she died. To hide something maybe."

"Could be," Agatha said. "But we've two more drawers to look through and then the boxes in the basement."

"Basement?" Summer's heart jumped. Spiders lived in basements. Summer didn't do basements.

"Don't worry, we'll bring the boxes upstairs."

"No! The spiders will travel in them," Summer said in a harsher voice than she intended. "You two will have to take care of it."

Agatha and Piper exchanged looks. They didn't have to say anything. Summer's cheeks heated, aware of what they were thinking—what everybody thought: Why is she so frightened of spiders?

Chapter Thirteen

"Where's your third wheel?" Agatha asked as Glads and Marilyn walked into the office.

"Doris's husband isn't having a good day," Glads said. "She needed to stay with him."

"What does that mean?" Summer asked, shoving the last of the folders from the second file drawer into the drawer. "Is he ill?"

Marilyn reached over the desk to where a group of box cutters hung on a nail. "Yes. Very bad. Who cleaned up in here?" She walked back out of the office.

"We were hoping you'd know." Summer said, following her into the storeroom, with her own box cutters in hand.

"No. I was here a couple of days before Hildy—" She stopped when Summer's eyes met eyes met hers. "I'm sorry." She plunged the box cutter into the seam of the box and yanked open a box flap, then pulled out brightly colored books. "Oh, it's the new Jessica Walters." She held it up as the bright sunflowers tattooed on her forearms caught the light. "I've been waiting for this one."

Summer opened another box full of books with bright covers and cats. "Must be a cozy mystery."

"They're so much fun!" Piper said as she came into the storage room. "I love a good cozy."

Summer held her tongue. As far as she was concerned, the word *cozy* was enough to put her off. Then again, she felt the same way about most popular fiction and hated romances. But she had to admit to a slight warming up to the book she was reading for her mom's book club. *Nights at Bellamy Harbor* was very well written, which she hadn't expected at all. There was no flowery language. No out-of-date euphemisms. And the main female character was kick-ass.

"Hand me those books, Summer," she half-heard a voice say. "Summer Merriweather? Where are you?"

"Right here. Just daydreaming a bit." She smiled. About *Nights at Bellamy Harbor* she kept to herself. Piper and Agatha would never let her live it down. She'd been so vocal and adamant about "trashy" books in her youth. Um. And maybe just last year at Christmas. She aspired to be one of those magnanimous teachers and people. You know, the kind who would say, "As long as your son or daughter is reading" . . . but no . . . just no. Her philosophy: Read the good stuff. You have so much time on this planet, don't fill your head with badly written books.

However, *Bellamy Harbor* was . . . not bad.

"They're too clean for me," Marilyn said. "I like sex and violence. Love me some good romantic suspense."

Summer flinched at the word *sex* coming out of the town librarian's mouth. She didn't know why. It wasn't as if she hadn't seen her dancing naked around in a circle of women.

"And I love the new dark suspense books," Marilyn said as she opened the box. "Although I do like a few cozy series too. I like a good puzzle to solve."

"Then solve this." Agatha entered the room with another sheet of black construction paper. "Look what I found."

"Not another one," Summer said.

"Hildy didn't pay any attention to them," Glads said. "But I wish she had." Her jaw stiffened. "She and Doris both considered it a joke. I told them she should go to the police."

"I agreed," Marilyn said.

"Doris?" Summer imagined her in her mind's eye: pink-haired, double-chinned. "Why would Mom listen to her over you two, her most trusted friends?"

They exchanged glances and went back to work. Enough said. Or not said, as it were.

Out of the mouths of babes . . . or old women, as the case may be.

"*Oh time, thou must untangle this knot. It is too hard a knot for me to untie!*" Summer said in sarcastic jest.

The two women looked as if they'd been caught with their hands in the till, not in a box of books. But they said nothing.

"If you don't have anything nice to say, it's best to not say anything at all," Piper said, allowing them to exhale and go back to work.

"Something is rotten in Denmark," Summer muttered.

"I've never been to Denmark," Agatha said. "They say it's lovely this time of year." She giggled and walked out the room with an armful of books. "I'm off to shelve these books. It's Piper's favorite shifter series!"

"What?" Piper lifted her head. "Bring those back." She dropped what she was doing and ran after her mother into the store.

Summer smiled and shook her head. Those two would never change. And she wouldn't want them to.

She mulled over what they'd learned today, and tried to process and come up with a plan. They'd found another note, an offer on the bookstore, and—most telling of all—her mother's office was neater than she'd ever seen it. Evidently it was still a mess a few days before Hildy had died. Summer figured someone had come in the day of or the day after and cleaned up. But why?

"Why would someone clean Mom's office?" she said out loud to no particular person.

Marilyn shrugged. "They were being nice. People sometimes go in and clean a house when someone is sick or dies. Maybe that's it."

"But wouldn't someone know about it? Who would?"

"We can ask Poppy when we find her."

Summer's heart skipped a few beats. "You can't find her?"

"We've not seen her since the funeral. She took it pretty hard," Glads said. "Well, we all did." Arms full of books, she left the room for the front end of the store.

"It may be crazy"—Marilyn shrugged—"but maybe someone wanted to hide something that was in the office."

"You know what, Marilyn? That's exactly what I was thinking. I just didn't express it."

"'*You know you've got to express yourself, hey, hey, hey!*'" She sang a Madonna song.

Once again, Summer marveled at how strange her life had gotten, unpacking books she didn't care for in her mother's bookstore, discussing scenarios for her murder—and then a Madonna song enters the picture, sung by the town librarian with floral tats all over her body.

Summer grinned. A tableau her mom would have greatly appreciated.

Chapter Fourteen

Agatha and Piper meandered into the basement to sort out the books and files there, leaving Summer alone with Glads and Marilyn, who were unpacking and stacking books like pros. And every once in a while, Marilyn whooped and wiggled to the music.

"Your mother always said dancing while you worked was the key to happiness."

"I remember that, Marilyn," Summer said and smiled. She wasn't going to do a little two-step or the hustle or anything. Summer was all business.

"Hello, ladies." A male voice startled Summer. She looked up and saw Rudy.

"What are you doing here?" she asked.

"How did you get in?" Marilyn said, eyes slanted.

He laughed. "Door was open. You all need to be more careful." His patronizing tone was enough to make any thinking woman sick, let alone a feminist who'd just lost her mother, a very successful businesswoman.

"Perhaps, but you shouldn't be walking into a closed business," Summer said. "What can I help you with?"

"Help me?" He straightened, placing his hands on his hips. "Get the cops off my back. They came back over to question me about Hildy. She died of a heart attack. Why are they bothering me?"

Summer wanted to throttle him, to just blurt that out in front of Glads and Marilyn. "We still don't have the final autopsy results yet. We've got no idea what killed her."

"Listen, Rudy," Glads stepped from behind the box she was unpacking. "Everybody knows you and Hildy had words all the time. And we all know you wanted the bookstore."

"What's that got to do with anything?" He flailed his arms around. "She died of a heart attack. Unless there's something I don't know?"

Summer wanted him to leave. She didn't want the women to spread rumors or get strange ideas.

"It's best that you leave, Rudy. I don't want to discuss this here."

"Oh, you don't want to *discuss* this, hey?" he said, with air quotes around discuss. "Hoity-toity," he said, turning his back and storming out of the storeroom.

Hoity-toity. The word pierced through Summer. She blinked. That was it. That was the way most of her mom's acquaintances felt about her, wasn't it? She thought she was too good for them. Too smart. Too modern to live on St. Brigid. At home. Which is, after all, where she belonged. According to them. Her heart ticked in her chest as she felt her face heat.

She went back to work.

"Don't pay any attention to him," Glads said. "Sour grapes. That's all. Beach Reach is prime property. He wants it bad."

"Bad enough to kill?" Summer said without thinking.

Gladys and Marilyn both stopped what they were doing and looked at Summer.

"What's going on here?" Agatha said, interrupting the moment—for which Summer was grateful.

"We're just about done," Summer said.

"I see that. You've been busy."

"I'm so glad you didn't come downstairs," Piper said. "I killed about three spiders."

Summer's heart sped. "Good. Nasty little buggers."

"You missed Rudy," Glads said.

"Rudy was here?" Agatha squealed.

"I guess the police have been visiting him again," Summer said.

"But why?" Glads said. "Why Rudy? Do they think he—"

"I don't know what they think. I mean it's Ben Singer, right?" Summer tried to laugh it off. She wasn't sure what her mom's oldest friend would say about her mom's possible murder. She wasn't sure how to tell them.

And besides, even though she hated to admit it, they both were suspects. All the clues—as scant as they were—pointed to someone close to Hildy. It seemed a very personal gesture.

"Ben Singer always gave your mother a hard time, but I had a feeling that deep down he liked her," Glads said, reaching for her bag. "I'm off for a dinner date with my grandson."

"Nice," Agatha said. "Enjoy it now. When they get to be teens they don't have time for you."

As the women exchanged platitudes about grandparenting, Summer's mind was focused on Rudy. He just looked like a nondescript sort. Old man. Jowly, shaky double chin, thin lips, and beady eyes. There was something about the set of his jaw that troubled her. Something that made her spine cold.

Chapter Fifteen

After all the sorting and lifting and shelving, Summer didn't think she'd have a hard time sleeping tonight. Even Piper and Mia turned in early. Summer must have fallen asleep almost the minute her head hit the couch pillow. She dreamed of dusty storerooms and old leather books. Smoking. *Smoking?*

Summer's coughing woke her. Was she still dreaming? She fought for breath. Fought for sight. What was going on?

"Fire!" Someone's voice said.

"Piper?"

"Get Mr. Darcy!" Someone said.

"Call nine-one-one!"

Summer still coughed, realizing the reason she couldn't see. Smoke. It was everywhere.

"Summer, get out now!" Arms came out of the smoke.

The three of them, plus the bird, escaped the house just as the fire trucks were arriving.

They huddled together and watched as the firefighters tamed the fire, its flames small but menacing.

"Oh my God," Agatha said. "Thank goodness we escaped."

"Fire!" Mr. Darcy said.

Summer's head and lungs cleared. She wondered why the smoke alarm hadn't gone off. Had her mother kept good batteries in it?

"I don't understand," Summer managed to say. "How could this happen?"

"I expect the fire chief will tell us what happened," Agatha said.

"It may just be some fluke," Piper said, voice thick with emotions.

"Mom has a smoke alarm," Summer said. "Did either of you hear it?"

"No," Piper said.

A firefighter approached them, holding the fire alarm. "Looks like there were no batteries in this."

They all stood agape. That didn't seem correct. Hildy was a freak about fires. Very careful.

"I don't understand," Summer said. "This is my mom's place. She was always very careful about the smoke alarm."

"Maybe someone took the batteries out," Piper said. "There's been a lot of people in and out since her funeral."

"Brings up a good point," the firefighter said. "Whoever set this fire wasn't a pro."

Summer's heart felt as if it would burst out of her chest. Agatha gasped.

"Someone set the fire?"

"Most assuredly." He shook his head. "And they were sloppy about it too."

"Why would someone do that?" Piper said. "I don't understand."

"Did she have an insurance policy?"

"Of course she did."

"Who is the beneficiary?"

"I don't know, do you?" Agatha looked at Summer.

"Probably me," Summer said.

He took Summer in. "And you were in the house when it caught fire."

"Sleeping," Summer said.

"You'll be asked to give a statement," he said.

Great. She'd have to talk with Ben again, and she hated that. So much. He made her feel like an ashamed little girl. But she had witnesses, didn't she? They couldn't pin this on her. As Summer mulled over everything and her mind cleared, it hit her like a stone-cold thud. Someone had tried to burn down her childhood home. Why? There was something going on here. Had the person who set the fire also killed her mother? Were they trying to kill Summer? What would be the point to that? What was the point to any of it?

"The place will be okay," the chief said. "Significant smoke damage. You'll need to stay somewhere else."

"We can stay at my place," Agatha said.

Piper slipped her arm around Summer. "Are you thinking what I'm thinking?"

"What?"

"Someone was trying to kill you," she said. "Someone deliberately disabled the smoke alarm."

A disheveled Rudy stumbled along toward them, looking as if he'd just rolled out of bed, and he probably had, given that it was three in the morning.

"What's happened? Are you okay?" He approached them, visibly shaken.

"We're fine," Piper said.

"Oh, thank God," he said. "I heard the sirens and wondered what the hell was going on."

Evidently others had heard it too, as a small crowd was gathering on the beach, dressed in various states of disarray. Some were in bathrobes.

"I'd hate for anything to happen to you," Rudy said to Summer. "Your mother . . . would kill me if I let anything happen to you."

"What happens to Summer is none of your concern," Agatha said.

His mouth flung open. "Agatha—"

"I mean it, Rudy. You've got no business here."

"I just wanted to help," he said.

She stared him down.

He turned to Summer. "If you need anything at all, please let me know. I'm happy to help. Despite what Agatha thinks, I didn't hurt your mother. I never would." He paused. "I loved her."

The roaring hush of the waves filled Summer as she examined him. He was sincere. Suddenly a warmth spread through her. Summer realized that this man had harbored feelings for her mom, even though they had seemingly been enemies over the years. Was he one of her mom's many lovers? Could he be . . . her biological father? He had blue eyes and sandy hair. She doubted it, with her large almost black eyes and thick black hair.

Agatha wasn't having it. Wasn't having his sympathy. "We don't need your help."

He shrugged.

"Thank you, Rudy," Summer said.

What more did Agatha know about Rudy? Summer made a mental note to ask. It was clear something had happened between them—or between Hildy and him.

Rudy shot Agatha look of disgust before he walked off.

"Well," Agatha said, "we should be going. Let's go over to my place and try to get some rest."

"Away from all the gawkers," Piper said.

More people had come along. Odd since it was in the middle of the night.

Suddenly, Doris came hobbling up to them. "What's going on? Are you okay?"

She was dressed in black sweatpants and a T-shirt. But her hair still looked great. She must use a lot of hair spray. It struck Summer as odd because she had noticed the bedhead of most of the community members.

"We're just on our way to my home to get some rest," Agatha said.

"Good idea," Doris said. "Shall I bring you some cinnamon rolls in the morning?"

"Please don't bother. I have some I just picked up from the grocery store," Agatha quipped.

Chapter Sixteen

S ummer had gotten very little sleep, but she gave up trying and
went for a walk on the beach around sunrise. She used to do
this when she stayed at home as a student. It helped clear her mind
to focus on whatever paper she was writing or book she was reading.

She had thought this was the only part of living here that she
missed. But last night, the risk of losing her childhood home, her
mother's tiny beach cottage, filled her with fear and dread. Why?
She'd planned to sell it anyway, hadn't she?

Then there were the people. Her life had become so full of other
academics and students that she'd somehow forgotten the kindness
of St. Bridget's people.

She walked along the edge of the surf in her bare feet as the sun
rose and its colors streamed across the sky. Soft blue. Bright orange
and golden yellows.

She glanced up along the beach's edge, toward a dune. She may
have sat at the very dune when a teenager.

She made her way to it and sat down, breathing in the salty air.

Someone killed my mother. And someone tried to kill me.

After searching her heart last night, she didn't think she had
anything to fear from Rudy.

So who wanted the bookstore and or her mom's house so badly they were willing to kill for it?

Who was interested in buying the shop? Several people had mentioned it to her. Someone had said she should offer it to the member of the book club. She'd mention it when attending the meeting on Wednesday.

If only the police would listen about the murder claim. She recalled the phone number she'd written down of the person who'd made the offer five years ago. Maybe they'd know something. Anything might help.

She brightened a bit when she remembered the fire chief. He might be the only hope of getting the police involved so that they'd take all of this seriously. It was clear the fire was started by someone—an amateur. Someone who had been in her mom's house and disabled the smoke alarm.

Who was in the house?

Agatha, Mia, Doris, Marilyn, Rudy, Piper, Glads, and herself.

Were there others Agatha allowed in to deliver food?

She needed to check with her.

Doris, Glads, and Marilyn were dear friends of her mom's. She couldn't imagine any one of them hurting a fly, let alone killing someone.

"There you are," Piper said as she came up alongside Summer. "I thought I might find you here. Breakfast is ready."

"Thanks."

"What happened last night was pretty wild," she said.

"Yeah," Summer said. "I couldn't wait to resolve matters with the estate and get that place sold, along with the bookstore. But now I'm not so sure."

"What? Someone tries to kill you, so you want to stay?" Piper joked. She tucked her hair behind her ears. Wispy blonde hair Summer had always envied.

"Something like that," Summer said and grinned.

"My mom's been on the phone all morning with various book club members—all wanting to make sure everything's okay. Sometimes I think they butt in a little too much."

"I used to feel that way too." Yes, the Mermaid Pie book clubbers were all up in each other's business. Summer didn't like it. And had taken the exact opposite tact in her life. She kept to herself. She had a few friends, but certain topics were off limits for sharing. The kind, she supposed, that forged good girlfriends.

But thinking about her mom and her life, the book group had been the one constant. Men came and went—so did other friendships. But those women always survived. Together. Summer found herself thankful Hildy had had these women in her life.

"Now, I don't know. It seems like these women cared about her. So I'm perplexed."

"God, the book group has been going on for years. She and Marilyn started it what—twenty-five years ago?"

"Marilyn? I don't know why I thought it was Doris."

"No, Doris is the newbie. She's only been in the club a few years. She's from Richmond. Not local," Piper said. "She makes a mean mermaid pie. I always look forward to the meeting when it's her turn to make the pie."

Summer had almost forgotten about that tradition. Each meeting was another member's turn at making the pie—a fluffy, sugary pie that Hildy had made for the first meeting, coming up with the name on her own. Summer shifted her thoughts from pie—a daunting task to be sure. "Have you talked to Mia?"

"Yes, and told her to stay where she is. That things would be crazy here today. It's best for her to stay out of the way.

"I'm guessing the chief and the cops will be along today."

"Yes, and god knows who else."

A hunger pang jabbed at Summer. "We better get fortified then." She stood.

"Yes, *something wicked this way comes.*"

Summer chuckled. "Macbeth? Really?"

"Sometimes, I feel like I'm living a Shakespearean farce," she muttered.

"Better than a tragedy," Summer said.

The two cousins walked arm and arm back to Agatha's home, a couple blocks away from the beachfront. Not many people were out and about this early. Summer was glad—she was certain she was as dreadful looking as she felt.

A shower, breakfast, and plenty of coffee were called for.

A cop car and another official-looking car sat in front of Agatha's home.

"Already here. See I told you," Piper said. "Wicked."

"I'm hoping that now they will look more seriously into Mom's death."

"You'd think they'd have to, considering the fire."

Fire Chief Levi Jensen grimaced when he saw Summer and Piper coming. But Ben Singer sneered.

"Well, Ms. Merriweather, have you gone from stealing hearts to arson?" he said.

"Now hold on—" Chief Jensen said, grimacing.

"I'm not sure what you're accusing me of Singer, but you better get your ducks in a row before you start making accusations."

"Besides, as I told you, she was asleep," Agatha said.

"People lie to police all the time, Agatha. Check yourself."

"Honestly!" Piper wailed. "Summer was sleeping. Someone set her childhood home on fire. What you should be asking is who would do such a thing. And perhaps it was the same person who'd killed Hildy."

"What?" Jensen said as Ben guffawed.

"Calm down, please," Agatha said to Piper. "Let's just look at this logically. Why would Summer burn down her home?"

Home. The word rolled around in Summer and settled in the center of her chest. Was the place still her home? After all these years of thinking Staunton was now her home, maybe she was wrong.

"The truth of the matter is, evidence does not point to Summer or either of you," came a voice of reason from the fire chief. "It's clear you all were in bed when the fire started."

He looked directly at Summer when he said *bed*, which made her blush. Just a little.

"Someone was definitely outside the house and worked to start the fire from there," he said.

Summer looked at Singer. "What did you think of that?" One eyebrow lifted.

He didn't answer.

"There are all kinds of reasons people start fires. This may not have had anything to do with you personally," the chief said. "When we find the arsonist, we'll call you."

"Do you ever find arsonists?" Piper asked, blinking at the handsome firefighter.

"Sometimes. It's easier to find an amateur arsonist than it is to find a murderer."

Piper's eyes slanted, and she looked at Summer. A chill traveled through Summer. Perhaps this fireman would turn this investigation around. Maybe her mom's killer would be caught and justice found. Was it too much to hope for?

"Do you see much arson in St. Brigid?" Summer asked.

"From time to time. But we see little fire here at all. We consider that a success. We keep busy with our education programs and fundraisers so that when we do have a fire, we know how to fight them and to investigate the cause of them." He stood, nodded to Ben Singer, and turned to Summer. "I'm so sorry about all of this, Ms. Merriweather. We'll do our best for you."

Something about the confident glint in his green eyes told her he would.

Chapter Seventeen

After the law left, the three women sat down to a huge breakfast prepared by members of the book club and brought over by Marilyn; Summer was liking her more and more.

"Why don't you stay?" Summer said.

"Oh, I can't, but thanks for offering," she said. "I'm on my way to my hot yoga class."

Summer almost choked on her hash browns. "Hot yoga? In St. Brigid?" And the thought of Marilyn sweating and stretching in yoga poses gave her pause.

"Hell yes," Marilyn said. "The instructor is pretty hot himself. I may be old, but I ain't dead." She wriggled her eyebrows.

"The class is too hard for me," Piper said. "I've tried it once or twice. I like regular yoga. I just don't like all that heat. "

"Very good for the muscles," Marilyn said. "But I agree that it's not for everybody." She turned to go. "Bon appétit!"

"She's like a whirlwind," Agatha said after Marilyn left. "Your mother used to go to that class with her. Marilyn forced her to go the first few times. It was hard to get Hildy out of the bookstore for anything. But she started to love that class."

"Was this a new thing?" Summer asked, thinking her mom had never mentioned it to her. Her mom had practiced yoga her whole life, but hot yoga?

"I'd say she started it a few months ago," Agatha said.

"A person with a bad heart couldn't get through one of those classes," Piper said and stuffed a piece of biscuit in her mouth.

"No." Summer tapped her fingers on the table. "But if she had an underlying heart condition, a class like that could put her over the edge, right?"

The three of them sat silent for a few beats.

"I'd like to think my mom wasn't murdered."

"But look at what happened last night," Piper said. "Someone definitely tried to kill us."

"Your mother was in great shape. You should ask the teacher about her. She was one of his best pupils," Agatha said.

Summer grinned. *Of course she was. Mom had to be the best at whatever she did, didn't she?*

Her smile vanished. She had to face the reality. Someone had killed her mom. No matter how she tried to talk myself out of it. It seemed so clear to her. Why wasn't it clear to Ben?

"Who would've taken the battery out of Mom's smoke alarm? The only people in the house were book club members—you know, people bringing food in."

"That's the million-dollar question," Piper said. "One of them had to do it. I know I didn't. I'm certain Mia wouldn't even know how to do it. So that leaves the book club ladies."

Agatha made a noise of incredulity. "Those women loved Hildy. It makes little sense that one of them would want to burn down the house."

"Maybe Aunt Hildy started to replace the batteries and was interrupted and forgot. And never got back to it," Piper said.

"It's possible, I suppose. But she was so vigilant," Summer said.

"Indeed, she was," Agatha said. "We survived a house fire when we were kids. We are both vigilant."

"I never knew that," Piper said. "What happened?"

Agatha shrugged. "My dad was a stubborn old coot who insisted on making all the house repairs himself. Best that we figured out, he screwed something up with the electricity. We lost the house. But we all survived. Things were never the same for us after that."

"What do you mean?" Piper asked, as she slid her plate slightly away from her, as if to say "I'm done."

"Well, we did have insurance, but there were a lot of problems getting it, and by the time we'd gotten it, Mom had passed away. Dad never rebuilt. He bought a double wide with the money, and we moved into it."

Summer loved that place, with its neat flower gardens, above-ground pool, and front-porch swing. "I remember that place."

Agatha nodded. "Unless you'd grown up in a lovely Victorian home. It was hard on us. We were teenagers, lost our home, then our mother. Rough times."

Summer knew the story from there: Hildy set off for college with an undecided major and returned pregnant. Agatha stayed on in St. Brigid, took a home course on midwifery, got some training, and married an island boy—Summer's Uncle Fred. Lost at sea, years ago.

Everybody wondered where Hildy had gotten the money to open Beach Reads. But Summer always suspected it was her own long-lost, secret father who gave it to her. Hard to prove. She'd given up finding him years ago—nothing would upset her mother more than the subject of Summer's father.

Which reminded her.

"Aunt Agatha?"

"Hmm?"

"Who is my father? Is it Rudy?"

Agatha laughed uproariously. "No. He creeped your mom out."

"But he seemed very protective of me."

"He loved your mother and is aware of how much you meant to her. That's all, dear."

But Summer sensed an undercurrent of tension.

"What about her father?" Piper persisted. "Do you know who he is?"

Agatha's smile vanished. She quieted. "I have my suspicion, but no, I never knew. And Hildy wanted it that way."

"Suspicions?"

"Yes," she said in a clipped voice. "Let's just leave it at that."

Her tone made Piper and Summer look at each other in a sort of fear. There was more to this story, and perhaps it was best left untold for now. Another matter was more pressing. Hildy's life—and death.

"I don't think Rudy has it in him to kill anybody. I don't like him, but I can't imagine him killing. So I don't think Rudy killed her. Do either of you?" Summer said.

"No," Piper said.

"I'm not so certain," Agatha said and sighed. "But if he didn't do it, who did?"

Chapter Eighteen

After covering her face with her nylon mask, and the bedding with her special blanket, Summer tossed and turned in her aunt's guest bedroom that night, finally falling into a deep sleep. But not before she ticked off things she had learned about murder from reading up on the internet. One, the killer is almost always someone the victim knows—even someone in the family or a friend. In fact, family members were often the first suspects. That left Summer, Agatha, Piper, and Mia. An unlikely group. But Hildy had friends, mostly those book group ladies, and Summer planned to talk with each one of them alone.

She also wondered if her mother had had a boyfriend or someone she'd been seeing or just sleeping with, as her mom was wont to do. More so when she was younger, but she'd never given up her belief in free love.

Summer finally drifted off to sleep, only to dream of spiders.

She awakened with a sweaty start, in confusion. *Where* am I? A pink floral wallpaper wall with photos of Piper made her grin. Okay, she was at Aunt Agatha's home.

The scent of breakfast lured her downstairs, where all suspects gathered. Mia looked the most suspiciously murderous, with a scowl that could kill.

"Good morning," Summer muttered.

"Morning, dear," Aunt Agatha said. "Help yourself to some breakfast. You must load up on food. We have a full day of cleaning ahead of us."

"I thought they were going to bring in professionals," Summer said.

"They are, but they won't get in until Monday. I thought we should take the weekend to gather whatever valuables we can, along with the bedding and clothing, and get started on washing them."

"I've been reading that if you wash smoky clothes in mouth-wash, it will take the scent out," Piper said as she looked up from her computer.

"More coffee, please." Mia held her cup up as Agatha freshened everybody's coffee and poured Summer's first.

"Also, charcoal. I have a bag in the shed. I understand if we lay it around the house, it will absorb odors," Agatha said.

Summer's head was cloudy from not sleeping well and a lack of coffee. Piper and Aunt Agatha must have gotten up early and were ready to forge ahead. *I'm such a schlep.*

As Summer sipped her coffee, she remembered what she had planned to do today. Visit all of the book club members on the auspices of getting to know them better, when in reality she'd question them, slyly. But today she couldn't let Agatha, Piper, and Mia do all the dirty work, could she?

She moved over to the stove and filled her plate with cheesy scrambled eggs and sat back down at the table.

"I've been thinking about the possible murder suspects," Summer said after a few moments of quiet eating.

Everyone's attention focused on Summer. "The thing is, most people know their killers. Since we know nobody in this room killed Mom, I'll snoop around among her friends." Summer used air quotes around *friends*.

Agatha gasped. "I can't imagine!"

"That's what people have said throughout history about serial killers," Mia said. "They all seem like such nice quiet men, and there they were . . . killing over and over again."

"Okay, Mia," Piper said. "We get the picture. But I don't think Aunt Hildy was killed by a serial killer." She paused. "But you're right. Most murders are committed by people the victims knew. I thought about that last night. But all of those little old women in her book club? I don't know . . ."

"Certainly not!" Agatha said. "You can't go around accusing your mother's dearest friends of killing her." Her face reddened and her eyes watered.

"Okay, okay," Summer said. "First, I was planning to be very subtle about it. Second, if it wasn't her book club friends, who else? Was she seeing someone?"

"You mean a man?" Agatha stammered, setting her teacup down with a clank.

Summer nodded with her mouth pulled into a twist. She hated the idea of her mom seeing one of these old farts on the island.

"I don't think so," Agatha said. "But she didn't tell me everything."

"She told me she was done with old men," Mia said. "She liked young ones."

Summer blinked that image out of her brain, but not without some trouble. "But was she seeing a younger man?"

"No," Mia said, shrugging. "If she was, she'd didn't tell me."

Thank god for small favors. Piper's eyes met Summer's. They were thinking the same thing. Both were glad that Hildy hadn't told Mia the sordid details of her love life, the way she sometimes had with them. But years later, she'd laughed it off, saying she had just been kidding, that she'd never seen half the men she'd told them about.

"I liked telling stories," she'd said. "I still do. Let me tell you about the man who—"

"No!" They'd both scream at the same time.

Summer finished her eggs and coffee, and walked upstairs to change into the sweatpants and T-shirt Aunt Agatha had laid out—just like the good old days.

She glimpsed her haggard self in the mirror. Summer didn't recognize the reflection gazing back at her—but she looked nothing like her beautiful mom, sorry to say. She breathed in deeply. She'd probably never learn who it was she resembled, assuming it was her mysterious, unknown biological dad, but she knew and loved her mom. She owed her justice, if nothing else. And even though Aunt Agatha considered it a terrible gesture, Summer vowed to speak with her book club members. Just not today, evidently.

Chapter Nineteen

T he good news was that the fire had barely touched the house. Most of the damage was smoke, which was bad enough. Summer, Agatha, Mia, and Piper spread bowls of charcoal around the place, dumped books in bins of rice and covered the containers in the hope that the scent would vanish and gathered clothes and bedding. They were all getting headaches and called it a day.

"Have you opened the bookstore yet?" Piper asked as we were loading the second or third round of clothes into a washer at the laundromat. Aunt Agatha's washer was not big, and besides, she didn't want to drag all the smoke smell into her home. Summer couldn't blame her.

"No. I should," Summer said. It wasn't as if she'd been putting it off. She'd been busy. Her attention was focused first on the funeral, then the realization that her mom had been killed and trying to figure out who did it, then the fire. She'd been way too busy to open the bookstore—even if it was her mother's pride and joy. It wasn't as if she wanted any of the books in there, although she had to admit she was enjoying *Nights at Bellamy Harbor*. Kind of. And was slowly starting to see the appeal of a happy ending, which every romance novel gave readers. *If only life could give that to you.*

"Everything is under control," Agatha said. "Poppy would be happy to open, if you don't want to."

"I need to think about that."

"I can't believe how the mouthwash just zapped the smoke scent right out of these towels," Piper said as she folded the last of her pile.

Marilyn and Doris bounded into the laundromat.

"We bought you a little lunch," Marilyn said.

How did she know Summer was famished? How did they track them down?

"Thanks, girls," Agatha said. These women had not been girls in fifty years. At least.

"I'm starving!" Mia said, as she shut the door of the mammoth dryer, which held several loads of clothes.

Chicken-salad sandwiches on whole-wheat bread had never tasted so delicious.

Summer drank from her bottled water as she sat on the bench next to Marilyn.

"How are you holding up, dear?" Marilyn said.

"I've got to admit. I'd be better without all the drama of the fire and the smoke."

Marilyn nodded.

"How long did you know Mom, anyway?" Summer asked. Nonchalant.

"We grew up together," Marilyn said. "I'm a few years older than your mother, but we lived next door and liked similar music and books." She laughed at what seemed like a private joke. "We used to sneak our mothers' romances out, then trade with each other when we were done. We talked for hours and hours about those books."

"How did you find out about her death?" Summer said.

"Well, that's an odd question."

"It's just that I'm trying to make sense of things. I want to know, like, were you with her? Was anybody?"

"Oh no, dear. I was out of town when it happened. My husband and I traveled to Charleston for a few days. Agatha called me, sobbing, and we cut our trip short."

"Had Mom been sick or anything?"

"No," she said and sighed. "I'd always considered her the healthiest one of all of us. She walked every day, did yoga classes, and was a strict vegetarian."

It wasn't just Summer who thought she'd been healthy.

She was on the right track. "You know someone tried to kill me. Someone set the house on fire. Whoever it was is going to get caught."

"I hope so. Why would someone do that? If they were trying to kill you, why? How stupid. And mean," she replied.

"I think whoever killed Mom wants me dead too," Summer said in almost a whisper.

Marilyn's heavy-lidded eyes widened into saucers. "What? You think someone killed your mother?" Her voice was also a whisper. One eyebrow lifted. "Have you told Ben?"

Summer nodded. "Please keep this to yourself." She finished her sandwich. "I found threatening notes. Someone wanted the bookshop—wanted her out of the way and figured I'd sell the minute she died."

"We all figured that, dear," Marilyn said.

"You all figured wrong," Summer said, standing, hoping she'd stirred up enough with that conversation to get the rumor mill churning. After talking with Marilyn, she mentally checked her off her list of possible suspects. She'd been in Charleston with her husband. "I'm keeping the bookstore."

She didn't even realize it herself until that moment. Whether she'd run the place, she didn't know. But she wasn't giving it to whoever wanted it—the person who most likely had killed her mother and tried to kill her.

She might go back to Staunton and teach, if she still had a job. But she would always come back here—and always keep the store and the house. Bill collectors be damned. She'd figure out another way. Maybe she'd rent the house or use it as an Airbnb.

Agatha handed her a basket of more towels to fold. "Why did Mom have so many towels and sheets? She lived alone. Why did she need all of these?"

Agatha turned around and gave her the once-over. "She always imagined you'd come home, and she wanted to be prepared."

A hollow feeling erupted in the center of Summer's chest and sank like a stone to her stomach. Breathe. Breathe. Breathe. She slipped out of the laundromat. *Air. Please.*

Chapter Twenty

Mom had thought she'd be back, which tore at Summer's heart. Her mom had died while not speaking to her because she was so angry and ashamed at Summer for running away from a sticky situation. "I didn't raise you to be a coward." Yet she stocked up on towels and bedding just in case Summer moved back. Her mom must have forgiven her in her own way but just hadn't gotten around to telling Summer.

But what would make her think she'd leave her dream job teaching Shakespearean literature to return home to the island? She'd worked so hard at getting that job, then getting tenure, with the constant push to publish constantly. She loved every minute of the research, writing, and teaching. Shakespeare fired up her synapses—she adored turning students on to him. It was just that academia wasn't as inviting as she had hoped.

So, was her mom afraid she'd get fired and preparing for the inevitable? Or was she just living in her own mother dream world, hoping that someday her wayward daughter would return home to St. Brigid?

She'd never know now. Maybe her mom had had a premonition. She'd always had them—and most of the time they were right. Summer girded her loins, almost certain she'd lose her job.

Mom and her premonitions. Summer tried to recall a time when she was wrong and couldn't. Which used to irk her, but now it fascinated her. Was her mom one of the few real psychics in the world? She used to call herself a witch, but Summer, with the ignorance of youth, never paid much attention to what that meant or if she was serious. Her witchiness had something to do with a goddess and monthly meetings with a group of other women.

Now, Summer's mind sorted through the possibilities. Was her mom still a part of that witch group? If so, who were they? Would any of them know anything about the way her mother had died?

Agatha walked over to her. "Are you okay, dear?"

Summer was sitting on a bench looking out over the parking lot. She nodded. "It just comes in waves. The grief."

Aunt Agatha sat down beside her. "I know."

They sat quietly for a few beats.

"I thought getting some fresh air might help, but it didn't. I've been sitting here wondering why Mom thought I'd be back." Summer smiled a twitchy smile. "And then I remembered all of her premonitions."

"Yes," Aunt Agatha said. "Always on the money."

"Then I remembered her witch group."

Aunt Agatha sat straighter.

"I wondered if they might know something about her death."

"Like what?"

"I want to know details, like where was she when it happened. Who was with her?" Summer sucked in air. "Was she alone?"

"Summer," Aunt Agatha said in a singsong tone. "Are you certain you want to know those things?"

"I do," Summer said. "I hate the idea of her dying alone. Or of her spending her last breaths in the presence of a killer. Her killer."

"Here's what I know," Agatha said, lowering her voice. "She collapsed at the bookstore, surrounded by friends and customers. She was taken to the hospital, where she later died. I was there, along with Mia and Piper. Your mother left peacefully. It was as if . . . she had just gone to sleep."

Agatha shrugged. "As far as that goes, it was a good death." Her voice cracked. She swallowed. "But I don't for a minute think it was natural. We need to keep digging."

"What about the witches?"

"Oh, they disbanded years ago. Hildy became what she called a solitary practitioner. But she introduced some of the book club ladies to her practices. I think you'll see proof of them on Wednesday."

"Are any of the witches still around?"

"One, I think. She lives over near the coves in a small rock house. Name's Posey. She was not at your mother's funeral, which I found odd since they were close. But perhaps they had a falling out."

Summer's right eyebrow lifted. "Maybe they quarreled, and she killed Mom."

Agatha shook her head. "I doubt it. These witchy women are all about gentle ways. Taking care of the earth, one another, the sacred feminine. You know? I doubt Posey ever harmed anything."

A good friend of Hildy's who didn't go to the funeral? Well, to be fair, Summer wouldn't have gone either, except Hildy was her mom, and if she didn't go, it would look horrible. But Mom would not have wanted a funeral in a church. Too patriarchal for her.

Perhaps Posey was honoring her by not going. Or maybe she didn't want to show her face because she'd killed her.

Okay, that was a stretch. But then again, it was all beginning to feel like a not very well plotted mystery novel.

Chapter Twenty-One

S ummer told the others she'd meet them back at the house. She wanted to walk.

"Do you need company?" Piper asked.

"Thanks, but I don't think so."

Summer needed to mull things over alone. Sort it out.

Who had killed her mother and tried to kill her?

Her head was spinning. Was any of it real?

As she turned onto the beach, the sky opened up. No buildings in view—only sand and sky and ocean. Hildy always said the beach healed. *Take your problems to the beach.* And Summer had. But this was more than a problem. More than a decision over what college to attend. Or which boy to go to the prom with. Or whether to get married. This was life and death and justice. Summer wanted to be careful. She wanted to nail whoever had stolen her mother's life. The person who took her mother away from her.

She slipped off her shoes and relished the warmth of the sand. Her hair blew in the wind. She drew in the scent of the sea air as she walked, one foot in front of the other.

At one point in her life she'd known every sway and dip, every rock and cove on this part of the island. The patterns of the waves

on the sand helped to form her thought process. Clear away the cobwebs.

Rudy didn't kill her mother. She was certain about that, no matter what Aunt Agatha said. But what about the book club members? Aunt Agatha had felt certain none of them would harm Hildy. But people could surprise you.

Marilyn was in Charleston, so Summer scratched her off her suspect list. That left Glads and Doris, the members of the inner circle of the book club. Then there was Posey, the witch who suspiciously had not come to Hildy's funeral.

Summer needed to follow up with her investigation of the book club members, along with make a call to the people who'd made her mom an offer on the bookstore.

She'd approach this methodically, as if it were a research project. She'd try to keep her emotions out of this. Ben would need to be on board at some point. She drew in another breath, exhaled slowly. She needed to discern the official cause of Hildy's death. She wasn't buying a heart attack. Not at all.

She strolled by a group of women spread out on the beach, soaking in the sun. One laughed at the book she read. Summer checked it out—a cozy mystery. Of course. She'd bought it at Beach Reads.

She'd open the store back up soon. Maybe tomorrow? Perhaps the killer would come back to the scene of the crime. Surely, Aunt Agatha was right. The book club members wouldn't have offed Hildy. They loved her. Summer was being foolish. Emotional.

The killer may have been a customer, though. A disgruntled bookstore customer? Why hadn't she thought of that before? Some disturbed customer?

She walked along until the Agatha's house came into view, beyond the grassy dunes. It looked like there was a strange car sitting in the driveway. Who could that be?

As she drew closer, she saw that it was some kind of official car. Police?

A sun-kissed girl tended to a tiny sandcastle, meticulously. She was covered in sand but intent on the castle, lining up seashells along its edges.

A Frisbee flew overhead and a young man ran to catch it. Summer narrowly escaped a tackle.

"Sorry," he said. "Didn't want it to conk you in the head." He smiled a flashy grin.

"No worries." She kept moving.

The scent of beer and body odor emanated from him, and she found it distasteful. She moved away from him fast to evade the stench.

* * *

She kept her eyes on the house as she drew closer to it. A seagull landed in front or her, almost as if it were trying to prevent her from moving ahead. She took in the bird and stopped walking. She didn't care what anybody said. They were beautiful creatures. Finally, it flew off with a caw to the breeze.

As she got closer to the house, she saw it wasn't a police car, but a fire car. Hmm. Her heart sped in anticipation. The fire chief must be there. Maybe, just maybe he'd found answers about the fire and who set it.

She picked up her pace.

Chapter Twenty-Two

Levi, the fire chief, sat on Aunt Agatha's front porch, waiting for her.

He looked up at Summer and smiled. "I just wanted to inform you how things are progressing." His eyes took a long view of her.

"Do you visit all of your cases in person?" Aunt Agatha snipped.

"Uh, I try to," he said, smiling politely, ignoring her jab. Summer made a mental note to ask Aunt Agatha what that was all about.

Summer sat down on the porch swing. Aunt Agatha sat next to her.

"We've gotten some prints off the smoke alarm case," he said. "And they match the prints on the gasoline can we found on the beach."

"On the beach?" Agatha said.

"Yeah, looks like our perp is not a local. We're all aware that if your throw anything out there, it's going to come back around Robin's Point—and that's where we found it. The prints are subtle, but they're there and match up."

"So what does this tell us?" Summer asked.

"Just that whoever set the fire was in your mother's house and disconnected the alarm," he said, crossing his arms. "Unfortunately, we've not found any matches in the system."

"So it's a pointless exercise," Agatha said.

"No," he responded. "I'm confident we will start finding suspects, and when we do, we'll fingerprint them, which will be all the proof we need. I have a few questions for you, Ms. Merriweather."

"Call me Summer," she said, almost blushing. Not quite. He was, as they say, a very well put together man. And he seemed to like her, which hadn't happened in a long time. But perhaps he was just being professionally friendly.

"Okay, Summer," he said. "Who is the beneficiary on your mother's insurance?"

"I am."

"But you were in the house and would have died if the fire had escalated."

"Correct."

"So who would get the place if something happened to you?"

"I have no idea," Summer said. "We're still waiting on a meeting with Mom's lawyer, who might help."

"Usually these crimes are money based. You know? I can't tell you how many times fires are nothing more than insurance fraud. So I have to rule that out," he said. "I'll talk with your mother's lawyer."

"Good luck with that," Summer said. "We've been trying to get an appointment. He's a busy guy."

"He's one of two lawyers on the island," he offered. "But when he sees me coming, he always makes time."

I bet.

He cleared his throat. "The other question is, do you have any enemies on the island?"

Summer laughed. "I haven't lived here in years. But the only enemy I can think of is Ben Singer. He despises me."

"Welcome to the club," he said and grinned. "I know why he doesn't like me, but any reason he doesn't like you?"

Aunt Agatha touched my thigh.

"You go first."

"Singer is intimidated by me. I have a background in criminology, worked briefly for the FBI before I decided to investigate fires. He doesn't think I'm necessary here." His strong, square jaw angled upward.

"Knowing him, you're probably right," Agatha said. "Can I get you something to drink?"

"No, ma'am. I'd like to hear what Summer has to say."

"I broke his son's heart," she said after taking a deep breath. "I left him at the altar."

"But that was a long time ago, right?"

"It was, but the family has never forgiven me," Summer said. "I'm not sure they should. It was . . . unkind of me." She tried to smile at him, but failed when she saw disappointment plastered over his face.

"Oh, Summer," Agatha said in her soft voice, which reached in, boosting her.

"I handled it all wrong."

He sat forward, uncrossed his arms.

"But people like Singer have no idea what it's taken for me to be here today. Utterly ashamed."

"I never would've guessed," he said, glancing sideways at Summer. "But it adds depth to the possibilities."

"What do you mean?" Agatha said.

"Maybe someone on the island has a vendetta against you."

"Perhaps it's time I talked with Cash after all these years? To hold that against me?" Summer laughed.

He stood. "Don't laugh. Believe me. Stranger things have happened."

Stranger things, indeed. Summer's face heated at the thought of Cash. Shame. Guilt. Dread.

"More likely someone had a vendetta for my mom, since she's the one who was killed and it was her home they were trying to destroy. I doubt it has anything to do with me. I've not lived here in a very long time."

He stood, as if he were getting ready to leave. His brown eyes momentarily held a note of emotion. Compassion? Understanding? But he blinked a long, slow blink and turned his head before he walked away.

Chapter Twenty-Three

What a day. Summer couldn't wait to get back to her home, but in the meantime, she lay in Aunt Agatha's guest room, snuggled beneath a comforter. She didn't want to think about leaving Cash at the altar. She had just been too young to marry. But she might've handled it with compassion and maturity. Even so, she didn't think Cash was behind any of this. He was too lazy. It would take way too much effort for him to create notes and try to burn the place down, let alone kill someone.

She reached for *Nights at Bellamy Harbor*, and as she did so, she did it with a measure of disbelief. Was she actually reading a romance? A few years ago, she'd not have been caught dead doing so. She'd ranted against them.

But as she held the book in her hand and cracked it open, she felt a mix of comfort and excitement. Comfort perhaps because this very book had been in her mom's hands. She'd been reading it, thinking about it. Plus, no matter how difficult it looked for the characters, a happy ending was imminent. *You didn't get one of those in reality—might as well enjoy them on the pages.*

An alpha male who owned the development corporation and the smart, feminist conservationist? He was a Muslim, to boot.

Pleasing his family was everything to him. It drove the character. How was it going to work out?

As she read, her eyes grew heavy, and she slipped off, only to awaken with the sun the next morning, with the book splayed across her chest.

She stayed there for a few moments, planning her day: breakfast, bookstore, investigation. The next person on her list to talk to about her mom's death was Posey, the one person still around who used to be in her mom's women's group. She also needed to call this person who'd made an offer for the store several years ago. She'd call them from the bookstore.

* * *

When she entered the store, already opened by Poppy, one of her mom's employees, she was happy to see it crawling with customers.

"Hi," Summers said to Poppy. "I'm Summer. Pleased to meet you. How's everything going?"

"I'm so busy, I haven't gotten a chance to update the blog or to make more coffee," she said, exasperated.

"I'll make coffee and see about the blog. Don't worry about that," Summer said. Blog? Surely she'd figure that out. She had a PhD in Shakespearean lit, for God's sake.

A few women dressed in cover-ups, hats, and flip-flops lined up at the cash register.

"Where's Glads?" Summer asked.

"Doctor's appointment. She should be back soon."

Summer made her way to the empty coffeepot. She threw away the grounds and rinsed the basket out.

"You shouldn't throw all of those away," a voice from behind her said.

She turned to face a customer.

"Really? Why?"

"It's good for the garden."

"Garden? I don't have a garden . . . so . . ." She continued with dumping the coffee grinds.

The woman waved her hand. "I do, and if you want to save the grounds for me, I'll take them."

Summer scooped coffee into the filtered basket. She imagined saving all the grounds from their daily coffee and considered this woman might be a bit crazy.

"Are you a local?" Summer asked. "I don't recognize you."

"Yes, I've lived here for years. But this is the first time I've been to the bookstore. Very cute."

Cute? Hildy hated when people called the store cute. Summer herself didn't like the word. But as she looked at the new-age hippy gardener person standing next to her, she decided not to hold it against her. Yet. She seemed kind of . . . lost and forlorn. Heck, if she wanted the grounds, Summer could devise a way. Perhaps it would save the store some hassle. Track costs? Summer shrugged. "Okay, give me your number and I'll call you about the grounds." *Or not. We'll see.*

The woman dug into her crochet bag and produced a card with her name and phone number on it. She handed it to Summer, who stuck it into her pocket. "You'll hear from me soon."

"Thanks," she said, smiling. "Hildy used to give me all the grounds from here."

Summer's heart stopped. "You knew my mom?"

Her face broke into a smile. "Are you Summer? I've heard so much about you. I'm Rowan." She extended her hand.

Rowan? Should Summer know her? Something seemed familiar about the name.

"I'm so sorry about Hildy. I loved her. She was one of a kind."

Summer laughed. "Yes, she was. How did you know her?"

"I'm in the book club. I wasn't much into romances, but I like them now. And I adore the other members. I can't believe this is the first chance I've gotten to actually come into the store. Hildy used to bring me the books."

"Will you be at the meeting next Wednesday?" Summer asked as she flipped on the coffeepot switch.

Rowan nodded. Her dark blue eyes watered. "I'll be there."

"We'll see you then," Summer said. Here was a new book club member. How many were there now? She needed to find out.

Rowan wandered off into the shelves of books.

With the coffee brewing and the scent filling the store, Summer ambled into the backroom to make her phone call to Xanadu Corporation, to talk to the man who'd made Hildy the offer. And she also needed to call Posey, the one person left in the witch group, and she'd just added one more task—getting a roster of all the book club members.

Call Posey.

Contact Xanadu corporation.

Get a complete roster of book club members.

Call the school.

What? Where did that business about the school come from? She'd not call the school. She refused to go back with her tail between her legs. They said they'd call her—and she'd wait for it. Wouldn't she?

Chapter Twenty-Four

B each Reads was so full of people it was difficult for Summer to sneak away into the office to make a call. But she did.

She sat in her mother's desk chair and dialed Xanadu.

After she explained why she was calling, they transferred her call to a man named Rex Garfield.

"Yes, sure I remember Beach Reads. Great place. But I never could convince Hildy to sell," he said.

"When is the last time you tried?"

"Hmm. Let me think. Hang on. I can look that up. Do you mind holding?"

"Not at all." Summer's heart raced. He'd give her the information she needed. Just like that. He had nothing to hide. Apparently. Maybe this call wasn't such a good idea. Perhaps it would be a waste of time. No, she needed to make a proper deduction. Every new fact was a good one, as it freed her up to move on to the next item on the list.

"Summer? It looks like I contacted her a few months back. She said she'd had a few other offers but wasn't interested in them either."

Summer's heart raced even faster. "Any idea who the others were?"

"No. She mentioned that there were a couple of locals. One was an English teacher at the high school."

There was only one English teacher at St. Brigid High School. He wasn't difficult to track down. No, indeed.

"She said nothing about the other local?"

"Nothing that I wrote down, and my memory is not so great. That's why I write everything down."

"I see." Summer drew in a breath and slowly let it out. "Well, thanks so much for your time. I appreciate it. You've been a big help."

"Great. Hildy was a character. I'm going to miss her."

Character, indeed. *Oh, Mom, what kind of a mess did you get yourself into? Who did you anger so much that they killed you?* Henry Chadworth had always gotten under Summer's skin, even though they had a great deal in common, including their alma mater. But was he a killer?

Poppy poked her head into the office. "I need a break. Can you cover the register for me?"

So much for her next phone call. She sighed. It would have to wait. "Sure."

There was already a small line forming at the register, so Summer hopped behind the counter.

"Did you find everything you need?" Summer asked the first customer, a bleached blonde with blue eye shadow. Stuck in the 1970s by the looks of things.

"Yes, what a great bookstore," she said, sliding books toward Summer. Five books. An avid reader.

"Thank you," Summer said with something like pride filling her heart. *Whoa. Where did that come from?*

"This is my first time," she continued. "And I have to say I don't think I've ever been in a store where you can see how much the owner loves books. Just the whole vibe of the place."

"Mom worked hard at that," Summer said while scanning the books.

"Well, it's very clear." The woman reached into her bag and pulled out a bank card. Summer totaled her purchase.

"Are you here on vacation?"

"Yes, I'm here for two glorious weeks. I might return for more books." She handed Summer her card.

"We'll be here."

Two mysteries. Three romances. *What are people thinking? Why don't they read good books?* Summer bit her tongue.

"We come back every year," the next customer said while sliding her purchase onto the counter. "This year, I'm into the billionaires."

"I see that." Three books with the word *billionaire* in the title.

She batted her eyes. "Now, if only I could meet one."

Summer laughed. "I hear ya."

If only Summer could *be* one. She'd given up on finding any man, let alone a rich one.

An hour later, Poppy was still not back from her break, and Summer continued checking people out.

Piper sneaked in behind the counter. "Poppy's sick. She's not coming back today. She called me to help out."

"Oh boy. Just like old times."

Summer and Piper had worked every summer in the bookstore. They'd worked hard, but they'd also had a blast.

"I'm here to give you a break."

"Okay, I need a bathroom break, and then I'll walk the floors, if you want to take over here a bit."

"Sure." Piper stepped forward and reached for the book a customer handed to her. "Good choice. I read this a few months ago."

* * *

Summer bounded off for the restroom. She couldn't remember ever needing a bathroom break when she'd worked summers here. Now, she was almost at the point of bathroom panic after working behind the register for an hour and a half.

Walking the floors was an exercise of making sure the customers were finding what they needed, plus tidying up. An empty coffee cup here, a napkin there. A book out of place.

Summer ambled upstairs and started from the back of the store. As she rounded the corner, she spotted a book out of place and shoved it back into the right spot.

"Hildy was so stubborn," Summer heard a voice say. "She'd never sell this place."

"Why would she?" another voice said. "She built this store, worked hard for years. It's her dream. Why would anybody think she'd sell?"

"Money, of course."

"A woman like Hildy? She didn't give one hoot for money."

True. Summer's heart swelled as she looked around at her mother's realized vision. Whether she liked the books here or not, Hildy had built something real. Something that touched people's lives. Something that people traveled to. Something that people talked about. You just couldn't get more meaningful than that.

Chapter Twenty-Five

A few days later, they were all back in Hildy's house. The cleaners had come in and left not a whiff of smoke odor.

Aunt Agatha, Piper, and Mia were slowing getting back to their own lives. Though now that it was officially summer, nobody's lives were normal. The tourists were already making a splash, filling up trash bins, leaving toys on the beach, and crowding restaurants. No wonder many longtime residents left for the season.

Mom never had. It was high beach book reading season. And she loved all the hubbub the tourists created. "Life," she'd say, "you need to be in the thick of it!"

Today, Summer prepared to dive into the depths of it. She planned to visit Posey. Summer had called her, and Posey was expecting her. She seemed happy to hear from Summer, though that could be a ruse.

None of the others had returned her calls. Henry hadn't even returned Summer's call. Well, she'd not be ignored. She might have to pop in on him and catch him off guard.

After she traveled to the other side of the island and found Posey's house, she took a deep breath. Could this woman know something about her mom's death? Or worse, could she be the killer?

When tiny, mocha-skinned Posey opened the door, warm memories spread through Summer, and she held back tears. Where did that come from? It was as if she was standing in front of a warm, glowing fire—one full of sweet memories.

"Come on in, Summer," Posey said after hugging her. "I have tea in the living room."

Summer followed her through the small kitchen into the living room, which stretched the length of the house and looked out over a swampy marsh area.

"I suppose you're wondering why I didn't attend your mother's funeral," she said after they sat down in overstuffed wicker chairs.

Summer didn't respond. She lifted her chin, trying to speak.

Posey waved her hand, as if to say never mind. "I just couldn't imagine walking into a church—a church, of all things—knowing how she felt about them. I felt bad. I wanted to say goodbye. But it felt all wrong."

"I felt the same way," Summer said. "I have nothing against church. I'm a member of one back in Staunton. But Mom?"

"How did that happen?" Posey poured cream into her tea, and Summer watched the milky clouds form into a solid brown puddle.

"I really don't know." Summer drew in a breath, stirred her tea, stiffened on the chair. "Someone tried to set the house on fire a few nights back. We were all inside. Me, Mia, Agatha, and Piper."

"I'd heard about it. Read about it in the paper," she said, lifting her teacup to her lips and sipping from it. "I'm so glad that nobody was hurt."

She was calm, steady. Either she was a psychopath or completely at peace with herself and the universe.

"I have to ask if you know anybody who would want to do such a thing," Summer said after a few beats.

She gestured with her hands and shrugged. "I'd not spoken with your mother in a while. We'd both just gotten very busy. There was no great falling out or anything like that." She sighed. "I wish I'd seen her before she died. I really do. I know she was having trouble with someone sending her notes about leaving town . . . selling the bookstore . . ."

"Yes," Summer said. "I've seen those notes and handed them over to the police."

One of her bushy gray eyebrows lifted. "The police?"

"I think someone murdered Mom," Summer said.

Posey clutched at her ample bosom and gasped. "Why? Why would someone kill her? "

"Why does anybody kill anybody?"

She leaned forward, the chair squeaking, "What do the police say?"

"At first, they didn't buy it. Thought I was not thinking clearly because of my grieving. I'm not sure what they think now they know someone obviously tried to kill me."

Posey quieted.

"I've not talked with the police again, but I've been dealing with the fire chief."

She smiled. "He's delicious."

Summer laughed. Yes, he was, but it was odd hearing it come from this elder woman's mouth.

"So you're talking with her friends to see if anybody knows anything?" Posey asked after a few moments.

Summer nodded. "What you've told me lines up with what everybody else says. I just keep thinking we're overlooking something. Some piece of the puzzle that will lead us right to her killer."

"Good luck."

"Did Mom stay in contact with any of the other members of your group?"

"I'm uncertain. Most of them are gone, moved far away. I'm afraid I don't practice the craft much anymore. It takes too much out of me. I'm diabetic. Now I go to diabetic support groups and recipe exchanges instead of monthly meetings in the moonlight at the beach. If you catch my drift."

"I'm sorry to hear that," Summer said, feeling ashamed that she even remotely considered that Posey could have anything at all to do with her mom's death.

"Oh, it's not so bad most of the time. I've met some wonderful people in my groups. There's a friend of your mother's . . . Doris?"

"Doris? I didn't know she's diabetic," Summer said, thinking of the very sweet cinnamon rolls she'd made for them. "I'd heard that her husband has diabetes. Not her." An image of the cinnamon rolls sprang to her mind. She willed it away before she drooled all over herself and Posey's lovely tea service.

Posey nodded. "No. She does, and she's got her hands full with her husband."

Summer remembered another person mentioning his illness. "What's his condition?"

"He's got a bad liver. He's on a transplant list."

Summer must be misremembering—or someone else had gotten it wrong.

"Well, that's a good thing—surely they'll find him a liver soon."

Posey opened her mouth to say something, then looked as if she thought the better of it. "I hope so," she eventually said.

They sat for a few moments in silence. Summer wondered what Posey had changed her mind about saying. But then she leaned forward.

"I'm not making any promises," she said. "But I used to be a fabulous tarot card reader. I'll do a reading later to see what the cards have to say about this murder business. I do hope you're wrong. I'd hate to think of Hildy going that way. But she was so healthy. The heart attack story just never made sense to me."

Speaking of not making sense: tarot cards? Summer wondered how that would go down in a court of law.

Chapter Twenty-Six

So much for Posey—Summer crossed her off her list of suspects or witnesses. She cared about Hildy enough not to pretend that sitting in a church was honoring her. That said something about her integrity. And she hadn't even revealed anything new except about Doris and her husband, which had nothing to do with her mom's death.

Back to the drawing board—or her checklist, as it were. Summer stopped by the bookstore on her way back to the house. She wasn't scheduled today, but she just wanted to check on it. She tried to sort through her wild mix of emotions toward the store. Proud of her mom and what she'd built on the one hand; on the other, why did it have to be just romances and mysteries? How many hours had her mother forced her to work here, shelving, unpacking, waiting on customers? And oh, how she'd hated it with every ounce of a rebellious teenage attitude mustered.

She'd developed a love of other books—the ones she was not surrounded with every day. Once she'd discovered Shakespeare at school, she hadn't looked back.

She stood in front of the store, drawing in a breath. The door opened, with its familiar bell alerting the clerks that a customer was entering or leaving, and the person glanced at her and smiled, with her parcel in her hands. A satisfied look on her face, like a cat finishing a bowl of thick cream.

Well.

Summer caught the door before it closed and stepped inside. She blinked. Glads was behind the counter, ringing up a few women who were laughing and chatting about the newest Nora Roberts book. Summer made her way in the opposite direction toward the first shelf of books—new romances lined up with their spines facing out. As she walked, the familiar creak of the old floors sent pings of comfort through her.

She strolled toward the corner shelf, where the staff picks always had been and still were. A couple of shelves with "Hildy's All-Time Favorites." Summer reached out and touched the books. Hildy loved this place. These books. What a remarkable achievement—to understand your passion and see its successful fruition. Joy welled up in Summer. Unexpected. Welcome. And it burst out of her with a strangled giggle and a prick of tears.

She turned from the shelves and continued walking along. The books—romances, all formulaic, all with happy endings and ridiculous sex scenes—looked happy. Odd. How could books look happy? She chided herself. *Get a grip, woman.*

But her mom had been the happiest woman she'd ever met. Her only unhappiness had been her problems with Summer. Guilt ripped at her as she became sharply aware of the emotional pain she'd caused her mom.

"Summer, dear, are you okay? You're not supposed to be here."

She turned to face Marilyn, whose face was full of concern and curiosity.

Summer tried to gather her wits, but her mind was reeling. Emotions were swarming through her, and she wasn't certain if they were happy, sad, angry, or shame.

"Summer?" Marilyn reached out and grabbed her hand. "Let's go in the back and get you a cup of tea?"

Summer nodded and allowed herself to be swept through the store and into the back room, where the staff took breaks in between boxes of books and stacks of magazines and papers.

"Have a seat, dear," she said and poured Summer hot water from the electric kettle. "Constant Comment?"

She remembered Summer's favorite tea.

"Yes, please." Summer managed to find the words.

"Hildy always said you and she loved your Constant Comment," Marilyn said.

True. They'd whiled away hours drinking the brew. No other brand of tea ever quite hit the spot.

Summer held the tea to her nose, allowing its spicy orange fragrance to soothe her even before her first sip.

"So she talked *about* me, even though she wouldn't talk *to* me," Summer muttered.

Marilyn sat next to her. "She talked about you all the time." She paused. "Mothers and daughters have tiffs." She shrugged, placing her hand on Summer's shoulder. "She was working it out, believe me."

It was as if Marilyn's purple-iris hand sprinkled Summer's shoulder with a bit of magic. Suddenly she felt more comfort than anger or shame.

"Were you there when Mom . . . fell over?"

"No," she said. "She and Doris were taking stock. I think they were in here alone when your mother collapsed. Doris called nine-one-one, and Hildy was taken to the hospital, where they worked on her for quite some time."

Doris? Her name kept cropping up. Summer made a note of it.

"Did you know offers were being made for the store?" Summer asked.

Marilyn laughed. "We all knew. To be fair, every single one of us would love to buy this store. Only a few of us ever could. I couldn't."

"But did you know about the warnings?"

Her eyebrows gathered. "What warnings?"

"Someone sent Mom threatening notes trying to get her to sell the shop."

"Yeah, I know."

"At first we suspected Rudy." Summer explained what had been happening. "And now, with the fire, we figure they were coming after me. They want the Merriweather clan gone."

"Well, whoever did that didn't know your mother very well. She would never give up that bookstore. She bitched and moaned about it sometimes. It was a lot of work. But she didn't plan to sell. As far as she was concerned, you would be the next owner," she replied.

"Me?" Summer said. "She knew how much I didn't like this place."

"Yes, but you are keeping it, aren't you?"

"I am," Summer replied, "but I'm not sure how it will work out. I have a job I love in Staunton." *Maybe.*

"It'll all work out," Glads said with confidence.

After drinking her tea, Summer walked back into the center of the store and spotted a man who looked vaguely familiar. He was moving directly toward her.

"Summer?" She recognized the voice, but when had Henry, the English teacher, gotten so hot?

He reached out and grabbed her as she stood dumbly considering things. She'd just called him yesterday. "I'm sorry I've not returned your call. My phone died. I mean, *just* died. Crazy how reliant I am on it."

"I know what you mean," she said. "Don't know what I'd do without mine."

Glads walked by them with a grin and a sideways glance. Oh no! Did she think that—

"Uh, listen," Summer said, pulling on his elbow to get him into a corner of the place for privacy.

"I'm so sorry to hear about your mother. What happened? I'd just seen her. She looked well."

Summer's eyes met his. "When did you see her?"

"I think it was the day before she died. We always had this healthy competition thing going. I wanted this store. I've made several offers. It became a joke between us." He smiled a kind smile, edged in deep dimples, then laughed. "The last offer I made was just ridiculous." He looked around. "I could never afford what this place is worth. High school English teacher. You know?"

They'd had this discussion before as well. Teaching English at high school versus college. Summer wasn't interested in the debate at the moment.

"I remember," she said. "So you gave up on buying it?"

His weight shifted. "Are you kidding? If I had the money, I would. I'm strapped these days. Are you selling? Is that what this is about?"

"No," she said. "I'm not sure it's mine to sell. We've yet to read the will."

"Then why did you call?" A note of something like hope tempered his voice.

"I'd heard rumors that you still wanted the place," she replied, not wanting to fill him in on everything yet, if ever. "So, um, I'm just exploring my options."

"Well, I can't help. A few years ago, maybe, but this place has escalated in worth. I'm not your guy," he said and walked away.

Had Summer offended him? It would not be the first time.

She walked out of the shop and he was long gone. She decided to walk home rather than take the car. She'd come back tomorrow to fetch it. For now, she needed to stretch her legs and inhale sea air, a balm to her soul. She hadn't realized how much she'd missed the beach.

As Summer walked along the snaking path, the sun setting in the distance, footfalls thudded behind her. She didn't want to turn around, for fear of scaring a harmless bystander. But as the footsteps came close, she picked up her pace—as they did. Were they trying to—?

Next, Summer fell to the ground, and her head thwacked against something hard. She tried to stand, tried to get a view of the person running away, but shadows were in the way. As she stood, dizziness overcame her, and she dropped into blackness.

Chapter Twenty-Seven

Gentle pats on her face awakened her. "Summer. Summer," a soft, soothing male voice said. She struggled to open her eyes. When she succeeded, the face in front of hers was a blur.

As it came into view, it surprised her to see Levi, the fire chief.

"What happened?" she said in a barely recognizable voice.

"I guess you fell?" He wasn't in uniform. Off-duty, then.

Summer struggled to sit up.

"Whoa," he said. "Let's take this slowly. Okay. Just get your bearings. You've got a nasty bump on your head."

He helped Summer sit up slowly, cradling her shoulders in his arm. Warmth spread through her, all tingly. She had either taken a harder fall than she thought, or she was living in a romance novel.

"How do you feel?"

"Like shit," she said. Nausea. Splitting headache. Sore. And warm and tingly. "How long have I been lying here?"

"I don't know," he said, shrugging. "I was just walking along here and saw you."

As her head cleared up and memory sharpened, Summer remembered being pushed. "Did you see anybody else?"

"No—why?" he said after a moment.

"Someone pushed me."

He grimaced. "Let's get you on your feet. I think we should have a doctor look you over."

"I don't need to see a doctor. I need to see the police," she said, standing, wobbly, dizzy, falling back into Levi's arms.

He cocked an eyebrow.

"Okay. Maybe both," she said.

* * *

St. Brigid Hospital was a small hospital, but adequate. The doctor took one look at her and pronounced that she had a mild concussion.

Agatha and Piper bounded into the exam room.

"My god! What happened?" Agatha said, coming over to Summer lying on the bed.

"I went to the bookstore and walked home on the path, and someone pushed me," she replied. "Hard. Hard enough that I fell and hit my head, along with a few other things."

"What's he doing here?" Piper said, nodding to the fire chief.

"He found her," Levi spoke up.

"How long had she been lying there?"

"As far as I've been able to figure, about fifteen minutes or so."

"You were just walking along and spotted her?" Agatha said with a touch of suspicion in her voice.

"Yes," he replied. "I was heading toward the beach from my place."

Summer noted that this was the second time Aunt Agatha had gotten kind of prickly with Levi. She'd have to ask her about it at a later time.

"Who the hell would have pushed you? Did they take anything?" Piper said.

"Nothing," Summer said. "I've checked my bag over and over again. Nothing seems to be missing."

Agatha sighed a long-drawn-out sigh. "First the fire, now this."

"I called Ben," Levi said. "He should be here shortly."

Oh boy.

"He'll be taking statements from both of us. Do you feel up to it?"

Summer shrugged. "I guess. When can I get out of here and go home?"

"You must ask the doctor," Agatha said. "I imagine you're here for at least the night. Do you need me to bring you anything?"

"Just a few things," Summer said, then listed off some items.

Piper cleared her throat. "Someone really wants you dead—or at least hurt."

"I have to agree it looks that way," Levi said. "But what I come back to again is the motive. Why would someone want Summer out of the way?"

"We don't know for sure," Piper said, "but Summer's mother, Hildy, had been getting threatening notes from someone who wanted her to sell the bookstore and leave."

"Did she get the police involved?"

"No," Piper said. "She didn't take them seriously."

"Was she interested in selling the place? Must be worth a good bit by now," he said.

"No," Agatha spoke up. "She complained about the work sometimes, but she never planned to sell."

"I'd assume with her gone, it's all going to you." He glanced Summer's way.

Summer nodded. "Can you hand me my bag?" she asked Agatha.

She rummaged through it and found what she was looking for—the book she'd been reading. The romance. She'd be stuck here all night. Damn if she'd lie there watching TV. A romance book was better than no book. And better than watching TV. Besides, she had to admit to thinking about the characters a good bit. How would they work things out? It seemed impossible. It had completely hooked her in—which also seemed impossible for a Shakespeare scholar and self-confessed literary snob.

"We haven't actually gotten to the will reading," Agatha said. "We're just assuming."

"Summer is her only child," Piper said, "so it stands to reason she inherits it all."

Summer bit her lip. *Lucky me.*

The door to her room swung open, and Ben Singer walked inside, with the nurse trailing him. "There are too many people in here."

"Okay, we're leaving," Piper said as she reached for her mother's arm. "But we'll be back with her things."

The two of them exited the room, leaving Summer with the nurse and two men. The nurse placed a blood pressure cuff on her and squeezed.

"Ms. Merriweather," Ben Singer said, "looks like you've brought trouble to the island. Yet again."

Summer was certain her blood pressure kicked up as the nurse looked at her with a cocked eyebrow.

She turned to Singer. "Sir, if you're going to upset my patient, I'm going to ask you to leave."

Singer lurched back as if someone had hit him.

Levi's voice rang from the corner. "Stick to the business at hand, Singer."

130

Chapter Twenty-Eight

After answering the police chief's myriad of questions about her attack, he took his leave, Levi still in the room.

"I hope we find who did this to you," Levi said. "Man, that Singer . . ." He smiled.

Summer laughed, even though her head was splitting, and she just wanted to sleep. "History with you too?"

"Oh yes," he said, folding his arms. "He's old school, and I don't mean that in a good way."

Not for the first time, Summer wondered what had gone on between them.

"I need to get going, but here's my card." he said, handing it to her. "Call that cell number anytime. I think something odd is going on here. I'm not sure if your mother was murdered, as you suggest, but you were attacked. Your house was set on fire. So, if Singer's going to ignore all this evidence, fine. I won't."

"Thank you," Summer said, fingering the card, then setting it on the table next to her bed.

A spark of ease fluttered in Summer's chest. He believed her. He was careful not to give her too much hope—and she respected that. Of course, he had to weigh all options and not completely believe the grieving daughter. But hard facts were not so easy to ignore, at least not to somebody with any sense. What was Singer's problem, anyway? Did he think she did this to herself? How crazy was that?

After Levi left, Summer picked up *Nights in Bellamy Harbor* and read it. Turned the page and saw that her mother had circled a few sentences about the alpha male developer wanting to buy half of the island. She placed exclamation marks off to the side of them. *Hmm. What was it about those sentences that bothered my mother? Was it because it was a pivotal part in the book, or was it something more personal?*

She blinked. Was there a developer snooping around the island? Is this why her mother had circled the sentences? Was there any recent news about a developer? When she was sprung from the hospital, she'd find out.

She proceeded with her reading. The alpha male developer, Omar, loved the environmentalist librarian. But just how was that going to work out? Silly, she knew, but she simply just had to find out. She read page after page until she drifted off. Then the book fell on her chest, waking her up. She scooted it off to the side and rolled over to sleep.

Through the night, she was awakened countless times by well-meaning nurses checking her blood pressure and temperature. She wondered how anybody could get rest in a hospital.

Aunt Agatha and Piper brought personal items for her the next morning.

"Thanks," Summer said. "I'm hoping to get out today."

"I think they'll keep you at least one more night," Agatha said. "You've got a very nasty bump on your head."

"I need to get out of here. I've got some sleuthing to do."

"You need to take care of yourself." Piper poured a glass of water. "Have a drink."

"Maybe the sleuthing you've already done is what's brought you here. Maybe we she just give up," Aunt Agatha said. "Your mother is gone. Nothing we do will bring her back. She wouldn't want you placing yourself in danger."

"Danger?" Summer couldn't believe what her aunt was saying. Was she ready to give up on finding the killer of her mother just because of a few incidents?

"So far, someone tried to kill you at least once, and someone attacked you. Is revenge worth it?"

Summer paused before replying. Perhaps Aunt Agatha was correct. This had all just gotten too dangerous. Maybe she should just leave and go back to Staunton, to her life there. Teaching. Reading. And Shakespeare.

"Visitors!" A group of women entered the room with food. Members of the book club. Marilyn, Doris, and Glads sauntered into the room.

"How are you feeling, dear?" Doris said, bringing the table across the bed. "We've brought you some food."

Summer's stomach waved at the scent of it. She looked up at the well-meaning Doris. "Maybe later. I just can't eat right now."

"She has a concussion," Piper said, "so she has a bit of a sick stomach. You can leave the food here until she feels better." She took the bags of food from the ladies.

"Poor dear," Doris said. Did she always look the same way? Her hair and makeup was always in place.

Marilyn moved forward. "I enjoyed your visit yesterday. I hope you'll be able to make it to the book group."

"Surely," Summer said, the bookstore entering her mind's eye. The rush of warmth she'd felt yesterday there comforted her.

"When do you plan to return to Staunton, or are you staying?" Doris asked.

Agatha, Piper, and Marilyn turned their heads to her.

"I don't know, Doris," Summer said. What an odd thing to ask someone who's lying in a hospital bed. But now that Summer remembered it, Doris had asked her that question more than once. "I don't feel very welcome here. I just might leave when I'm sprung. Perhaps it's time I consider heading home."

Summer rarely gave up that easily. But here she was, lying in a hospital bed, with a huge painful knot on her head. And her aunt and cousin appeared to have given up on it all. Why not head back home, where she was safe and secure?

Not only was Summer a failure at her life, having run away to England because of a little controversy, but she was also a failure as a daughter not being able to find her mother's killer.

"But this is your home," Aunt Agatha said.

Was home a shifting place? Or was it always the place you grew up? Summer felt the tug of her new life in Staunton, the one she had created with her education and independence. But she had to admit St. Brigid also had an undeniable pull on her heart.

Chapter Twenty-Nine

"We will have to keep you at least one more night."

"I don't understand," Summer said. "I can take care of myself and can do it at home." She folded her arms.

The doctor frowned. "I'm sorry. It's a new policy for concussions. We can't be too careful. The more we learn about head injuries, the clearer it becomes that we need to be more cautious, not less so."

His condescending tone made her want to scream. It was men like him who made her want to quote Shakespeare. Out loud. Maybe a whole act of one of his plays.

"Do you understand?"

"I may have a concussion, but I have a PhD in Shakespearean literature and understand English perfectly well, and let me tell you—"

"Summer?" Agatha walked into the room. "Are you giving your doctor grief? You need to calm down, dear."

There were only a few people Summer didn't argue with—Aunt Agatha was one of them.

"They want to keep me another day."

"I explained to her that—"

"You need not explain it again. Thank you. I got it the first time. I'll fill her in."

He nodded, smiled, and left the room.

Agatha sat on the edge of her bed. "It's best for you here, dear. Just get some rest."

Summer rolled her eyes. "I don't need to rest. I need to get out of here and find who killed my mom."

"It's getting a little dangerous, don't you think? First the fire, now this. I don't know . . . maybe we best leave it alone."

"I must be getting close." Summer's headache was getting worse.

"Why would you say that?"

"The fire and the attack. Someone is worried." Her hand snapped to her temple.

Agatha stood. "Have they given you anything to sleep? We just need to shut that brain of yours down."

"I just took something," Summer muttered.

"Thank goddess for that!" Agatha stood.

"I'm sure I'm getting close to something with all this poking around I'm doing. I called Xanadu Corp. Rex Garfield claims he's not made an offer in a long time. I visited with Posey."

"Posey? Why? She was a dear friend of Hildy's."

"I just wondered if she was aware of any strangeness in Mom's life."

"Was she?"

"No more than us."

"I also called Henry, who never returned my calls. Some excuse about his phone." she paused. "But I ran into him at the bookstore."

"And?" Her eyebrows rose.

"And . . . nothing. He's as strange as he ever was."

"You never liked him. Your mother was quite fond of him and all of his offers." She giggled. Summer's eyelids grew heavy as she tried to listen. "I've often wondered if, you know, they had some kind of affair . . ."

Now Summer laughed. Henry and her mother? He was Summer's age. Wait. Was he a bit older? But still. She laughed herself to sleep. The idea of Henry and Hildy rolled around in her mind and spun itself into a dream of her mother. Laughing. Suddenly serious. "What is so funny? Me with a younger man?" She looked as if she was upset, about ready to cry. "Mom? I didn't mean to upset you. Mom. Mom?"

"Sorry, I'm not your mother," Glads said, smiling. "I'm just here to check on you."

Glads. She was always popping up. Her and her purple glasses. Summer said nothing. Her cottony mouth kept quiet.

Glads had an armful of books. "I brought you some books in case you get bored."

"I'm still reading the book club book," Summer said.

Glads smiled. "Good, but take these for when you're done." She sat the books on the bedside table. "How are you feeling?"

"Like shit. And I'm so thirsty."

"Let me pour you some water." Summer hadn't realized there was a pitcher of water in her room, until that moment.

"How are things at the store?"

She handed Summer the water. "Good. As always. Things at the library are very busy these days with the kids' summer reading program."

Summer drank the water. Had water ever tasted so good?

"So Henry came back in the store the day you fell—"

"Was pushed. I didn't fall."

"Right. But anyway, he came back in, looking for you."

"He did?"

"Yes. He seemed agitated."

"I've already given the police my story. They're aware that I was talking with him just before this happened."

Glads head tilted in interest. "Do you think *he* pushed you?"

The nurse walked in and started fussing over Summer, took her blood pressure, gave her medicine. Then she walked back out.

"I can't imagine him pushing me," Summer said. "But then again, I can't imagine any of this. Someone killing my mom? Someone trying to burn down the house? Now this? I'll tell you someone on this island is not what they seem. And it could be him. Who knows?"

Glads's face blanked.

"What's wrong?"

She shook her head. "I sometimes feel as I don't know this place anymore." Her chin quivered. "Half the time I'm torn between crying or-or . . . beating someone up!"

"What's going on Glads?"

"Besides all this? As if this wasn't enough, there's a developer moving in. I saw the office sign. We've fought them off before. I just don't know how much longer we can keep our little beach town authentic."

Authentic. Summer was beginning to hate that word. But she knew what Glads meant.

Her eyes drifted to the book on the nightstand. "Just like *Nights at Bellamy Harbor*. They're fighting with everything in them to keep their town away from the developers."

Glads's face lit up. "Yes, it's kind of a trope. But there are reasons for it. It happens every day, so people relate."

"I wonder if our developer is half as hot as Omar," Summer said, promoting a giggle from Glads.

Chapter Thirty

After Glads left, Summer drifted into a nap. She awakened with a start because someone was standing by her bed. She attempted to open her eyes, but her vision blackened several times. The sun was streaming, obscuring the person's face. Then he moved. And his face came into focus.

She sat up and gasped. "Jesus! What are you doing here!"

Henry lifted a bouquet of flowers. "Just checking on you."

"Why? You scared me half to death!"

He shrugged, looking a little miffed. "I thought it'd be a friendly gesture. Since you're moving back. I kinda wanted to, uh, start things off on the right foot this time."

Summer's head was hurting and spinning. But the flowers were a nice gesture. "Okay," she said, not really buying this sudden friendly attitude from him. What was he up to? An awkward pause. "I think there're vases in that drawer."

He opened it, pulled one out, and arranged the flowers.

"Thank you. It was very kind of you."

"You're welcome. Your mother and I——" oh no, did she want to know this? She almost covered her ears—"had become very good friends." His voice cracked. "I lost my mom a few years ago and, well, I guess appreciated Hildy's overbearing motherly nature." He grinned.

Summer rolled her eyes, suddenly embarrassed at how she must look in the hospital bed. No makeup, surrounded by white. "I hear you." She paused. "So you became friends? That's so nice." *Mom didn't mention that to me.*

He glanced at the books on her table. "Looks like the book fairy has been here."

"Yes, and her name is Gladys."

"*Nights at Bellamy Harbor*?" He picked it up and grinned at Summer. "You're reading a romance?" He lurched back. "Miz Shakespeare professor?"

Okay, she deserved it, a bit, but how dare he come bearing gifts and now launch into this? "It's the book club's book. Mom was reading it when she passed away. There are notes scattered throughout. They invited me to come to the meeting. I just wanted to be prepared."

He laughed. "It's a good book, isn't it?"

"I have to admit that it's not as bad as I imagined." *And would you please leave?* "Are you reading it?"

"I finished it last night. In case you didn't know, I'm in the book club."

Okay, she needed a roster of those members. The high school English teacher was a member of her mom's romance book club?

He was local, in the book club, and wanted the bookstore. Something didn't sit right with her. He claimed he was a good friend of her mom's. But she'd never mentioned it. He was still definitely a suspect. She was not yet completely certain he wasn't the one who pushed her. Whoever it was definitely had strong hands. If she closed her eyes, she still felt the heave on the exact place where her assailant had placed hands on her back.

"Good for you."

He leaned in. "Shakespeare was a popular writer. He appealed to the masses. You know that."

"Of course I do. But there was a brilliance to his writing, outlasting all the other popular writers of the day. And such a brilliance in that he's inspired so many other authors that it's impossible to say how many. Story mechanics. Language. Tension. The list goes on. You can't say the same for Nora Roberts."

He stood, dumbfounded, then shook it off. "Not yet, anyway."

Summer stared him down.

"Well, I need to get going. I hope you feel better soon." He turned to go, then moved back toward her. "See you at book club." Then he winked. Winked! She threw a pillow at him, which he narrowly escaped.

But the doctor just walked in and lifted the pillow from the floor. "Everything okay?"

"Absolutely," she said, gathering herself. *And none of your business, Doc.*

"Well, I have good news, and I have bad news." He walked over to the bed and brought the pillow, which he set at the end of the bed. "You can go home. But no screen time for at least two weeks. And you shouldn't go back to work for at least that long."

Work. Hmm. She wondered if she should check in with the school. Then she thought again. And she supposed she'd not be going into the bookstore.

"Try not to think too much. That'll be hard for you."

Was that a jab?

"How can anybody stop from thinking?"

"Well, of course. What I mean is just try not to overthink, figure out problems, and so on. It's bad for a healing brain."

142

"But I can go home?"

He nodded. "If you don't take care of yourself, I'll know it because you'll be back. You don't want to come back here, do you?"

No, indeed.

Piper came to the hospital to fetch her and her flowers. "Flowers from Henry? Do tell?"

Summer shrugged while she was being wheeled away. "I wonder what he's up to. I don't quite trust him."

"You never liked him," she said.

"He says he and mom were close."

"Were they?" Piper said.

"He's in the book group."

"Oh yes. I'm aware. And as far as I can tell, it's worked well for him."

"What do you mean?"

"He's worked his way through several members of the group, including our Poppy."

"What?"

"Not the inner circle. But the new younger ones. Yes, indeed. Our Henry is quite the ladies' man."

Summer snorted. *Well, well, well.*

Chapter Thirty-One

Summer collapsed into her couch bed. She was losing track of time and days. Mr. Darcy flapped his wings and cawed. He had plenty of food, and his cage had just been cleaned. But he paced back and forth, agitated.

"What's wrong, Darcy?"

Piper walked into the room, with water for Summer. "He's been agitated since Glads and Doris came over to help me clean his cage. He doesn't seem to like them."

"He's getting old. He probably doesn't like anybody." Summer downed her medicine, hoping it would take away the nagging pain of a headache. "Is it Monday?"

Piper nodded. "I think he misses Hildy." She plopped down on the La-Z-Boy.

"I'm sure he does. Poor guy. She was his best friend."

"So my mom says you've been sleuthing."

"A bit."

"She's worried. She thinks someone is trying to hurt you, and she wants you to stop."

Summer set her half-empty water glass down. "I'm aware. But I'm not going to."

Piper sighed. "I figured. But listen don't go off alone anywhere. Just to be on the safe side. Mom is worried. She doesn't want anything to happen to you. Well, none of us do."

Something bloomed in Summer's chest. She'd almost forgotten what it was like to have family around. Or anybody around who cared about her well-being. She had a few acquaintances at the university and at her church, but mostly she was met with indifference. Especially at the University. If not indifference, then hostility. Being around her family used to make her feel stifled, but now it warmed her. Or perhaps strong pain medicine was messing with her?

"I appreciate that."

"Are you sure you don't want to sleep in one of the beds?"

"I'm fine here. I enjoy bunking with Darcy. Right, boy?"

He rocked back and forth on his feet. But no answer.

"So have you found out anything interesting?"

"Nothing. It's been more a process of elimination." She filled Piper in on everything she'd learned.

"What's next?"

"I keep questioning the book club members. Including Henry."

"Henry? I don't see it. I think you're wasting your time."

"They say that most murder victims know their killers."

"I've heard that, but it's so hard to imagine any of the book group hurting your mother."

"It's hard to imagine any of it." Summer snuggled down into the couch and pulled the blanket closer to her. "I spoke with Rex from Xanadu, who wasn't anywhere near the island. Who else wanted the bookstore? And who else had access to this place besides the book club members?"

"What if it has nothing to do with the store? What if they just wanted your mother to leave?"

Summer hadn't considered that. She'd been following a logical line of thinking. The notes mentioned the bookstore. Her mom had had offers. But maybe Piper was right—and this was personal.

"Mom could be kind of mysterious. There were whole parts of her life I know nothing about. Like my father. Who is he?"

"I wish I knew that too. But you're right. Hildy was very open about some things, but also very private in her way." She waved her arms around. "She loved you. Look at the place. It's like a temple to you and all the many goddesses she loved."

"She wasn't talking to me when I left for England. She thought I should stay and hold my head up and fight back."

"I'm aware."

"But that video went viral, and—well, it was a mess. I needed to get some distance and do something that would help keep my job."

"I get it. How's it going with the therapy?"

"Well, my therapist is in Staunton. We've had one conversation since I've been here. It's been okay." Summer paused. "We're looking at the root of my fear, and that's difficult."

The medicine was taking over, and Summer's eyes felt heavy.

"Some deep, dark childhood thing, no doubt," Piper said.

"Yes, but what?" Summer slurred her words and yawned.

Piper stood and placed the cover over Darcy's cage. "I think it's bedtime. Good night."

"Good night, Piper." She pulled her anti-insect blanket over her.

Summer closed her eyes and hoped her mom would visit her in her dreams again that night. Even an angry Hildy was better that no Hildy.

But Hildy wasn't in her dreams. It was a dreamless night, and when Summer awakened, she regretted it. She reached for *Nights at Bellamy Harbor*. It wasn't a bad book. But more than that. It was her mom's book. Somehow, it brought Hildy closer to her. The notes in the margin, the underlining of sentences. So, Hildy. And so Summer—as she did the same things.

Summer hadn't given much consideration to the mystery of her father these days. But now that her mom was gone, she wondered if she should. Agatha would not support her quest to find out who he was, understanding how strongly Hildy felt about keeping it secret. She'd had to do it on the down low. But it might be good to just know. She doubted she'd contact the man. She used to lie awake at night, imagining who he was. *Was he handsome? Was he a nice person? Why did he leave Hildy? Was he rich?*

Summer had been without her dad for her whole life—and yet sometimes she felt like she missed him. Had Hildy ever planned to tell Summer who he was? Maybe now was the time for Summer to use her research skills to find her own father.

Summer quoted a line from Shakespeare. *"'Then, good my mother, let me know my father—Some proper man, I hope.'"* She grinned. Summer doubted propriety had anything to do with it.

Chapter Thirty-Two

The next morning, Summer awakened early, made herself coffee, and sat on the front porch with it, watching the sun get higher against the horizon and reflect in the ocean. This was the same view she'd gazed at when making all the major decisions in her life. She'd said yes to Cash's marriage proposal, and then the day of the wedding, this was the spot where she'd planted herself, unable to move. This was also the spot where she'd decided on which college to attend. The porch swing was where she had whiled away her hours, reading one Shakespeare play or poem after another.

Now, she was here, with her mom gone, trying to figure out what had happened to her. Now, more than ever, she believed her mom had been murdered. Summer's life had been threatened with the fire and then the attack. She was getting too close to the truth. Someone wanted her gone too.

She took a long drink of coffee. She wasn't going anywhere. Not yet.

The door creaked open, and Piper came out onto the porch, sitting quietly next to Summer.

A few minutes later, she broke the silence. "How's your head?"

"Hurts a bit. But it's getting better."

"Good. Have you heard from Ben at all?"

"No. I've been thinking about following up with both him and Levi."

"Levi." Piper drawled as if he were a delicious dessert. "Now there's a man. He's put together very well."

"Yes, and all the women on the island seem to think so. Even Posey."

"Posey? She's what? In her eighties?" Piper laughed.

"Yes, but she's got it goin' on." Summer grinned.

Later that morning, Summer received a call from Al Pereles, her mother's lawyer. He had an opening that afternoon.

Summer. Piper, Mia, and Agatha piled into Piper's car and drove to the courthouse, where the lawyer's office was.

"This is kind of ridiculous," Mia said from the backseat. "Why do we have to go? We figure Summer's getting everything, right?"

"Mia!" Piper said.

"We were all named in the will—that's why we have to go," Agatha said in a clipped tone.

Piper parked the car, and the four of them found their way.

The courthouse was small, but it sufficed for the small island, with two lawyers and two, sometimes three, cops. There were no grand cement pillars. Instead, a green awning flapped in the breeze, flanked by two potted plants. Probably fake.

The lobby was cool and smelled of something floral. Maybe it was the receptionist's perfume.

"Hello, I'm Summer Merriweather," she said.

"Great," she said, smiling at Summer. "Follow me. Mr. Pereles will be right with you."

She led them down a long, narrow hallway and into a room with a conference table and chairs. The walls were lined with thick books. A familiar rush swept through Summer. Gorgeous books. Weighty. Legal books, no doubt. The real deal. Her eyes scanned them—beautifully aligned and arranged. So deep in her musing over the books was she that she didn't realize the lawyer had walked in and taken a seat at the head of the table.

"Hello. I'm Al Pereles, Hilda Mae Merriweather's attorney," he said, breaking the silence. "Which one of you is Summer?" He looked at Summer and Piper.

Summer raised her hand. "That would be me."

He shuffled the stack of papers in front of him on the table. "Hildy left everything to you. The bookstore and the house."

"Of course she did," Agatha said.

"But there are a few notable exceptions. She has some other items she wanted other people to have. Piper Merriweather?"

Piper raised her hand. Watery-eyed, frowning.

"She's willed her first edition Anne Rice books to you, plus a necklace that you've always admired."

She gasped, her hand went to her mouth, and tears streamed. The lawyer slid the box of tissues to her.

"You must be Mia."

"Yeah," she replied, with a little quiver in her voice. Tough girl Mia was a bit nervous.

"If your aunt Summer passes away without children to inherit, all the property goes to you."

Mia glanced at Summer, then to her mom. She opened her mouth as if to say something, then shut it. Agatha reached over and took her hand, smiling at her granddaughter.

"Agatha?" he asked.

"Yes."

"She left all of her first editions to you, except for the folio, of course, which goes to Summer."

Agatha nodded, trying to smile.

Summer's hand snapped to her chest.

"Folio?" Summer said. "What are you talking about?"

"A surprise for you," Agatha said in a hushed voice. "Your mother purchased a copy of a Shakespeare folio. She planned to give it to you for your birthday, I believe."

Stunned, Summer's brain reeled—and hurt. A headache was creeping back in. The damned concussion. "That would have been too expensive."

"Your mother handled her money very well," the lawyer said.

"What?"

He handed her a folder. "These are the stocks and the account your mother had. They go to you, of course." He paused. "There is one more thing to note, Agatha. She asked that you do not sell the first editions, particularly not to Henry."

Summer's heart skipped a beat. Why would her mom have stated that?

"As if I would," Agatha said. "He was always bothering her about it. Wanted her to sell them to him."

"I thought it was the bookstore he wanted," Summer said.

"He wanted both," Mia spoke up. "But he didn't give up on the books. He wanted them."

Funny he didn't mention that to me. Henry looked more and more suspicious. But would he—or anyone—kill for a collection of first edition books? People have killed for less. But she realized that perhaps they'd been following the wrong leads. Maybe the person who left the note was setting a false trap. Maybe they wanted the first editions—some of which would be valuable by now.

Summer cleared her throat. "We need to find out if anybody else made Mom an offer on the first editions."

Agatha's eyes met Summer's. "My thoughts exactly, my dear."

Chapter Thirty-Three

After the reading, the group progressed to lunch at Dixie's Diner, a favorite with the locals. The summer folks rarely discovered it until about midway through the season, so it was still a decent place to go for lunch—for now.

"Okay," Summer said after the server dropped off the menus and glasses filled with water. "We need to talk. I think we've been on the wrong track."

"I agree," Agatha said.

"What are you talking about?" Piper said.

"The first editions. I think Mom's killer was after the first editions, not the bookstore."

"What makes you say that?"

"Well, after snooping around I can't find anybody who's made a recent offer."

"Yes, but to kill—" Piper started but was interrupted as the server came up to the table.

"What can I get you?"

They listed off their menu choices, and the server left the table.

"It seems a small reason to off someone," Piper said with a lowered voice.

Intrigued, Summer leaned in. "What's a good reason to kill?"

"If someone is after a family member and you need to protect them," Agatha said.

"Yes, to defend of your family or yourself," Piper agreed.

"Is that the only reason?" Summer asked. She paused, waiting, but neither Agatha nor Piper came up with another reason. "Okay, we're agreed. So that means that any other reason is ludicrous. Money. Love. Greed. Anger. None of it makes sense. So someone killing Mom for her books makes little sense. Or for the store. Neither are really valid."

They sat quietly.

"I totally get it," Mia said, breaking the silence.

"Of course you do—I've trained you well." Summer ginned and took a drink of water.

She used to play a "game" with her niece, based on the characters of Shakespeare. At one point, Mia was the only fourth-grader who knew anything about Shakespeare, let alone was capable of listing all the major female characters in his plays.

"Your knowledge got the child in trouble, as I recall," Piper said with one eyebrow lifted.

"Pshaw. What did her fourth-grade teacher know about Lady Macbeth?"

"She knew it was inappropriate for a fourth-grader," Agatha said, grinning.

"I maintain the untruth in that statement," Summer said. "Look at her. She's fine. She's smart. She's sitting there quite undamaged."

Agatha harrumphed.

"So, can you name the character who loved her father according to her duty as a daughter and the bond between a parent and child?" Summer asked Mia.

"Cordelia." She didn't skip a beat.

"How about the female character who disguises herself as a male judge?"

"Portia."

"Okay, okay. We get it," Piper said. "Look, here comes our food."

When everybody's food was in front of them, Agatha cleared her throat. "I agree with you, Summer. There may be another motive and that motive could be the first editions. But does that mean they'll come after me next?"

Summer thought about it. "Only if they realize you have them."

"Well, we're the only ones who know that," Piper said and bit into her burger.

"Us and the lawyer. That's it." Mia said.

"Okay, then I suggest we don't tell anybody," Piper said.

"Won't Henry come looking for those books again?" Mia asked.

"If he does, we'll just tell him they aren't for sale and we've placed them in storage," Piper said. "Simple."

"What if I tell everybody?"

"Why would you do that, Gram?"

"Let's lay a trap," she said in a lowered voice as she stabbed at her salad.

"Could be dangerous," Piper said.

"I agree," Summer said, her stomach roiling. She'd just lost her mom and wasn't prepared to lose Aunt Agatha.

"What's life without a little danger?"

"A *live* life."

"Yeah," Piper said.

"Oh come now, we can figure out a way to do this safely."

"I don't know about that," Piper muttered.

"I won't have you risking your life," Summer said, voice cracking.

"But if it's in the pursuit of justice for Hildy . . ."

"She wouldn't have it," Summer said.

"She's dead and doesn't get a say. I'm doing this with or without you all." Her jaw set firmly. Stab, stab, stab at her salad.

After lunch, Piper and Mia left to run errands, and Agatha and Summer dropped in at the bookstore. The place was brimming with readers. As Summer walked in, a jolt of panic jabbed her. What did she understand about running a bookstore?

"It's all yours. What will you do with it?" Agatha said.

"I guess that depends on my job. If I don't have one, I'll stay here and manage the place."

"Well, I hope they fire you. It's the best thing."

"Aunt Agatha!"

"What fools they must be not to see your worth. They're making a big deal over a little video."

They walked toward the coffeepot.

Academia was a strange world. People on the outside didn't get it. There were the written rules, and then there were unspoken rules. The truth of the matter was that Summer had been disappointed with her job for a while. She'd always wanted to teach, to light young minds with a passion for the Bard. She hadn't counted on the inter-office politics. The way everything was easier if you were a male teacher. The way the dean was capable of making your life miserable. If your colleagues took a dislike to you, it was like working in a prison cell.

Summer tried to focus on the teaching, not the politics of the small university department. It was the only thing that got her through. And even teaching wasn't all that she hoped it would be.

Most of her students were there to fill an elective. Some of them came into her class with disdain for Shakespeare. But some students made it all worthwhile.

Summer poured herself some coffee as Agatha strolled over to the showcase of first editions. Not all of them were displayed. Hildy kept a few at home and a few in a safe deposit box.

"Hey, Agatha," Poppy said. "How are you?"

"We just came from the lawyer's office."

"For what?"

Summer stirred cream into her coffee as a woman with an armful of books moved by her.

"Hildy's will."

"Any surprises?"

"Well, she left me her first editions," Agatha said loudly. "Those books are mine."

Summer refrained from rolling her eyes. Aunt Agatha was so obvious.

But she was right. In a small island town like St. Brigid, the news would travel fast. Hopefully, they were wrong and nobody would bother Agatha. But in the meantime, Summer, Piper, and Mia were keeping a close watch on her.

"What are you going to do with them?

"I'm not sure yet. For now, I'll keep them where they are."

"Lovely," she said. "Oddly enough, people love to come and gawk at them."

If Summer were a dog, her ears would perk up. "Really? What do they do? Just stand there?"

"Oh yes. Some get a little emotional. Some come back every so often and look at them again. Henry, the English teacher? He's completely gaga over them."

Agatha and Summer exchanged knowing glances.

"Any English teacher or librarian would be, I imagine," Agatha said.

Doris and Marilyn walked out of the storeroom and over to the threesome.

"Well, hello there," Doris said. "What's going on?"

"Just back from the will reading," Agatha said. "Hildy left me her first editions. I was checking out the precious goods."

"Oh, I see," Doris said. "We were just going over the book club calendar. Hildy chose our books for the next six months, which was so typical of her."

"Is the bookstore yours now?" Marilyn turned to Summer.

Summer nodded. "Of course."

A woman passed by holding the hand of a child, who was not happy to be there. He wanted to be on the beach, building sand-castles or playing in the waves. Not in a bookstore that didn't even have any children's books. She dragged him along into the paranormal romance aisle. Poor kid.

So deep in her reflections was she that Summer didn't realize that the lull in conversation had prompted the others to look at her. "Oh," she said. "I'm keeping the bookstore. But I'm not sure if I'm staying to manage it. I do have a job back in Virginia."

"A very impressive job," Doris chimed in. "I'm sure it would be hard to leave it."

A queasiness came over Summer. She took a deep breath, then swallowed.

"Thanks, but I'm not sure about any of that." Summer stumbled off toward the bathroom as suddenly sickness thrummed through her. Was it the concussion? Was it the questioning? The idea of owning the bookstore? Her job? She ran to the bathroom, leaned over the toilet, and threw up her lunch.

A knock came at the door. "Summer, it's me—let me in. Are you okay?"

"Just a minute, Aunt Agatha," she said, splashing water on her face and wiping it off with a paper towel.

She unlocked the door.

"Are you okay? You look pale," her aunt said with concern.

"I need to go home."

Agatha nodded and took her by the elbow.

Maybe she'd pushed herself too far. The lawyer. The bookstore. After all, she did have a concussion. But she had hoped to stop by the police station to see if they'd gotten the final results back from her mother's autopsy. Or if they had any leads on her death. Were the police calling it a murder yet?

Summer climbed into the car. Agatha was unusually quiet as they drove back to the house.

"I must have eaten too much," Summer said as they walked toward the door.

"You probably did, with the concussion and all. But I'm sure it's been an emotional day." She paused. "It's going to take some time for you to sort through all of it emotionally."

Summer's legs felt heavy as she walked into the house. Her eyes focused on the couch, and her body followed her gaze. She slipped off her shoes and curled up on the couch, drifting off.

Chapter Thirty-Four

"Aww, Summer, Mommy loves you."

An odd voice awakened her. She opened her eyes.

"Aww, Summer, Mommy loves you."

She sat up on the couch, clutching her chest. Mr. Darcy was peering down at her. If a bird could express affection in its eyes, this bird did.

"Aww, Summer. Mommy loves you," he said again.

Fireworks exploded in her chest. The bird must've heard Hildy talking like that. He was a great imitator. "Aww, Summer. Mommy loves you."

She yanked off her mask. "I love Mommy too, Darcy."

Weird. The word *Mommy* coming out of her mouth. She'd not said it in thirty years.

"Love, love, love," he said and rocked back and forth, from one leg to the other.

"What a happy bird," Summer said, yawning and lying back down.

"Happy bird," he said and whistled.

She closed her eyes.

"Happy Summer? Happy Summer?" Whistle.

What an odd thing for the bird to ask. "I'm happy right now, Darcy. Lying here on the couch. Maybe not so happy elsewhere."

"Happy Summer?"

"Good question." She yawned again. "What is happiness anyway, Darcy? Money? A good job? Romance? I used to think I knew . . . but these days, I'm surprised by how little I know. Education or not." She paused, and the bird blinked, appearing as if he were enraptured by her speaking. "Like, I had no idea there had been so many offers made on the bookstore. Good offers too. And I didn't know people wanted Mom's first editions, did you?"

He cocked his head but didn't reply.

"And now there's danger everywhere I look. Someone set the house on fire. Then someone hit me. Now Aunt Agatha is courting danger. Mom wouldn't like that. At all."

"No," the bird said. "No, no, no."

"You've got that. Smart bird."

He quieted, lifted a wing and began cleaning it.

Well, she'd lost his attention—just like she managed to do with every man in her life. She refrained from rolling her eyes at herself as she pulled the covers closer around her. It was so quiet. Where was everybody?

Piper and Mia had gone off on some errands. But what about Aunt Agatha? Was she here?

Summer couldn't bother to lift her head and ask, let alone rouse herself off the couch to find her. She supposed it didn't matter. She didn't need a nurse. She just needed more sleep.

"*To sleep, perchance to dream,*'" she muttered to herself as she dozed off.

Her dreams had gotten vivid since returning home to St. Brigid, and it was almost like watching a movie of different times in her life. Scattered images, like scrapbook pages in no order. Holding her mother's hand along the beach. Walking along the shore, feeding the seagulls. The day the second floor opened at Beach Reaches. Sitting there with her mom, Agatha, and Gladys, drinking sweet tea beneath café umbrellas, a warm gentle breeze blowing through her hair. Her mom's laughter. If she could capture a sound to recall in any moment of need, that would be it: her mom's laughter.

She rolled over, facing the back of the couch, pressed herself against it. Drifted off again. Mom brushed the hair from her forehead. "Rest, sweet girl," she whispered. Her cool, smooth fingers felt good against Summer's warm skin. "Don't let it trouble you. It's all good. I'm okay."

"It's not all good, Mom. Who hurt you? Someone hurt you! They took you away from us!"

Drenched in sweat, Summer woke herself up with a start. Sat up. "Mom?"

"Summer?" Agatha said as she came into the room.

Aunt Agatha. Mr. Darcy. Couch. "Yes. I'm sorry. I was just . . . dreaming."

Agatha came and sat on the La-Z-Boy. "About your mother?" Summer nodded.

"I've yet to have a dream about her. I imagined I would, we were so close. They say spirits talk through their loved ones' dreams."

"That's silly."

"It's not." She shrugged. "But believe whatever you want. Did your mother talk to you?"

"In my dream, you mean? Yes."

Agatha sat forward. "What did she say?"

Summer reflected. "I think she said it's all good. Not to worry. That she's okay." She paused. "Which is ridiculous. She's not okay.

162

She's dead and the last time I checked, that's about as not okay as you can get."

"You're being way too logical, as usual, my dear. Death is not final. You should know that by now."

Not final? "How do you know? I mean, really know?"

Agatha raised her legs and flung them over the side of the chair. "There are two kinds of knowing. One is the kind where you've experienced it or it's a fact. Yes? The other is a feeling. And that might be the most important form of knowing."

Summer tossed her blanket off and sat up on the couch. "You're sounding like Mom now."

Agatha beamed. "I suppose I don't mind that at all. "

She studied her aunt, deep in her own memories and mourning. "Tell me something aunt Agatha. Would the Hildy you remember not want revenge if someone killed her?"

Agatha sighed. "I get it. She certainly would. But now that's she's gone, she might see things differently. It might not matter on the other side. If you will." She looked sheepish.

Summer kept her own counsel. She loved her aunt but had never heard so much poppycock in her life.

* * *

It had been a day since Agatha announced it loudly at the bookstore that she'd inherited the first editions. So far, nobody had stalked her, made an offer, attacked her, or set her house on fire. Thank the Universe.

Yesterday's outing had been too much for Summer, so she'd stayed home today. But that didn't mean she couldn't continue her investigating.

She scribbled down the motives.

1. Wanting the bookstore
2. Wanting the first editions

Those were the only two motives she could imagine. If there was another one, she had no clue.

Trouble was, those motives didn't give Summer much. Henry was the only person who'd expressed an interest in both the bookstore and the first editions. He was annoying and a cad, evidently, but was he a killer?

Summer reached for her laptop and keyed in his name. A string of things came up, mostly related to his teaching. He had a website and a blog. She clicked on it and read it over. The man was a good writer. He wrote about his students and his life as a teacher and on St. Brigid. Nothing about first editions or the bookstore. Nothing leading Summer to believe that he harbored dark murderous tendencies.

But it wasn't that simple. Most murder victims knew their killers. And if it was clear that they were killers, nobody would let them into their lives. People were complex.

She clicked on to another site where students rate their teachers. She knew it well, as she'd been rated there. Not one bad review on Henry. That in itself was suspicious.

She clicked on the Beach Reads Bookstore website—then to the Mermaid Pie Book Club page—and there they were, with his arm draped over her mother. Hildy was grinning but looking off to the side. What was she looking at? His gaze fell on her.

A tingle traveled up her spine. Was Henry sleeping with her mother? He was Summer's age. Could it be? Her mom had never gone for younger men, but that didn't mean she hadn't changed her mind.

She texted Piper. "Was Mom sleeping with Henry?"

While she waited on the response, she checked out Henry's Facebook page. Typical stuff. Yes, he was friends with her mom, but he was also friends with everybody else in the book club. So that didn't mean a thing. She scanned his friend list and stopped on Cash. There he was in all his glory. She couldn't help herself. She clicked on him.

He was married to Sonya. Summer didn't recognize her. Had two kids. He still looked good. In fact, it looked as though he hadn't aged at all. The children were healthy and beautiful. A wistful pang swept through her. This could have been her life. Staying on the island, being Cash's wife, bearing his children.

Thank God she left when she did. Her life in Staunton was far from perfect, but she'd needed to leave this island when she did. And she didn't regret it—except for the lack of time she'd gotten to spend with her mom. But that said, she'd assumed she would have more time. Someone had stolen it from her. Anger tore through her.

Was it Henry? One of the book club members? Someone else she had considered?

Her phone dinged. Piper. *I don't think so. Why?*

Summer texted back: *I saw a photo of them together on the website and just wondered.*

The answer came back right away. *Be over soon.*

Great!

Summer moved back to her research on Henry. She checked out the groups he was in. Classic Movie Buffs. Harry Potter in the Classroom, Gambler's Anonymous. What? *How could he be anonymous if it's on Facebook?* She clicked on it. Private. Hmm. So Henry had a gambling problem, which explained his remark about not having any money. Not having any money often led to a sense of desperation. He'd just moved up to the first spot on her list of suspects. A cad with a gambling problem.

The trouble was he'd not been anywhere around the house. He couldn't have taken the batteries out of the smoke detector. But she was assuming it had happened since she'd been home. Perhaps it hadn't. Maybe he'd been here before her mom died.

The other people who'd been in the house were herself, Agatha, Piper, Mia, Doris, Glads, and Marilyn. Could she consider all of them suspects? Certainly not her cousin or her aunt. That left Glads and Doris, since Marilyn had been out of town. Which made little sense. At all.

Chapter Thirty-Five

"Do you know if my mom had anybody over a few days before her death?"

Piper stood at the kitchen counter, pouring them both a cup of coffee. She brought the cups over to the table where Summer sat.

"I'm just not sure. Mia was in and out of here all the time. And your mother had this open-door policy. Everybody knew they were welcome."

Summer was aware of that. She didn't even have an open-door policy for her students. She shuddered to think of it. Half the island population could have been here. "I wonder if there's any way we could find out."

"I'll talk to Mia tonight and see if she knows. What are you thinking?"

"I'm trying to figure out who would have taken out the batteries—who would've had access. At first I thought of the women who've been here since her death. Then it dawned on me that it could've happened weeks before Mom died."

Piper frowned. "It seems unlikely, knowing how careful Aunt Hildy was, but it's worth looking into. So you definitely think the person who set the fire is also the person who killed your mother."

"Yes, but I need more proof." Summer took a sip of coffee. "That's so good." She took another sip.

"First, we need to know how she died. Have you heard anything at all from the police about the final autopsy results?"

"Nothing."

"Well, we recognize she didn't die of a heart attack, even though that's what they say."

"It seems impossible," Summer said. "It happens to people occasionally if there's some underlying issue." A thought occurred to her. "Was Mom still seeing the same doctor?"

"I believe so."

"I wonder how much information he'd give me."

"That's a good question."

"Let's go," Summer said, reaching for her bag.

"Now, wait a minute. You've got a concussion and last time you went . . . I sound like my mom, right?"

"You do. But I hear you. I think I pushed myself too hard. Traveled too many places—the lawyer's office, then the bookstore. And it was a stressful day."

Piper folded her arms. "I agree. But if anything happens to you . . ."

Summer shrugged. "Come on. You'll be with me the whole time. If I start to feel bad, I'll tell you."

Piper lifted an eyebrow with incredulity.

"I promise."

"Okay, let's go. I'll drive."

"Good idea."

* * *

The cousins drove the short distance to Dr. Chang's office. The parking lot had a few cars in it, and Summer hoped it wasn't a busy day. It wasn't a nice thing to do—just to pop in on a doctor. But a strong impulse drove her forward. She needed to get a move on this. She'd not considered this before. This thread warranted some plucking.

They walked into the office, which was cool and crisply decorated. Even the plants were well manicured.

The woman behind the counter considered them. "Sign the check-in form, please."

"I'm not a patient," Summer said.

Her eyebrows lifted in interest. "How can I help you?"

"My mom was a patient. She recently passed away. I was just wondering if the doctor might have some time to chat with me about her."

"Is your mother Hildy? Are you Summer, the Shakespeare professor?" She brightened.

"Yes," Summer said.

"I love your mother, and I'm going to miss her. When she came in, she always brought us a treat. Vegan cookies or cupcakes. Something. Such a doll."

"Yes," Summer said, pausing. "So is Dr. Chang available?"

"Let me see," she said, plucking at her keyboard and staring at the schedule. "He'll be back any minute. He may have some time then."

"Is he at lunch?" Piper asked.

"No," she said. "He'll be right back. Make yourself at home. There's coffee. Tea. Water."

"Thank you," Summer said.

Piper and Summer sat down next to each other and watched the fish in a huge tank swim around. Shocking bright orange fish. Summer's thoughts turned to spiders. She glanced around. Her heart raced. Anytime she ran into a small critter, spiders came to her mind. She stood and paced, trying to avoid the huge tank.

"What's wrong?"

She shook her head. "You don't want to know."

"You don't like the fish?"

Summer nodded again. "For some reason, they remind me of spiders."

Piper smiled. "What?"

"Right. It makes no sense. But what does anymore?" The pacing helped. Summer was breathing fine.

"Miss Merriweather?"

"Yes?"

"Dr. Chang is here." She opened the door back to the exam rooms. "Follow me."

They walked past several and sunk around into an office where the doctor sat, reading over papers on his desk. He stood. "Summer! So good to see you. You, too Piper." It was kind of uncomfortable to sit across the desk from a man who'd seen your bare butt, among other things. He shook her hand. Then Piper's.

"I'm sorry to hear about Hildy." He dropped his head and shook it. "I was shocked. Please sit down."

"Yes, well, that's what we're doing here. I'm inquiring about Mom's health before she died."

He sat back in his chair. "I can't give you access to those records."

"That's not what I'm asking. I just want to find out if she was healthy. Was she having problems?"

"Your mother was healthy. That's why I was shocked to hear of her death. She didn't have heart issues at all. In fact, she had great blood pressure. Which she would tell you was from years of not eating meat." He grinned.

Summer's brain twisted and turned. Her mom had been healthy, just as she suspected.

"You're verifying our feelings and, in fact, what everybody we've talked to says. Nobody was aware of any health issues," Piper said.

He lifted a finger. "That said, these things do happen. Science and medicine can only explain so much."

"Will you be viewing her final autopsy results?" Summer asked.

"If you want me to, you must request it with the chief of police." He rapped his fingers on the desk and stopped. "Can I ask what's going on?"

Summer drew in a breath. "We think someone might have killed my mother. She'd been getting threatening notes and phone calls. Other things just don't add up. Like the fact that she was so healthy. We're just checking into it."

Summer had exposed herself to more ridicule. But instead, he nodded in consideration. "If there's anything I can do, please reach out. I hate to think of anybody hurting her. But anything's possible. Have you talked with the police?"

"Yes, Chief Singer's not taking me seriously, but I think the fire chief is."

"Someone set Hildy's house on fire when we were inside," Piper said.

"This was after she died?" the doctor asked.

"Yes, which makes us think he or she might be after me next."

"From what I remember, if they get you, they'll get more than they bargain for." He grinned at Piper.

Her chin lifted and her mouth curled into a grin. "I'd agree to that statement."

Chapter Thirty-Six

"Let's stop in at the police department," Summer said. "It's on the way and I feel fine."

"You promised," Piper said. "I think one visit is enough for today. Besides, you can call the police from home."

Duly scolded, Summer agreed. But she felt fine. She did. The trip to see her mom's doctor had been a success. He'd verified everything she'd felt. Hildy was healthy.

At the same time, sadness washed over her. Someone had killed her mom. She was so loved on the island and was such a good person. It felt like a big screw-you from God. Anger welled up from her guts. One moment sad, the next angry. *Control yourself, woman.* She wouldn't be ruled by emotions. Not now. Not when her mom needed her to think as logically as possible. She swallowed her feelings. She knew how to do that. Was well practiced.

When the two of them arrived at the house, Aunt Agatha was there, hands on hips. "Where were you?"

"Calm down, Mom. We just went to see Dr. Chang."

"Hildy's doctor?"

"Yes, and he confirmed everything he could without revealing too much, that she was healthy," Summer said as she sat down at the kitchen island.

"Well, we figured," Agatha said, "but I suppose it's good to hear from a pro."

"Do you know if anybody was here the days before her death?" Summer asked.

Agatha looked perplexed.

"We're trying to figure out who took the batteries out of the smoke detector."

"Mia was in and out of here," Agatha said. "That's the only person. But you know your mother."

"Where is Mia?" Summer asked.

"Out with her friends. And that's a good thing. I've been so worried about her. She was so close to your mother."

"I'm going to text her and ask her to stop by later. She may know something and not even realize it," Summer said. "Also, I need to find out more about what her last day was like. Did she go straight from home to the shop?"

"Most of the time, yes. The only other thing she did was attend yoga classes some mornings. But I'm uncertain whether she attended that morning."

"She also volunteered a couple of places. The women's shelter and the library, of course."

"Women's shelter? I think we need to check and see when she was there the last time. Maybe she got involved with someone there."

"That could be," Agatha said.

"What did she do at the library?"

"She spearheaded a reading program where she and some others would go to terminally ill patients and read to them,"

Summer warmed. "Now that sounds like Mom."

She scribbled down *Glads*. "I'll call Glads to see if she knows if Mom was reading that day. And I'll call the women's center."

She had an action plan. Keeping busy was what she needed to do. She jotted down *Henry*.

"Aunt Agatha, have you heard from anybody about your new-found ownership of the first editions?"

"Only Henry."

Summer recalled his gambling problem and money issues. "Did he make you an offer?"

"Yes, but of course I didn't take it."

"He's got gambling problems. I'm assuming he also has the money issues that go along with that. So it's odd that he has the money to make an offer."

"Maybe his gambling turned around. Maybe he had a good night."

"He couldn't have waited awhile? Aunt Hildy just died a few days ago!" Piper said, face red with anger as a tear escaped. Piper was an angry crier. Always had been.

Her mother wrapped her arm around her. "Calm down." She paused. "But you're right. The more I think about it, the more suspicious that man is."

"He said he was a friend of Mom's, but she made special mention of him in her will—to not sell her books to him."

The wheels in Piper's head were turning. "But if he did hang out with her, he definitely could have been in this house. Nobody would have suspected."

"No, indeed. Plus, he's a member of the book club. Nobody would think a thing of it," Agatha added.

"How do we prove it?" Piper said, sniffing.

"We need to prove he was here," Summer replied. "And we need to know exactly how she died so that we can link the murder weapon to him."

Agatha's eyes widened into circles. "Weapon? There was no weapon."

"You know what I mean." She officially had a heart attack, but someone could have given her some drug or substance to induce a heart attack. Why hadn't Summer concluded this before? She dialed Ben, leaving Agatha to calm Piper down.

"Ben Singer, please. This is Summer Merriweather, calling about my mom."

"Just a moment, please."

The phone rang more than a few times. "Hello," he croaked into the phone. "What can I do for you, Summer?"

Have you gotten the autopsy and blood results back yet?" Agatha and Piper looked up at her.

"Should be any day now. I'm sorry it's taking so long."

"I want Doc Chang to review the results. Do you have a problem with that?"

"No. But why?"

"He claims Mom was healthy. He was her doctor. So I think if there's anything off, he'll be able to spot it."

"I see. Are you still—"

"Yes, I think my mom was murdered. I understand that there are several drugs and poisons that will mimic a heart attack, and I'd like to see if she ingested any of those."

"Well, you're within your rights to ask for these tests, but I don't want you to get your hopes up, Summer. As I've said before."

Summer clicked off the phone. She didn't want to hear anymore.

"Well?" Agatha said.

"Well, what?"

"What did he say?"

"He said the final tests aren't back yet but that I'm within my rights to ask for the results of them. But then he started down the same path as before. The sometimes-people-just-die path. I don't want to hear it. I want answers. I need answers."

Chapter Thirty-Seven

A phone call from Poppy interrupted their visit. "I'm sorry to disturb, but we've got a problem with reconciling the books and wonder if you could help. Now that you're the owner and everything."

Summer never reconciled anything in her life, but she supposed it couldn't be too hard. "Reconciling the books? Sure. I'll be right over."

Agatha and Piper looked at one another.

"They want you to do what?"

"You heard me."

Agatha looked frightened. "That's a very complicated process. Your mother hated it."

"Mom, she's got a PhD in Shakespearean lit. She can handle it," Piper said.

She replied with a snort. "Very impressive, but that has nothing to do with what they're asking of her. Spreadsheets. Figures. Databases."

Piper stood. "We'll come with you. Between all of us, we'll figure it out."

Agatha reached for her bag. "You'd think they could do it at the store. They manage this stuff."

"Let's walk," Summer said.

The three of them left the house and took the sandy path to the beach, shoes slipped off, heading toward the boardwalk.

"I need to find someone who knows what they're doing. I may head back to Staunton."

"They usually have it taken care of. Poppy knows what she's doing, but it must be a big problem. Computers!" Agatha said over the sound of crashing waves.

"Surf's getting stronger," Piper said.

She and Piper used to watch the cycle of the ocean and the moon tides when they were kids. But Summer lost track of all of that and could barely remember the names of the different tides.

They stood for a moment, watching the waves crash into the sand. Foamy caps left behind. The sun was sinking, though still far from setting. Summer and Piper continued walking.

The scent of funnel cakes and hot dogs hung in the air. The boardwalk was teeming with people in line for hot dogs and funnel cakes. Lemonade. Ice Cream. Young people spilled out of the arcade. The place was hopping.

Finally, the two of them arrived a Beach Reads. Summer opened the door as the mermaid looked on. Bloody thing—for some reason it always chilled Summer. It was just a carving, and it was intricate and beautiful, but Summer also found it a bit . . . well, creepy. In a *Titanic* kind of way. Sunken ships. Lost lives.

Poppy rushed toward them as they entered. Flustered. "I'm so glad to see you. I just don't know what's going on. If it's me. If it's QuickBooks or . . ." She shrugged. "I just don't know. This has never happened before."

"Okay, First calm down," Piper said. "We're here now. Just show us the problem and we'll take it from there."

Poppy led them to the computer in the back. There was a huge spreadsheet on the screen, which sent Summer's heart afire. Nothing like a beautifully organized spreadsheet. She scrolled over to the balances. "See?"

The bookstore appeared to be just over $6,000 in arrears.

"That can't be right," Piper said.

"I know."

"I need to get on the register to give Cally a break," Poppy said.

"Okay, we'll take it from here."

Summer and Piper scanned over each expenditure, each deposit. And a few hours later, they still had no answers. The money appeared to be gone. Had someone taken it? Who would have access to the money besides Poppy?

Summer groaned. "Who would do something like this?"

"I don't know, but we need to figure it out."

"We've been so focused on the murder investigation that we've taken our eyes off the store. I need to get my act together."

"I think, to be safe, we should hire an auditor."

"Hire with what money?"

"The bookstore will have to pay for it."

Summer mulled it over. "Maybe what we need is an IT guy. Someone who can tell us who's been on this computer and what they were doing."

"Probably more expensive than an auditor."

"Okay. I'm just thinking out loud. What about Mia? Didn't you say she's into computers?"

"She is," Piper said, "but I'm not sure how good she is or how much she can do. But she has a friend who's amazing. We start there." Piper pulled her phone out of her bag and called Mia.

Summer focused on the spreadsheet in front of her as Piper spoke with Mia on the phone.

Piper placed her phone on the desk. "She'll be right over."

Poppy wandered in. "Someone's here asking about a Shakespeare folio."

Summer had almost forgotten. She'd yet to even glance at it. "It's not for sale."

Poppy smiled. "Okay." She left the room.

Soon enough Mia was there with a friend and Agatha.

When Summer explained what the problem was, Agatha laughed.

"What's so funny? There's missing money."

"Have you looked under the desk pad?"

"Why would we?" Piper said.

Agatha lifted the corner and there were several checks dated the end of the month.

Agatha shrugged. "She wrote checks, placed them here for the end of the month. She waited until the last possible moment."

"Why didn't Poppy know that?"

"Nobody knew except for us," Agatha smiled. "I do the same thing. Our parents always had a corner they slid checks under."

Summer didn't know whether to be miffed at the innocence of such a practice or just happy that they weren't being ripped off.

"You look perplexed," Agatha said. "This is very typical of Hildy. The rest of this clean office is not, however."

Poppy walked into the room to grab some bookmarks.

"Did you clean this office?" Agatha asked.

"Me? No."

"Who did?" Summer asked.

"The book group. They were back here the night she died, almost all night."

"All of them?" Agatha squealed.

"No, just, you know, the inner circle." She held a stack of colorful bookmarks. "Can I go?"

Agatha nodded.

When she left, the room was silent. Even Mia didn't say a word.

"What exactly is 'the inner circle'?" Summer finally said.

"You know. It would be Glads; Marilyn; myself—and I wasn't here; Bobby Jo, who's on vacation; and Loretta. Sometimes Henry . . . It's not an official thing. The inner circle. It's just the longest members and her closest friends."

Summer had forgotten about Loretta. She's spoken with Glads, had yet to speak with Marilyn or Doris. And she would. She needed to understand why they were in this office cleaning. Who had told them to do such a thing? Would her mom have appreciated these women snooping through her things? They were her closest friends, but it still seemed a bit creepy and invasive. Summer didn't like it. Not one bit.

Chapter Thirty-Eight

S ummer strolled through the bookstore one last time before heading home. This was something her mom had always done. And Summer hated it because it meant they weren't going home just yet. Hildy always found something to fix—an out-of-place book, a left-behind coffee cup, a customer with questions. Summer was better off right now because the general public kind of customer didn't know she owned the bookstore. So she was incognito, traveling up and down the aisle, straightening books, picking up coffee cups, muttering to herself. What was she going to do? How would she manage the store from her home in Staunton?

Did she even have a job at the university anymore?

The school had sent flowers to her mom's funeral, but she herself had not heard from one person. She tried not to dwell on it—but it burned.

She needed a bit of clarity from her boss. She also needed clarity on her mom's death.

She paced the spent cups in the bin for cleaning and moseyed back into the office.

"Are you ready?" Piper said.

"As ready as I'll ever be."

They gathered their things and left the cool shelter of the book-store. The light and heat hit Summer like a slap in the face. "Good god. It's horrible out here."

"Funny, isn't it?" Piper said as she dodged a child running to keep up with his parents. "It's not nearly as hot as what we used to love. Remember, we couldn't wait for days like this. Now the heat makes me sick."

"Me too. I can't stand it." Was she thinking of coming back to her small beach town even though she hated the heat? She might not have a choice. She might not have a job. As stupid as it sounded, the spider incident might have been the last straw.

Her last review? She was too tough on the kids—kids sup-posed to be there for a college education, which these days, seemed to be something you bought, not something you worked at or earned.

She had also not published recently, had not served on enough committees, nor had she offered open office hours. She was also the only female Shakespeare professor in the program. She refused to believe that her troubles were because of that.

As they walked along, Summer spotted the old lemonade trailer that she'd loved as a kind. Best lemonade ever. "Do you want some?" she asked Piper, who was trying to tame her blonde hair by pulling it back into a ponytail.

"Yeah, sure."

As they walked along with their lemonades, toward the house, a welling of emotions bloomed in Summer's chest. The lemonade brought her straight back to her youth, a time when she'd had no worries, when all she had was time on her hands, and she still had her mom. She blinked away a tear and gathered herself. *Get it together, Summer.*

"So good," Piper said as they walked along, past the church where the funeral had taken place.

"Ah, yes . . . so what's the scoop on Poppy? I just considered it strange that Mom's assistant didn't know about those checks."

"Poppy's sweet. But she's not the brightest bulb in the pack, if you get my drift."

"So why did Mom hire her?"

"I'm not sure. She is very good with the customers and knows mysteries. I think she's started a mystery book group." She slipped off her shoes as they started walking on the sand toward the neighborhood. "She's also a single mom."

Summer slipped off her shoes. The sand felt good and familiar. "Mom was like a beacon for all the single mothers. Which reminds me, I need to visit the women's shelter. Perhaps she got involved in something there. A domestic dispute?"

"You know she also read to ill people. Kids. Older folks. But mostly people who were terminally ill." Piper paused. "I don't understand how she did it. She became very close to people, even though they were going to die."

Summer warmed. "That sounds like Mom." She drew in a breath, then released it. "So I doubt any of those folks or their families murdered Mom. But I'm wondering about the women's shelter. Could she have stepped into something there?"

"That's a good question. It's had a hard time of it—lost a bunch of funding and it's not big enough for state funding. The last I read, it's very close to being shut down."

Hildy had said that it was a luxury and a necessity to have the shelter on such a small island. She'd helped get its original funding and volunteered there from the start. Summer needed to stop by and find out if her mother had been involved in any bad domestic situations.

"I'd forgotten how good these lemonades are," Piper said.

A kite flew across the sky, a young boy trailing after it. Piper and Summer were just about at the path toward the house. As they turned down the path, a rushing movement from one of the seagrass-covered dunes startled Summer. She jumped. But soon enough, a cat revealed itself and set off on its merry way.

Chapter Thirty-Nine

S oon after they entered the house, a knock came at the door. Glads and Marilyn arrived with even more food. When Summer opened the door, the two of them entered like it was their home, sashayed straight to the kitchen and found places for the food, rinsed off dishes, and placed them in the dishwasher.

"Ladies, you don't need to go to all this trouble," Summer said.

The two of them ignored her as they finished putting things away.

"How are you doing?" Glads said.

The question stopped Summer dead in her tracks. How was she doing? Someone had killed her mother and probably tried to kill her. And she was trying to find a killer. She didn't have time to worry about how she was doing, did she? Summer shrugged. "I've been busy."

"How's the concussion," Glads persisted.

"Oh that. Yes, it bothers me off and on. I'd like to do more. I have things to do. But I have to watch myself."

As they women moved around the kitchen like a well-oiled machine, Summer remembered her mom's office.

"Why was my mom's office cleaned after she died?"

Piper stopped pouring a drink and looked up. Glads shut the refrigerator door and spun around. "I told them not to do it. They wouldn't listen."

"It was Doris's idea. She said she didn't think Hildy would want to leave behind such a mess. It's a time-honored Southern tradition to clean after someone passes away," Marilyn said.

"It is?" Summer said. "I never heard of that. But in any case, what happened to all of her stuff that was there?"

"It wasn't anything . . . just junk. Most of it we pitched because it was stuff nobody needed."

Summer felt her pulse in her temples. She tried to choose her words carefully. "Who decided what to trash and what not to trash?"

Marilyn wiped off the counter with a paper towel. "It was clear what was trash and what wasn't. Your mother hung on to everything, and these days a lot of it is on the computer. We pitched nothing important. We filed it all. So if there is something you're looking for, it should be in the file cabinet."

Unless it's something I don't know I'm looking for, Summer inwardly fumed.

"Did we overstep? I'm sorry. We were trying to be helpful," Marilyn said. "I'm sorry I can't stay. I've been corralled into cleaning the library tonight. Our service is on vacation." She placed her hands on her hips, and an iris peeked out from her collar bone.

These women were always cleaning or cooking or delivering food or helping in some other way. Summer felt a pang of guilt for any thread of suspicion she held against any of them And yet . . . they were some of the people who had direct access, and things were not always as they appeared.

"I'm sorry if I seem ungrateful. It was startling to walk in and see such a clean office, realizing what a mess Mom was."

"It wasn't a dirty mess, though. It was a happy mess, you know?" Glads said with a winsome note in her voice. Red splotches forming on her cheeks, around her eyes. She was trying not to cry.

"Oh, Glads," Summer said and reached out for her. "We're all just doing the best we can. It's okay to cry." Marilyn buried her head into Summer's shoulder. Finally, sniffing, she pulled away.

"I just don't see how things will go on without her. She was the center of everything . . . one of my best friends," she argued with wildly gesturing arms. "I don't understand any of it." She sniffed again and Piper handed her a box of tissue.

Summer wanted to pull them into the fold. But she wasn't sure how to approach it. "Do you two have time to sit down?"

"No, no, we've got to go. But we'll see you at the book club meeting tomorrow, right?"

"Is that tomorrow? I've not finished the book."

Summer felt a brief surge of panic, as if she realized she'd not studied for a huge test.

Glads laughed and waved her off. "It doesn't matter. Sometimes you just can't do it. As long as you've read most of it, you can take part in the discussion. No worries."

Summer smiled back at her. Well, that was good to know, but she definitely felt the urge to finish the book now. Besides, she wanted to know how it'd end, and she despised other people telling her. She even despised that she wanted to know how it ended. It was like good chocolate candy—she couldn't stop herself. Was it like an addiction? Was that the secret sauce for romances selling so well? She wanted to research it. And she would. But now, Piper was reheating crab cakes that Marilyn and Glads had brought, and the scent was distracting.

"We've got to run," Glads said. "If you need anything, let us know."

Summer nodded. "Thank you, ladies. Those crab cakes ought to hit the spot."

After they exited, Piper spun around to face Summer. "I noticed a few things. Did you?"

Summer reached up into the cupboard for plates. "Like what?"

"Doris is never with them anymore, and it was her idea to clean the office. I wonder if they had a falling out."

"I don't think so. Her husband is ill. She may just be busy."

Piper placed the crab cakes on the plate, the scent filling the room. "There's something about Doris I don't like. I always talk myself out of not liking someone. But . . ."

Summer shrugged. "You can't like everyone. No matter how hard you try."

"I had no idea your mother was so close to Marilyn." Piper sat down at the table.

"Oh yes. Marilyn, Glads, Posey, Aunt Agatha. They formed the romance readers book club twenty-some years ago. Mom was close to all of them. They were like an army, the way they worked together, stood up for one another, had each other's backs. It was pretty amazing."

Piper cleared her throat. "Mom used to say you're lucky if you find one true friend in your life. Seems like these women are a lucky bunch."

"Indeed."

* * *

Many women weren't so lucky. Summer stood in front of the St. Brigid women's shelter. Its parking lot was forlorn, with only three cars, and one of them looked dangerously dilapidated. The green paint on the building was peeling and cracking.

Summer pushed the door open. The lobby was clear, but there was a brown-skinned woman at the reception area. She looked up at Summer. "Hello. How can I help you?

"I'm here about my mother."

Her head tilted, and she leaned forward. "Is she in some kind of trouble?" She reached for papers.

"No. Well. Sort of. My mom is dead. And she was a volunteer here."

"Do you mean Hildy Merriweather?"

"Yes, she was my mother."

"You must be Summer. I'm Keri. Have a seat," she said, cracking a smile. "We'd not seen your mother in a while. I was so sorry to hear of her passing."

Summer sat. "Thank you."

The phone rang. "Just a moment, please."

Keri answered the phone, and Summer tried not to listen to the conversation. She looked around the office. There was a poster titled "Is It Abuse?" Another poster had the title "Suspect Neglect?"

"You need to come in," Summer overheard the receptionist say. "I know it's hard."

Summer busied herself with a piece of lint on her jeans. Finally, the woman hung up.

"Sorry," she said. "Now, how can I help you?"

"I was wondering if my mom had gotten involved with any—I don't know— dangerous situations?"

Keri's brows knitted.

"She received threats before she died," Summer continued.

"All the work we do here is anonymous. She never used her real name."

Oh.

"Well, I didn't know that." Summer paused. "But this island is small, and my mom was sort of popular, out in the community a lot. Bookstore owner. You know."

Keri nodded. "I suppose it's possible. But most of the population here are victims, not perpetrators. I don't know if she ever met any of the perps. In fact, she mostly just provided books. We have a whole library stocked by your mother."

Summer's heart flicked.

"She took women to doctor's and lawyer's appointments—things like that."

"Can you think of anybody here she came into contact with who might have wanted to hurt her?"

Keri frowned. "Not specifically, no. and as I mentioned earlier, she'd not been around in a while. Months, I'd say."

Strange.

"But Mom loved it here. Why wasn't she around?"

The woman shrugged. "Sometimes we counsel our volunteers to take time off. It gets to be hard on them. Your mother volunteered here for a long time. Maybe she just needed a break."

"Did you counsel her to take a break?"

"No, I didn't. Not specifically. Look, what exactly do you need to know? I've got an appointment coming in about fifteen."

Summer leaned in. "I think my mom was murdered."

The woman's face drained of blood. "What makes you say that?"

For the first time since Summer had begun this investigation, here was a person who took her seriously.

"She received these threats on her life. She was a healthy woman, and they are trying to say she died of a heart attack. I think it was something more."

The woman leaned back into her chair. "Hmm. "

"Do you think I'm crazy, like everybody else?" Summer tried to smile.

"One thing I've learned in this business is that people are troubled and do awful things. Another thing I've learned is to trust your instincts." She paused. "I can't tell you how many women come here saying if only they'd listened to that little voice in their head from the start. So, no, I don't think you're crazy."

The phone rang again. "Excuse me."

Was she the only staff member here? Summer didn't see or hear anyone else. There more offices tucked back inside the building, she was sure. But were there people in them?

"I told you the center is having some difficulties, but the check is on the way," Keri said and hung up. She glanced up at Summer. "Now, where were we?"

Summer didn't want to take up much of her time, so she spit it out. "Was Mom involved with anybody who could have hurt her?"

Keri's eyes slanted, as if she were deep in thought. "Your mother worked with victims. I don't think she ever came into contact with anybody else. But I'll check on that for you and get back with you."

A sliver of hope.

As Summer drove back to the house, she worried about the women's shelter. It sounded like it was in a financial struggle. If she could see her way clear of her debt, she'd like to help them out. She vowed to herself that she'd try to use whatever money her mom had left to help them.

Her phone dinged, reminding her she had a phone appointment with her shrink. She should be home just in time.

Chapter Forty

"I don't think you're dealing with your emotions," Dr. Gildea said. "Losing a parent is an extremely difficult matter. You seem to be focused on this being a murder and finding the killer rather than giving yourself time to grieve."

This wasn't quite true. "I'll admit that I'm not sitting around beating my chest and crying, but I've had my emotional moments."

"And what about this murder case? Have the police even deemed it that?"

His question hung in the air. "Are you seeing things that aren't there as a way of diverting your attention?"

"You might have been on to something, except since the last time I talked with you, someone tried to burn the house down and I was attacked and ended up with a concussion. I understand someone wants me off this island and is trying to harm me."

"Then what are you doing there? If your life is in jeopardy, you need to leave and let the police deal with your mother's death." He paused. "It would be best for you to come back to Staunton and resume your life."

Her heart sank. "That's impossible right now. There's just too much to settle here. Along with my mom's murder, I've inherited a very busy and successful bookstore. I have decisions to make about it."

"Have you heard from the dean?"

"Not at all."

"I'd suggest you give it a few days and then call him. Fall is right around the corner. You can't keep hiding from this."

God, her therapist sounded like her mother. She didn't consider herself hiding—not now, and not when she left for England. She was removing herself from the situation to get distance so she could think.

"I'm not hiding. I'm dealing with the fallout from Mom's death."

"Okay then." He breathed into the phone. "Resolve to call the dean tomorrow. That's your assignment. I need to go. I have a call coming in. But Summer, please, call the dean. You need resolution."

And how. She needed resolution everywhere. Her job. Her mom's death. The bookstore. The job situation wouldn't be complicated at all if she were well liked and successful. She couldn't think of one of her colleagues that would stand up for her when push came to shove. Her mom had said she was paranoid, but her mother didn't understand what academia was like. Summer hadn't understood until she'd gotten there. The backbiting. The pressure to publish. The pressure to keep the students happy. Which wasn't an issue when she was in school.

Somehow today's students had become customers, not students—at least not in Summer's book.

Maybe she should seriously give up the academic life. But it was what she'd always wanted. A popular Shakespeare quote came to her mind: *"All the world's a stage, and all the men and women merely players. They have their exits and their entrances; And one man in his time plays many parts."*

Many parts. What if she didn't give them a chance to fire her? What if she quit? As a kind of pause. She could look for another university position while managing the bookstore. Nothing wrong with that.

She'd definitely phone the dean tomorrow.

Had she made a decision about her life? Maybe. Maybe she had.

She was so tired of trying to fit in. Trying to please everyone. Giving her energy to unappreciative people.

She lay back on the couch, picked up *Nights on Bellamy Harbor* and read until she fell asleep.

She dreamed of Omar, the main character, who, in the dream, had an office next to Beach Reads. Their eyes locked from the moment she entered his office. And the next thing she knew, they were on the thickly carpeted floor, tearing the clothes off each other.

Summer awakened in a sweat, startled by the ferocity and passion in her dream. Then she found herself laughing. Perhaps this was one thing that kept the women in the book club coming back for more romance.

She rolled over and drifted back to sleep.

* * *

The next morning, while on the porch, with her coffee and a notebook, she scribbled a list of to-do items to follow up on hunches she had about her mother's death.

1. *Check up on the women's shelter*
2. *Talk with Henry again (only suspect?)*
3. *Call Levi, the fire investigator*

4. *Call Ben Singer*
5. *Continue to question book club members*

The last item on the list bothered her. As she contemplated it, she couldn't believe any of them would hurt her mother. But maybe they knew something she didn't know.

The phone buzzed, and she picked it up. "Summer, you need to get to the bookstore. There's been a robbery." Poppy's voice quivered.

Fear and confusion pierced through the center of her. "What? Come again?"

"Robbery—Beach Reads. Come now."

Summer drew in air and released it slowly. "I'll be right there."

Beach Reads had never been robbed. Never. It was a measure of pride with Hildy, who would've been turning over in her grave if she had one.

Chapter Forty-One

Summer rushed to the bookstore. The beach and the boardwalk, along with the people dotted on it, all blurred as she hurried toward Beach Reads. Her mom's lifetime project. Her dream made into reality. *Someone had the audacity to rob it!*

Her heart thundered as she approached Ben Singer, who was standing outside the store, looking at the door.

"Summer—"

"What happened?" she managed to say.

An odd look came over his face before it returned to its normal, stone-cold expression. "I'm trying to find that out. But there wasn't any breaking and entering. If there was, I can't find it."

"What was taken?"

"Five hundred fifty dollars, petty cash. And the first editions." He frowned.

Pings of anger zoomed through her. "Henry is the only person on this island who cared about those books—other than us, her family."

"We already have him down at the station. The girl who manages things here told us that."

"Okay." Summer turned to enter the store.

"Summer, wait. Before you go in, there's something you should know." He grabbed her arm to stop her from moving any further.

Her eyes met his, and he let go. "What is it?"

"There was some vandalism. Graffiti."

Vandalism? That hurt and angered her almost more than the robbery. That someone would mar this lovely bookstore galled her. She took a deep breath and walked through the door.

There on the wall behind the register were spray-painted words: *"Go home or die, bitch."*

"I've already called a painter to take care of it," Poppy said as she came up to Summer.

Summer's head swirled with anger, fear, and confusion. "How did someone get in?"

"It looks like they had a key or picked the lock so well that there wasn't any damage," Poppy said, folding her arms. "I hope they catch him. I'd wring his neck myself." Her voice quivered. "How dare he?"

A strong waft of patchouli breezed past Summer. Stronger than normal. The store held patchouli in every crack and crevice, but it was a lingering scent. This time it was stronger. Usually the scent annoyed her, but right this moment, it comforted her. *Mom.*

She spun around to find Ben chatting with a man in a suit. Forensics? Did St. Brigid even have a forensic team?

"Ben? I'm sorry to interrupt. What do you make of the graffiti?"

"Summer, this is John Quincy. He's here to take paint samples for the lab in Wilmington," Ben Singer said.

Summer eyed him. "Good. Thank you. Nice to meet you."

"Nice to meet you as well. I'll get my equipment and get to work." He smiled and then left.

"Summer, I know what you're thinking," Ben said after a few beats.

"I doubt that, Ben."

He stood awkwardly and folded his arms. His leather belt and holster squeaked as he moved. "Okay, I admit, all this activity put together is very suspicious. Your mother's death. The notes. The fire. Your attack. Now this."

Summer tried to feel warm and fuzzy toward him. But this robbery might never have happened if he'd listened to her in the first place. Instead, he'd patronized her.

He held his hand up. "I don't conclude all of this means murder. But I'm going to find out."

Summer fought the urge to strangle him. "We might start by finding out who had a key to this place.

"That won't do very much good," Poppy spoke up. "Hildy was always giving people copies of the key. I tried to maintain a list, but I gave up on it last year. Half the time, she didn't even tell me when she had copies made." Poppy's voice was edged in emotion—frustration, fear, anger.

Singer shook his head. "That's Hildy for you."

"She didn't know she was going to die, and we'd need to know her every move to be able to figure out what happened," Summer quipped. As she did so, bells and whistles popped in her head. It would be difficult because Hildy was such a flibbertigibbet, but Summer had a new plan. She planned to trace her mother's footsteps her last day. Why hadn't she thought of it before?

"We?" Singer said. "I appreciate your concern. But I'll take it from here."

"Now you're getting involved?" Summer voice rose in a crescendo. A warm hand touched her shoulder. She spun around.

Agatha stood, looking barely awake. "Now, Summer, let him do his job."

"There no evidence of a murder." He lowered his voice. "But there have been plenty of suspicious circumstances since she passed. So much so, I'm going to check into it. Me. Not you."

Summer opened her mouth to object but decided not to waste her breath. Since when did Ben Singer's opinion hold sway over her life? If she wanted to continue with her own investigation, she would. Besides, how would he know?

"Let's keep the shop closed this morning until we can get that mess cleaned up," Agatha said.

"They took your first editions," Summer said. "Looks like your trap worked. Kind of."

Agatha growled. "I hadn't gotten the cameras set up yet. I planned to film with a nanny-cam."

"Too late," Summer said. "They're gone. Every one of them."

"Except for the ones in the safe deposit box."

"I didn't know Mom had one."

"It's where that Shakespeare's thing is, plus some other books."

"Oh, I see. How do we get into it?"

Agatha shrugged. "I have no idea. Perhaps her lawyer knows."

"Aunt Agatha, why didn't you tell me about this sooner?"

"I thought I had. I'm sorry."

If her mom had a safe deposit box with books in it, what else could be in it? Could there be clues to what was happening in Hildy's life? How she'd spent her last few days? Who would have had the means and the motive to kill her?

* * *

After they put the shop back in order, Summer took off to the police station to file a report. Ben Singer was nowhere around. Which pleased her. Even though he'd come over to her way of thinking, she wanted to throttle him. All of this time lost. He could have already found the killer. Instead, he refused to believe Hildy had been murdered.

Even though he'd told her he planned to investigate, Summer had no intention of stopping her own inquiries. No, indeed. She didn't trust Ben Singer.

She made her way back to the bookstore to check on things and to talk with Poppy.

Poppy stood behind the register, checking out a customer. The scent of fresh paint lingered. From the looks of things, nothing had happened. Which was good.

"Poppy, when you get a moment, I'd like to talk with you," Summer said after the customer left.

Poppy's eyes widened. "Okay."

Summer figured she made Poppy nervous. She had that effect on young women. She was a woman with agency, who wasn't into the niceties—hair, jewelry, fashion. It threw some people off balance, mostly young people.

"Doesn't appear to be anybody ready to check out. Let's slip in the back for a moment."

Poppy nodded and followed, reminding Summer of a doe. Long, lean, with huge innocent-looking eyes framed in long lashes.

When they entered the back room, Summer was surprised to find Glads and Marilyn unpacking books.

"Hi, Summer! Are you okay? What an awful thing to happen. Who would do such a thing?" Marilyn said.

"Ben Singer is working on that."

"Pshaw, Ben Singer," Glads said. "Waste of space."

Summer laughed. "What are you doing here? Did Mom have you on the payroll?"

"Heavens, no. We're just helping. Both of us love checking out the new books. We're thrilled to do it." She paused, grinning. "It takes so little to thrill us."

Wheels clicked in Summer's brain. "Well, since the three of you are here, I'll tell you all what I'm trying to do."

They all stopped what they were doing and looked at her.

"I want to retrace Mom's footsteps, as it were, on the day she died. I'm hoping it will lead me to her killer."

"Killer?" Poppy said.

Summer nodded. "What time did Mom come in that day, Poppy?"

Poppy blinked nervously. "I need to think."

Lord. It looked like it pained the young woman to engage her brain.

"She was a little late. She's stopped at the bank first."

"Perfect. That's exactly the kind of thing I need to know."

Poppy looked relieved.

"Were you two around that day?"

"I was in Charleston," Marilyn said, "so I didn't see her. I wish I'd been here."

Glads stepped forward. "Both Doris and I were here. Plus Poppy was here."

"So you two, along with Doris, were here when Mom died?"

"Yes," Marilyn said.

Summer's "So what happened?" was met with silence.

Glads finally turned her head. "I don't want to talk about this."

"I get it. We all loved my mom. But if someone hurt her . . ."

"Who would hurt her?" Glads snapped.

"That's what I'm trying to find out." Summer paused. "I just need a little help here, ladies."

202

Glads spun to face her. "It was dreadful, Summer." Fear and sorrow played across her face. "I don't want to revisit that scene."

"No. Wait," Marilyn said. "They told me all about it. I'll tell you what happened, if you promise not to speak of it again."

What the heck? Summer nearly rolled her eyes. But she felt as if she'd stepped into something tricky here and held her own counsel. "Certainly."

Marilyn swept her arm. "They were all right here, shelving books in the vampire section. Poppy in and out. Glads and Doris."

Summer took in Poppy. "Where were you?"

"When she first came in, we were all right here, chatting about the weather. It had stormed the night before," Poppy said. "Then I had a customer and stepped back into the front of the store."

"Leaving you, Glads and Doris?"

Marilyn and Glads nodded, almost in unison.

"There was a huge box with books in it right over there." Poppy gestured. "We all gathered around and emptied it. Those lovely historical romance books. What was it? The Earl of something or the other . . ."

"*The Earl of Cambridge*, wasn't it?" Glads said.

"It doesn't matter what the name was." Summer tamped down her impatience.

"Oh, okay," Glads said. "Then Poppy came back in and asked for help upstairs. So I joined them."

Summer imagined the scene. "Is that right, Poppy? What did you need help with?"

"Yes, that's right." Her eyes were still as wide as saucers. "Someone had knocked over an end cap. It was quite a mess.

"Didn't Mom usually tend to these things?"

"Yes, but she was busy," Poppy said. "I just asked for help. And then Glads followed me."

"Okay. So that left Mom here with . . . who? Doris?"

"Yes," Glads said.

Silence for a few beats.

"Then what?"

"We were upstairs when we heard her scream." Poppy said with a hush in her voice.

"She screamed?" Summer's heart raced.

"Yes, it was . . . bloodcurdling, dear. Are you sure you want to hear this?" Glads said, pale, gray.

Was she? Her mother had screamed. That must mean that she had been startled or in pain or . . , both. Would she scream if she were having a heart attack?

"Then Doris yelled for help. But we were already on our way." Glads paused. "I don't think I felt one step. I flew down those steps." Her blue eyes bulged.

"When we got here, she was on the floor. Doris was cradling her and trying to give her CPR," Poppy said. "I called nine-one-one."

"I tried to call you, but the number I had was wrong," Glads said quietly.

Summer felt the air leave her lungs. "I wasn't home." *I was in England, insisting on space, not allowing phone calls because of my bloody research. And I was running away from the joke my life had become.*

Chapter Forty-Two

Summer needed a breather. Going through the last few moments of her mom's life had taken more of a toll than she'd expected. She thought the goal of finding the killer would help her plow through the emotions. But she couldn't get over the fact that her mom had screamed. She had been hurt, which was disturbing. Intellectualizing was Summer's way of getting through things, through life, but it didn't work with this.

If her mother had fallen over and passed out quietly, would it be any easier?

She rarely heard her mom lift her voice, let alone scream. It was so not Hildy. Soft-spoken, vegan, tree-loving Hildy.

Besides, having a heart attack would seem to take your breath away and not allow you to scream.

She opened the door to the house and made straight for her computer to research heart attacks. Why hadn't she considered this earlier?

Well. She wasn't aware her mom had screamed, for one thing.

Do people scream when they have heart attacks? she keyed into the search engine.

Alas, some people did. There was a case of a man in a hospital in Great Britain who lay writhing in pain for some time before anybody helped him. But that didn't seem to be what had happened with her mom. The ambulance was called, and they took her to the hospital. No one said anything about her crying or writhing in pain after that initial scream.

And then, from everything Summer was reading, heart attacks without previous symptoms were very rare. Her mother may have been nauseous or had chest pains. Had she mentioned it to anybody?

Summer dialed Poppy.

"Beach Reads Bookstore," Poppy answered.

"Hi, Poppy. It's Summer. I'm sorry to bother you again."

"Hi, Summer. Can you hang on? Customer here."

"Sure."

Summer waited a few minutes until Poppy returned.

"How can I help you, Summer?"

"I need to ask you again about that morning."

"Okay."

"You said Mom was late because she'd been to the bank."

"That's right."

"Was she feeling okay?"

"If she wasn't, she didn't mention it to me."

"How did she look?"

Poppy didn't answer right away. "Your mother looked as healthy as ever. The whole thing was shocking."

"It just that I've been reading about heart attacks, and now I'm even more suspicious. It makes no sense."

"I agree," Poppy said. "Is there anything else I can do to help?"

"No, thank you. I'll let you get back to it."

Summer moved to her laptop. But found no answers. Frustrated, she set aside her computer and slipped her flip-flops on. Time for a walk. Walking along the beach always helped. She had some stale crackers she'd been saving to feed the birds, and grabbed them before heading out into the early evening.

The waves rolled in roughly. Almost high tide. Birds walked along the edge of the surf, and she scattered crackers. They launched themselves at the crackers. She loved watching the seagulls. A deep sense of comfort came over her. Home. Walking this beach. Feeding the birds.

Her emotions spun in so many directions. Her mom screaming had set her off. That didn't seem right. Not at all.

Tomorrow, she'd go to the bank and talk to them to find out why she'd been there, whom she'd talked to, and if she looked well. Surely a healthy woman would look sick if she was having heart problems?

The sun sank into the water—or at least that's what it looked like. Pink and bright orange spread across the sky. A breeze chilled her skin.

She didn't comprehend what had happened to her mom, but she was bound and determined to find out. And someone didn't like that fact. The bookstore break-in, the fire, and her attack. They were all attempts at hurting her—or getting her to leave.

She wasn't going anywhere. She was so close to figuring this out. So close she could almost taste it on the salty air.

When she returned home, there were two messages on her cell phone: one from Piper saying she'd be over in about an hour, and the other from Dr. Jones, the dean of her department. Damn! Summer couldn't believe she'd missed that. Why hadn't she taken her cell phone with her?

She listened to the voicemail: "Hi, Summer, this is Dean Jones. Please call me back at your earliest convenience."

Summer's heart nearly stopped. What did that mean? Had they come to a decision? Were they going to fire her? How would she ever find another decent job if she got fired from one of the best Shakespeare programs in the country?

She stared at her phone for a few minutes. Finally, she picked it up and hit the call back button, heart racing.

"This is Dean Jones. Sorry you've missed me. Please leave a message and I'll get back to you as soon as possible."

Beep.

"Uh . . . Dean Jones, this is Summer Merriweather returning your call. I'll be waiting for you to call back."

Of course. She'd missed the call she'd been waiting for weeks and had to leave a message. Who knew when the dean would get back to her?

Chapter Forty-Three

The next morning, Summer dressed and made her way to the bank—the one bank on the island. A few years ago, there had been two, but since online banking had become so popular, one of the banks just couldn't compete and shut its door a few years ago.

When she walked into St. Brigid Federal Bank, she caught the eye of the manager, Cecilia Garfield. She walked over to her. "Summer? How good to see you. I was so sorry to hear about your mother."

Summer smiled and nodded her head. "Thanks. It's good to see you too. Is there somewhere we could talk?"

There weren't many people around—just a few tellers and some early morning customers—but Summer didn't want anybody to hear her spiel.

"Sure. Come into my office." Cecilia was dressed in a sharp, slightly out-of-style gray suit.

Summer followed her down a short hall, with pictures and paintings of previous bank presidents. A whiff of something flowery caught Summer's nose. When she walked into Cecilia's office, she saw why. A fresh floral arrangement sat on her desk.

"So pretty," Summer said, holding back a sneeze.

"Thanks," Cecilia replied. "Now what can I help you with?"

"I'm retracing my mother's footsteps on the last day of her life."

Cecilia frowned.

"She came here before she went to the bookstore that morning. Any idea who she spoke to?"

Relief washed over her face. "Oh, I thought you were here on business." She paused. "I helped your mother that day. She was just making a deposit, I believe."

Bingo.

"Okay, Cecilia, I want you to think about this next question before you answer. It's very important to me."

"Okay."

"How did Mom look? Did she mention not feeling well?"

Confusion played out over Cecilia's face. "No, she didn't mention it. In fact, I think she'd just come from a sunrise yoga class and she looked great."

"I didn't know that."

This retracing of her mother's footsteps thing was trickier than Summer had imagined.

"Can I ask why you're asking these questions?" Cecilia said.

"They said Mom had a heart attack. I think that's hard to believe. Most people have symptoms. She didn't. So, I'm just trying to make sense of it all."

Cecilia sat forward, her long brown hair falling onto the desk. "She seemed healthy to me. She looked good. But looks can be deceiving. She didn't seem to be the type to talk about her aches and pains. So if she wasn't feeling well, I'm not sure she'd have said anything."

True. "But you'd know it if she looked bad."

"Sure," she said. "It shocked me to hear that a few hours after she left here, she died. It freaked me out, to tell you the truth."

It freaked us all out.

* * *

After Summer left the bank, she looked up the yoga center on the island on her phone. There were three. Three? Only one bank and three yoga centers? Summer rolled her eyes. So typical of St. Brigid.

She dialed Aunt Agatha.

"Yes, Summer. How are you?"

"I'm retracing my mom's footsteps on the day she died."

"Come again?"

"You heard me."

"Summer, you need to be careful. The store was just robbed and vandalized. What else will happen if you keep poking your nose in this?"

"Only one way to find out."

Agatha laughed. "But seriously, be careful."

"I will. So I just left the bank, and Cecilia told me that Mom had been to a sunrise yoga class that morning."

"That sounds about right."

"Which yoga center did she go to?"

"Susan's Center of Yoga Arts."

"Okay—that's all I needed to know."

"What have you found out so far?" Aunt Agatha asked.

Summer told her aunt everything she'd learned.

"This was such a good idea," Agatha said. "Keep me informed."

"Will do," Summer said.

"But how are you feeling?"

"I'm okay," Summer said. "No headache. No dizziness. Nothing."

"Good."

Summer slid into the car after saying goodbye to Agatha. She googled Susan's Center of Yoga Arts and drove to the place. It was not the closest yoga center to Hildy, so she must have really liked this place. Summer pulled into the parking lot, which had a few cars in it, and sat in the car for a few minutes. Took a drink from her water bottle.

She exited the car and walked to the front door. *Damn.* The place was closed. But, according to the sign, it would be open tomorrow. Okay, then, Summer could wait one more day to talk with the yoga teacher. Besides, she had an inkling of what she'd say—the same thing everybody else had said. Hildy Merriweather was healthy, and she'd not been feeling sick that morning at all.

As soon as Summer entered her car, her mobile phone buzzed. She glanced at the screen. It was the dean. Her heart jumped.

"Hello, this is Summer."

"Dr. Merriweather," Dean Jones said.

Uh-oh. When he used *doctor,* he meant business.

"Yes, Dean Jones. How are you?"

"I'm well, thank you. Very sorry to learn of your mother's passing."

"Thank you," Summer said.

Pleasantries done, Summer wondered what would be next.

"We've been discussing your position. While you don't have the best reputation or record, objectively I don't want to see you let go. I'm aware you're getting help for your arachnophobia. The incident, though, was almost beside the point at this juncture. You need to serve on more committees. Publish more papers. And make efforts to pass your students more often."

Summer had known that was coming. If they planned to give her another chance, she'd have to pass more students. She dared not say a word about how her students were coming to her with barely average reading skills and less than average writing skills, and she had so little time with them.

"If you agree to that, the next step is a sabbatical."

A forced sabbatical?" Summer said.

"A preemptive sabbatical for you to consider what I've said and whether you want to move forward."

"Okay," Summer said weakly.

"Summer, you're a brilliant woman. We're pleased to have you on staff." He paused. "But personally I've always wondered if you were cut out for academia. Not everybody is." Another pause. "Please take this time to reflect on what you want to do, and if you do come back, bring it on."

Bring it on made Summer smile. "Thank you, Dean. I appreciate the chance you're giving me."

"Certainly."

No, this wasn't too much to think about. What to do with the rest of her life. She'd dreamed of being a Shakespearean professor for as long as she could remember. What else was there for her? That decision, along with figuring out what had happened to her mom, weighed heavily on her as she flicked on her turn signal and headed for Beach Reads.

Chapter Forty-Four

A brisk shopping crowd had gathered in Beach Reads. Poppy was busy behind the register, but when Summer waved, she waved back. She continued on upstairs, as she wanted to set her computer up outside and investigate further. She believed her mom had been murdered and that all clues were leading her in that direction. But it helped to keep her mind occupied with the research—for now. Soon she would need to turn back to Shakespearean research. But she could get there. Not yet.

She walked upstairs to the light-filled room and out onto the deck. A blue and white table umbrella flapping in the breeze.

How many times in her young life had she sat at this very table, reading or chatting with Piper or just thinking as she watched the waves roll in. This view. This island. This life. She had wanted out of it so badly. Wanted the life of an academic. Yet, at this moment, this place didn't seem so bad.

"Hey, Summer!" someone from behind her called. She turned to see pink-haired Doris and Marilyn.

"Hello, ladies." She should probably ask them to sit down. "How are you?"

They sat down.

Bother. Was that an invitation?

"We're looking forward to the book club meeting tomorrow. Have you finished *Nights on Bellamy Harbor?*" Doris said, bubbly.

"Not yet." But she wanted to. Which irked her. How had she gotten so hooked into this book?

"It doesn't matter," Marilyn said. "As long as you've read enough to discuss."

"So, Doris, I hear you were with Mom when she collapsed."

Doris's face fell.

"She doesn't like to talk about it," Marilyn said.

"Oh, I'm sorry," Summer said. "Didn't mean to upset you. I'm just trying to figure out what happened to her. I mean, she was healthy on all counts. She had no symptoms at all."

"She mentioned to me earlier that she felt sick," Doris said.

Summer's skin prickled. "She did? You're the first person to say that."

Doris nodded. "She said she felt sick at yoga—got dizzy too."

Summer was dumbstruck. If her mom had gotten sick in yoga class, why had she gone to the bank? And why wouldn't Cecilia have noticed it?

"That's odd."

"I thought so too," Marilyn said.

"No, I mean if she was sick, why did she go to the bank? Why didn't she seem sick to Cecilia?"

"It came and went is what she said," Doris explained.

The three of them sat quietly. Summer allowed the sound of the ocean's waves to lull her momentarily. To calm her racing heart. She needed Doris to tell her more about her mom's death. But the poor old thing couldn't do it.

"When you're ready to talk about it, please let me know. It's important."

Doris's jaw tightened, and she gave a quick nod, looking into the distance.

She was torn up. Summer imagined anybody would be. Doris had been right there when Hildy died. If it had been Summer, she'd have had nightmares about it for the rest of her life.

"How's your husband?" Summer asked, wanting to change the subject.

Surprise came over Doris's face. "He has good days and bad days. Liver cancer."

"I bet he misses Hildy," Marilyn said.

"What? Why?" Summer said.

"She used to read to him," Marilyn said. "She read to a lot of sick folks." Marilyn paused. "I'm not sure who's going to step in and take care of those people now."

"I've finished reading the book they were reading. I'll continue to do it with my husband," Doris said.

"Yes, but it's good for you to get away from him."

"But he's my husband. He's very sick. Sometimes I don't want to miss a moment." She blinked, as if she were trying not to cry.

"So Mom was giving you breaks by reading to your husband?"

"Yes," Doris said and quickly looked away. "She insisted."

Such a Hildy thing to do.

Summer had wanted to change the subject, and she had. But she wasn't sure this one was any better. Doris was one of the newer people in the group, and Summer didn't know her well. But she had always been the most bubbly and vivacious of all of them. Summer hadn't had any idea the woman had all of this heaviness in her life. She felt a pang of guilt for asking about the day her mom died. But still. Doris would have to talk about it eventually. At least Summer hoped she would. It was too raw right now.

But Summer needed to know. There were no two ways about it. If she were going to figure out who'd killed her mom, she needed to figure out every detail. She eyed Doris, with her pink hair and crazy-looking jewelry, and pity swept over her. It could wait for another day.

"Can I get you something, dear?" Marilyn said. "I'm going to get myself some coffee. Anything?

Summer smiled. These women were so kind. "Yes, sure. I'll take a cup."

She sank further into her chair, with Doris at her side, and drank in the scenery. Memories washing over her. Good ones. Bad ones. Slippery thing, these memories.

Chapter Forty-Five

After Summer finished her coffee, mostly in silence, with her mom's best friends, all enjoying the view, she headed into her mother's office to check out the events she had planned over the next few months. If Summer was stuck here, involved in the shop, she needed to know. She needed to keep involved in something— anything other than the murder investigation, which was ever on her mind.

Hildy had planned several upcoming events. She and Marilyn were hosting a romance writers workshop at the library in a few months. They'd scheduled an author to be here in a few weeks.

Poppy poked her head into the office. "Someone is here to see you."

"Who?"

"Someone named Posey."

"Posey? Yes, please. Send her in."

Poppy nodded.

Summer stood and walked to the office door. Soon enough, Posey made her way in. She reached out and hugged Summer.

Posey looked tired, seemed winded. Summer remembered she wasn't in good health. Why did she bother herself to come here?

"It's good to see you," Summer said. "Please sit down. Can I get you something? Coffee? Water?'

"I'm fine darlin'. I won't stay long."

"What's up?"

Her smile turned into a frown. "I'm afraid I have bad news. I told you I'd do a reading. And the cards are warning you. Very strongly."

Summer stifled a nervous giggle.

"You may be a bit of a nonbeliever, but I came all the way here because I've never seen such a complete and strong warning."

Summer swallowed. "Oh, Posey. Why didn't you just pick up the phone?"

"I needed to see you in person. I needed to inform you this is serious." Her voice lowered. "There is someone very close to you who wants to harm you. The same person who killed your mother. Make no mistake about it. She was killed."

Summer's skin prickled. *Come on, Summer, this is ridiculous. Isn't it?* She leaned forward. "The cards told you that?"

"No. The cards told me that you are in danger."

"How do you know about Mom?"

She laughed. "You think I'm a crazy old woman. You're such a modern, sophisticated woman. Your mom was so proud of you."

"Don't try to change the subject. I need to know."

She paused, then took a breath. "There are things in the universe . . . that make little sense. Unexplainable things."

"Posey, I'm losing my patience. If you know something about who killed Mom . . ."

"Oh no. All I know is it was someone very close to her."

Summer's heart sank. How awful. "And how do you know this?"

"She told me."

"Come again?"

"I had a visit from your mother. It was very brief."

"But, Posey, Mom is dead."

"You know what I mean. Her spirit visited me."

Oh dear. Is Posey okay?

"I had a very vivid dream. Sometimes spirits come through into dreams. She didn't stay long, and she didn't get specific enough for my taste. She is worried about you. She wants you to be careful. Her warning was very clear. Along with the cards."

"Okay, I'll be careful," Summer said. "I thought I had been." She didn't believe a word of this. She'd played along because she liked Posey so much. But she wondered if her diabetes had addled Posey's mind.

"She also said not to worry about her. She's fine."

"What? She's dead. How can she be fine?"

"On the other side. She's fine." Posey had a matter-of-fact tone in her voice that unsettled Summer.

Summer's stomach twisted into a knot. She didn't like this conversation. She didn't want to think of her mother being on the other side. She wanted her here.

"There's one more thing," Posey continued.

Summer leaned in even further across the desk.

"She said to tell you to sleep, perchance to dream." Posey shrugged and laughed. "I have no idea what that means."

But Summer felt the blood drain from her face and her body go cold. "How?" she stammered. "What? I don't understand."

Her mom used to kiss her every night at bedtime and had whispered that very phrase to her. A quote from Hamlet.

"Are you okay?" Posey said.

220

Summer couldn't speak. How had Posey learned this? Had Hildy mentioned it to her? Or had the spirit of Hildy visited Posey?

"Summer?"

"I'm sorry, Posey." Her mouth felt dry. "It's a bit much. Isn't it?"

"I know it is. Your mother and I used to talk about how smart and logical you are. But she hoped that one day you'd see the universe was not just a logical place. It's full of magic and wonder, and sometimes the inexplicable things are the best things."

Summer's head spun. That definitely sounded like Hildy. She felt she might be beyond words. Summer Merriweather always had words. Words to answer questions. Words to explain. Words to come back with a quip. But words . . . she was out of them now.

"I can see you're struggling, Summer. I know it's a lot." Posey stood up and sighed. "I might be as crazy as I seem, but my ways have never failed me. Spirits have always guided me since I was a small child. You need to heed my warning."

She started to walk away, then stopped. "One more thing, Summer." Summer looked up at her. "Your mother says she loves you. Always has. Always will."

Tears burned in Summer's eyes.

"No reason to cry," Posey said. "Love turns the universe. And there ain't no love like mama love."

Chapter Forty-Six

*S*hake it off, Summer. You know all of that new-age hippy stuff is nothing more than mumbo jumbo. But how did Posey know about the quote from Hamlet? Maybe her mom had mentioned it to her at some point. The mind is a tricky thing. Memories surfaced at odd times, and especially in dreams. She'd had some dreams about Mom since she'd been home. Wouldn't it have been odd if she hadn't?

She waved off the chill she felt creeping along her spine, but she couldn't wave off the sudden exhaustion.

She picked up the photo of her mom and her on what must have been the other side of the island, as it didn't look familiar at all. They both looked happy and content as they smiled at whoever was holding the camera. Summer didn't remember that day at all. She was much too young in the photo to have remembered. She set it back down on the desk. Another wave of exhaustion came over her, along with the prickling start of a headache. Time to go home.

She walked along the boardwalk, past the bells and explosive sounds coming from the arcade, and followed her nose to the hot dog stand. She ordered two to go.

"Mustard and relish, right?" Wanda winked at her.

"You remembered me!"

"Sure. You're Hildy's daughter, Summer. Sure was sorry to hear about your mother's passing."

She handed Summer her hot dogs, and Summer paid her. "I'll never forget your mother stopping here and trying to tell me not to give you any hot dogs. Remember that?" Wanda laughed.

Summer grinned. "Thank goodness we didn't listen to her."

Wanda drifted off to help other customers lining up as Summer walked away. She felt like a glutton, what with all the good, healthy food back home in the fridge. She just couldn't resist the hot dogs one more day. They'd been taunting her since her arrival.

She walked to the end of the boardwalk and continued walking through the sand toward the house.

The sun was sinking low in the sky, but it was still as hot as blazes. She mulled over her day. Going to the closed yoga place. Talking with her dean. Then Posey's visit. She respected Posey, one of her mom's oldest and dearest friends, so Summer had bitten her tongue. Not her forte.

But if she could do it here, she could do it with her students and other professors, couldn't she?

It was extremely hard for her to see students squandering their education. She wasn't sure how much biting her tongue she could muster.

As she drew closer and closer to the house, it came into view behind the clumps of seagrass and sand dunes. A gust of warmth spread through her chest. Her home.

This place where she'd grown up. This place that she'd always despised. Now it stood like a beacon of warmth and comfort. *Odd, that.*

She walked the path to the house and opened the front door to her aunt Agatha and Piper sitting in the kitchen.

"Hello! I'm sorry—I didn't know you were here, or I'd have brought you some," she said, holding up her hot dogs.

Agatha and Piper just looked at her.

"What's wrong?" she said and shoved a bite into her mouth.

"It's Mr. Darcy."

"Is he okay?" Summer said after swallowing.

"We had to take him to the vet. He's okay now," Agatha said. "But he was quite sick."

Summer started to march into the living room.

"Wait—we need to talk with you about him," Piper said, voice lowered.

"You don't want him to hear?"

She nodded.

"The doctor thinks he's depressed. And because of his advanced age, it's making him sick," Piper explained.

Summer mulled that over. "He misses Mom."

Agatha and Piper both nodded.

"Oh God. Have I not been—" She fed him. She cleaned his cage. She even talked to him. Wasn't it enough?

"It's your mother he wants. But it would be good if we could all give him all the affection he needs," Agatha said. "Your mother was very devoted to him. Took him out of the cage and loved him up. Let him fly around a bit in the house. Talked and sang to him."

Summer took another bite of her hot dog as she listened.

"Okay," she said. "I think I can manage."

Had she been a bad bird babysitter? She felt awful. She remembered the way her mom had bonded with the bird and how much she'd loved him. Hildy had always wanted cats, but she was so allergic to them and couldn't be anywhere around them. When she and Mr. Darcy found one another, it was true love.

"I think we all can," Piper said. "We'll pitch in with it all. Poor bird. He was quite distressed—threw up everywhere."

"And he kept asking for Hildy." Agatha said. "It's heartbreaking."

"Animals do mourn," Piper said. "They mourn each other. They mourn their people."

Summer recalled conversations she'd had with her mom about animals. Her mom, the typical animal-loving vegan. Summer, the typical rebellious, thinks-she-knows-it-all daughter. "Animals are not people," Summer would say.

An image came to Summer: she and Piper feeding the birds, no matter what their parents said. Maybe, just maybe, there was more of Hildy in her than Summer acknowledged.

She tiptoed into the living room, where Mr. Darcy was sleeping. Even sleeping, he looked ruffled. Poor bird. She'd love him up when he awakened.

She moved back into the kitchen. "Any special advice from the vet?"

"He gave us some vitamins for Darcy and just said to monitor him. It's a big change for him with Hildy being gone. He was used to her routines, her attention. And he's an old bird. Change is harder for old birds."

"Ain't that the truth," Agatha said, grinning.

Chapter Forty-Seven

The three of them gathered around the kitchen table, with heated casseroles and soup.

"You're not eating much," Agatha said. "Are you okay?"

"Just not very hungry. I just ate two hot dogs. I think that's enough."

"So how did your investigation go today?" Piper asked and then shoved a bite of Mexican bean casserole into her mouth.

"The yoga studio was closed, but I did get to talk with the woman at the bank yesterday. She said Mom looked great, not sick at all that morning."

"Of course," Agatha said.

Summer hesitated to tell them she'd found out that her mom had screamed. She also didn't think it was wise to tell them about Posey's visit. They were all weary from their day. She didn't want to add to that.

"I spoke with Ben today about the robbery," Agatha said. "He has no leads yet."

"Has he gotten the final autopsy report on Mom?"

"He didn't say."

Surely it was in by now. Summer made a mental note to call him first thing in the morning.

* * *

She also kept the news from her dean to herself. Nothing was written in stone. He was just proposing that Summer not be terminated, that she be given a sabbatical to get it together. If the board granted her the time, it would be a reprieve, but it would go fast. She felt like she needed to have a plan for it. She should finish her paper that she'd started in England.

But she couldn't think about that now. She needed to figure out what had happened to her mom. She was getting close. She could almost taste the answer. But with each step she made, her mom's loss hurt even more. She theorized that by finding out the facts, she'd feel better. So far, all her investigations were just picking at her open wound.

But she wasn't ready to give up. No matter how much it hurt. Or freaked her out. Finding out that her mom had screamed at the bookstore before she collapsed was like a dagger in Summer's chest.

Then Posey's visit had done nothing to calm Summer in the least.

She shuddered.

"Summer, are you okay?"

"I've overdone it a bit today. Think I'll turn in." Her voice sounded whispery and weary.

Agatha reached out and grabbed her hand. "This is a lot for your to deal with. Take tomorrow off. Rest."

Was she kidding? How could she rest? How could anybody rest with a killer loose on the island? A killer who had murdered Hildy

Merriweather, one of Brigid Island's most beloved citizens. No, she wouldn't be resting soon. But she would not argue with her aunt. She didn't have any arguing left in her. "Maybe I'll do that," she said as she rose from the table. "But for now I'm off to the couch."

"Good night, then," Agatha said.

* * *

Summer readied for sleep and headed to the couch. She just wanted to take a glimpse at Mr. Darcy. She lifted the drape. The bird was wide awake. He blinked. What was it about the blink that made her heart rush into her throat? She opened the cage door and reached for him, rubbing his head. He purred—a noise that Hildy had taught him. He was so light and soft feeling. She began to remove her hand, but he leaped onto her finger.

"Okay, Darcy. I'm tired, but you can come out for a little while," she said. He eyed her and blinked again. "Oh, Mr. Darcy!" she said and grinned.

She pulled him close to her. He rested his head on her chest, purring.

Summer lay down on the couch and continued to stroke the bird. She'd no idea it could be this comforting and relaxing to have a huge parrot curled up on her neck.

Summer's eyes felt heavy as the bird's warmth heated her. She continued to pet him until she fell asleep.

The two of them—Mr. Darcy and Summer slept all night wrapped in a bird-human cocoon.

* * *

"Look at that, would you?" a voice said. "The bird is asleep with Summer."

"Never thought I'd see the day," another voice said.

Summer's eyes opened to Agatha and Piper, standing in front of her grinning brightly.

The place on her chest where the bird slept was hot, but she didn't want to disturb him. "Can you get him?"

Agatha nodded and lifted the sleeping bird, placing him on the bottom of his cage.

"He looks cold and lonely there," Piper said.

"We should get him one of Mom's sweaters or something."

"Good idea." Agatha strode off upstairs to fetch a sweater.

"Did you sleep with him all night?" Piper said.

"I guess I did."

Piper cocked an eyebrow. "I guess you found your Mr. Darcy."

Summer grumbled. "And he's no Romeo." She brushed the feathers off her comforter and nightshirt. "But then again, who is?"

"Speaking of Romeo . . . have you finished *Nights on Bellamy Harbor*? I see the main character is nothing but a modern-day Romeo. Want some coffee? It should be done."

"No, I've not finished the book. Let's hope he's not a Romeo. He was a first-class idiot."

"What?"

Summer stretched. "Romeo and Juliet is no more a romance than my a—"

"Here we are!" Agatha said. "A sweater for Darcy." She held a stubbly brown sweater in her hands. Summer placed it around the bird, who slept as soundly as a baby. Or an old bird, as it were.

Chapter Forty-Eight

After Summer showered and dressed, she phoned Ben Singer. He didn't pick up, so she left a message asking if he'd gotten the autopsy result in. Hildy had wanted to be cremated, and they couldn't move forward with her wishes until the autopsy was complete—and Summer was satisfied that it was accurate.

Nothing had gone according to what Hildy had wanted since she'd died. She wouldn't have wanted anything to do with a church, for example. She hadn't even wanted a memorial service.

Summer quickly brushed her hair, grabbed her car keys and bag, and headed to the yoga studio.

When she opened the door, it surprised her to find Rudy skulking around outside.

"Good morning," she said.

"Yeah," he muttered. "Did you see a cat? I'm trying to find my granddaughter's cat. It got out, you see. She's heartbroken."

"Oh no. Did it come this way?"

"There it is," he said, squinting. "How did she get up there?" The cat perched on the porch roof. "Do you have a ladder?"

Summer didn't want to miss the yoga studio. She had a slim time frame. "I have no idea if we have a ladder. If we do, it's in the shed in the back. It's open. Help yourself, Rudy."

He nodded. "Thanks. My granddaughter . . . she means the world to me, and she loves this cat." He shrugged and headed toward the backyard.

So old, curt Rudy had a soft spot. Summer would tuck that away for further use in the future.

She slid into her car, flipped on the ignition and radio, and was off to the yoga studio. As she drove along, past familiar places and some unfamiliar ones, warmth came over her. The warmth of familiarity. She knew every inch of this side of the island. As a kid, she'd traveled everywhere on foot. She knew the businesses and the landscape with its dunes and coves, along with its marshy area, which she used to have bad dreams about. All of these things she wanted to get as far away from as possible. And yet here she was.

She turned into the full parking lot of the yoga studio, parked, and exited the car.

She opened the door to a class that was just finishing. She'd timed it perfectly.

She glanced around at all the yoga students, looking blessed out, dressed in different varieties of exercise clothing. Finally, her eyes spotted the teacher. She walked over to her. "Are you Susan?"

"Yes," she said. "Can I help you?"

"I'm Summer Merriweather."

"Oh! You're Hildy's daughter." She opened her arms and hugged Summer. "I'm so sorry to hear about your mother. I loved her. She was fabulous. What happened?"

"I'm glad you asked that question because that's what I'm trying to find out. She was here that morning, taking a class?"

"That's right," she said, waving goodbye to a student as she exited.

"Did she seem ill in class?"

Confusion swept over Susan's face. "No, not at all. That's why I was so surprised to hear she had a heart attack later that morning. She looked healthy and strong. That particular class is strenuous. And she did well."

Prickles of excitement ran through Summer. Everything she was learning supported her theory that her mom had been healthy and was murdered. But how? She'd collapsed in the bookstore. It had looked like a heart attack, for all intents and purposes.

"Are you okay?" Susan asked.

"Oh yes, just thinking. Trying to make sense of my mom's death."

A calmness came over the yoga teacher's face. "It rarely makes sense. I know. I lost my mom a year ago, and I'm still grieving."

"I'm sorry." Summer was torn between leaving and staying. A part of her wanted to reach out to this young woman. But she was uncertain.

Susan's eyebrows knit into a V shape. "She was sick for a long time. We had plenty of time . . . but it still feels like we didn't have enough. But Hildy's death was so sudden. I understand you trying to make sense of it."

She didn't want to tell the woman that she wasn't trying to make sense of it—she was trying to find her mom's killer. Summer nodded. "Thanks for talking with me. I better get going. Busy day."

"Thanks for stopping by," Susan said. "Why don't you take a few classes? Your mother was a paid lifetime member. I can transfer that membership to you."

Yoga? Hmm. Summer didn't think so, but she didn't want to be rude.

"We have a beginner's class that starts this Saturday. You should come," Susan continued.

"I might do that," Summer said. "Have a great day."

She couldn't get out of there fast enough. Summer Merriweather did not do yoga. Was there anything more undignified than a downward dog? She used to do it as a child because her mom did it. It was just a way to be close to her mom. As a child she loved being a part of her mom's grown-up world. And yoga was a part of that.

But she'd not done it since before she became a rebellious teen, when she began eating meat, only reading great literature, and embracing the academic lifestyle. As she opened her car door, she rolled her eyes at herself. She was such a cliché. *Academic lifestyle. Puhlease.*

Summer drove toward the bookstore, brightening as she recalled her mom's last day. She'd experienced things she loved on that day—yoga and the bookstore. And she hadn't been sick. Summer supposed she should be glad of all that. But she needed a happier ending for her mom.

Hildy had gone to yoga class, to the bank, and then straight to work, where her employees and friends helped her with a new shipment of books. That's where it all turned.

She was shelving books, screamed, and collapsed. The paramedics were called, and she was taken to the hospital. The hospital. That's where Summer needed to go next.

She drove by the bookstore, noting its full back parking lot.

Chapter Forty-Nine

St. Brigid Hospital was small. It was barely a hospital. Serious medical issues were transferred to the mainland hospitals. So when Summer walked in the door, it wasn't unusual that the receptionist remembered her. After all, she'd just been there with a concussion.

"How are you feeling?" the nurse asked.

"I'm fine, but I have some questions about my mother, Hildy Merriweather. She was brought in here with a heart attack last week."

The woman behind the desk paled. "Yes, I remember."

"Were you here?"

"Not when they brought her in. No. My shift started later that day." The phone rang. "Sorry, I have to get this."

While she was on the phone, Summer scanned the hospital. The waiting area held couches and big chairs. They looked as if someone had purchased them from the local Goodwill, which didn't inspire confidence.

When the receptionist hung up the phone, Summer turned back to her. "Who is the person I should talk to about when my mother was brought in?"

234

"I can't give you too much information, but I can tell you that." Her fingers moved over the keyboard. "It was Dr. Flather."

"Is he here? Can I talk to him?"

"*She* will be here tomorrow. Today is her day off."

She. Well, that was good. A woman doctor. Summer found that comforting.

"Okay, I'll stop by tomorrow."

"She won't be able to say much. Privacy laws and so on."

"I get that," Summer said. "But whatever she can tell me."

The woman looked at Summer with sympathy. "I understand."

"Thank you. I'll see you tomorrow."

*   *   *

Summer left the cool, air-conditioned hospital and walked out into a hot, muggy day. Gray clouds gathered on the horizon. She better get to the bookstore. When it rained during tourist season, the bookstore filled with tourists. She couldn't leave Poppy to deal with it all alone.

By the time she pulled into the back parking lot, lightning crackled. Trees swayed. The air smelled of rain.

When she walked into the store, Summer was pleased to find Agatha and Glads helping Poppy out. Mia was also there—upstairs, helping clean. It was a constant work in progress trying to keep the store picked up and clean. People left their trash. Summer often wondered if they did it on purpose or if they slipped into the world of books and completely forgot about their coffee, croissants, or tissues. Sometimes people left the oddest things behind. Once, Summer found a pin that read "Jesus Loves Bicycles." She considered keeping it, just because it was so odd. The thought of it made her smile.

"Excuse me," a small voice from behind Summer said. "Do you work here?"

Summer turned to find a young woman wearing a Kurt Cobain T-shirt.

"I guess you could say that, yes."

"I'm looking for something to read. Something I can sink my teeth into. I see nothing like real literature. Some Shakespeare?"

Summer's jaw dropped. Of course. If she were the owner of this store, she'd stock a shelf or two of what she considered good books. "I don't have anything like that now, but I can order something for you. We'd have it by tomorrow."

The young woman pushed her glasses back up her nose. "Well, I've not decided which Shakespeare play I'm in the mood for. "

"In the meantime, we do have a classic romance and mystery section. Jane Austen. Agatha Christie."

"Okay, I'll check that out."

"It's upstairs," Summer said. "In the far-right corner. If you decide to order something else, please let me know. It's no bother at all."

She smiled as she made her way to the stairs.

Even as the skies were darkening, Summer brightened. Of course. This store was hers. And while it would be foolish, business-wise, to get rid of the romances and mysteries, there was nothing preventing her from stocking some good literature. This young woman proved Summer was not the only person who might sit on the beach with a copy of *A Midsummer Night's Dream* in hand.

A group of older women entered the store, laughing. "I love cozy mysteries. Where's your cozy section?" Summer pointed her in the direction. The others she came with headed for the erotic romance section. Erotic romance. Summer refrained from rolling her eyes. She didn't understand what that meant. Was *Nights on Bellamy Harbor* considered erotic romance? There were some steamy scenes. More than steamy . . . Summer remembered a dream she'd had last night. Had she been dreaming about Omar, the main male character? Her face heated. Why, yes, she had.

"Summer? Are you okay?" Poppy asked as she walked over to her. "Your face is red."

Summer stiffened, stood straighter. "I'm fine. It's just a bit warm in here. I'll go get some water. If you need me, I'll be in the office for a little while."

"Okay. Oh dear. Another storm heading this way," Poppy said.

Thunder boomed in the distance.

Summer slipped off to the office for some water. How ridiculous to dream about a fictional character. Especially to dream that intimately. She took a swig of water and sat down at the desk. Dang, she must be getting desperate. She tried to remember the last time she'd had a date, let alone . . . well, anything more than a date. She gave up.

She flicked on the store computer. Her mom loved the thing. It made her life so much easier, for the most part. Only when it didn't work, it screwed everything up. Summer forced herself to think of other things besides her dream. What was wrong with her? She needed to get a grip. She needed to find out who'd killed her mom.

She clicked on the email program and started clearing out the obvious spam. As she did so, she mulled over what she'd found out. Nothing more than what she had already known—that her mom appeared to be healthy until she suddenly dropped dead. After screaming.

That scream said something. Summer shivered. She just wasn't certain what it meant.

Chapter Fifty

Summer shut off the computer and moved on into the store to help with crowd control, as her mom used to call it. Days like these, people were looking for something to do, and sometimes all they wanted to do was browse. Which was fine. Hildy welcomed browsers. But she wanted buyers. So, ever since Summer had been a kid, her mom had tutored her on how to sell books to browsers. Sometimes it worked—and sometimes it didn't.

But being present was key. Not on your cell phone. Not in the stockroom. And if you were behind the register, you were otherwise engaged.

Summer approached a woman who was wandering down the rows. "Can I help you find something?"

"I'm just looking," she said.

"Okay, but if I can help, please give me a holler."

The woman didn't respond but kept walking. *Okay, then.*

Summer turned to find Henry Chadworth on her heels, and she almost ran into him.

"Henry!"

"Sorry, Summer. I didn't know you'd turn around like that."

She straightened. "Obviously."

They stood in a weird silence for a moment.

"What can I help you with, Henry?"

"Call the cops off. Every time I turn around, they're at my doorstep. They think I stole the first editions. And you know I couldn't do such a thing."

A customer shimmied by them.

"No, Henry. I don't know that. And I have nothing to do with the cops. If they're looking at you, there must be a reason."

His voice lowered as he led her to one of the book nooks. "That's insane, Summer. I'm a high school English teacher. A whiff of scandal could cost my job. Why would I do such a thing?"

Summer hadn't considered it from that perspective. "I don't know, Henry. All I know is they were stolen. You're one of the few people on this island who appreciated those books."

"Well, that's true enough," he said with a sarcastic tone, "but I'm not a thief. And I loved and respected your mother. I'd never steal anything from her—or her store."

Summer folded her arms. "People do all sorts of things, Henry. Things you wouldn't imagine. Husbands kill wives. Women steal from their husband. Human nature isn't as cut and dry as you seem to suggest."

He rolled his eyes. "Okay, Summer, we all know how smart you are. Stop trying to show off."

"What?" Her voice rose. Anger and humiliation spun through her.

"You heard me."

"Get out, Henry."

"What?" His face reddened.

"You heard me."

His hands balled into fists, and his arms stiffened at his sides. "I didn't steal those books."

"I hear you. Now, get out."

He spun around and charged out of the bookstore.

When he left the space, a tiny woman appeared. Had she been there all along? She grinned at Summer. "Spurned lover?"

"What? Who?"

"The good-looking man who just left. If I were a few years younger . . ."

"Henry?" Summer's face turned red. "Not at all. He's just . . . an acquaintance."

The woman held her books to her chest. "Pretty heated conversation." Her eyebrows lifted.

Summer breathed in and out. "Can I help you find something?"

"Oh no, dear, I've got everything I need right here." She gripped her books close and then moved on.

So, the woman had been listening. Summer would have to be more careful.

But what she'd learned from Henry was gold. Ben Singer was investigating him for the theft of the books, but she wondered if he was also a person of interest in Hildy's death. Ben hadn't officially come out and said it was a murder investigation, but the last time they'd talked, he'd acknowledged that something was fishy. Should she call him?

"Excuse me, do you work here?" A woman with startling blue eyes asked Summer.

"Yes, can I help you?

"Do you have *Nights on Bellamy Harbor* in stock?"

"Yes, we do. Please follow me. I'm reading it right now. It's our book club selection."

"I've heard it's very good."

Summer led her to the place where the books were. "I'm enjoying it." She handed her a copy.

"Thank you," the woman said, eyes skirting the shelves. "Looks like she's written a lot of books."

"Yes, she's very popular. Please take your time and have fun," Summer said. "If I can help you with anything else, please let me know."

"Thank you." The woman was wide-eyed as she perused the shelves of books. Summer felt a ping of pride. She'd helped this young woman find what she wanted. It was a romance. But at least it was a book. She caught herself. Had she just had that thought? Was the ghost of her mother taking over her body? Summer laughed at herself. What was going on with her?

* * *

That night, Summer fell into bed, or onto the couch, as the case might be. Darcy tapped on his cage. Tap, tap, tap. She tried to ignore him. Tap, tap, tap.

"What's wrong, Darcy?"

She opened the door to give him a rub, and he flew out of the cage onto the couch.

Did the bird want to sleep with her again? She'd thought last night was a fluke. She wasn't sure she could manage sleeping with him again. But as he curled up on her shoulder, his soft warmth lulled her—even as she told herself this couldn't be a good thing. *You can't make a habit of sleeping with birds, Summer Merriweather.*

Chapter Fifty-One

Summer awakened with an intense longing that became an ache through her whole body. She wanted her mom. The feeling was beyond crying; it was beyond any kind of nameable emotional pain. *Mom. What happened to you?*

Why?

Summer had expected to have many years with her mom just a phone call away. Just a five-hour trip away.

It felt so unfair. As if it were some kind of a sick joke from God. Her mother, one of the most beloved people in the community, had been murdered, struck down by a backstabbing friend.

Summer drew in air and sat up slowly, so as not to wake the sleeping bird. She lifted him and placed him gently back in the cage.

She made her way to the kitchen to make coffee, surprised to see Piper already there. "Good morning," she said. "I see you were sleeping with Darcy again." She picked a silky gray feather from Summer's shoulder.

"Yeah. Pitiful, right?" She reached in the cupboard and pulled out a coffee cup. "Coffee. The elixir of the gods."

"Indeed," Piper said.

They sat and drank their coffee in silence for a few beats.

"What are you going to do today?" Piper asked.

"I'm going to check in with Ben about the robbery and about Mom's autopsy report."

"Sounds like . . . fun?"

"I feel like I'm getting close. Like the answer is just around the corner but just out of reach. I've got pieces to the puzzle, but they don't connect."

"Mom still thinks Rudy has something to do with it."

"I don't think so. But people surprise you. He was outside yesterday looking for his granddaughter's cat." Summer smiled. "That was a surprise."

Piper lugged. "Doesn't sound like a killer to me. Do you have any other suspects in mind?"

"I don't know about Henry. He stopped by the store yesterday and told me to call the cops off. I heard they were talking with him about the robbery, but maybe there's more to it."

"I can't see it," Piper said. She took a sip of coffee. "I can't see anybody hurting her. That's the odd thing. She didn't make enemies."

Summer's stomach wavered. "But it had to be someone close to her. If the same person set the house on fire, they were in this house. It had to be a friend. That hurts more than anything. That my mom's last few moments on earth might have been pained by betrayal."

"Don't go there. She wasn't aware of it. She was in the bookstore and collapsed. It wasn't like anybody attacked her."

"I tried to follow her footsteps, and all it did was make me think what I already thought. Mom was healthy. It's very rare for a woman not to have signs of sickness before a heart attack. That's why those autopsy results are so important."

243

"So how could people think she had a heart attack if she didn't?"

Summer placed her coffee on the table with a thud. "What are you getting at?"

Piper shrugged her shoulders. "I'm not sure what I mean. It seems like . . . I guess . . ."

"Whoever killed her intentionally made it look like a heart attack," Summer finished the thought.

"Exactly! And what could do that?"

"A poison? A drug?" Summer stood and started pacing. "We need to find out what could either mimic a heart attack or cause one."

"And then we need to figure out how it was given to her," Piper said, eyes wide. "What did she have to eat that day?"

"She usually had oatmeal and berries or fruit for breakfast," Summer said.

"Oh no, not anymore," Piper stood up and took her empty coffee cup to the sink. "She was drinking protein shakes in the morning."

"What?"

"I have no idea how or why she got on to that. But you might want to talk with Mia. She drinks the same ones."

Summer had read that some protein shakes had energizing substances, like caffeine. Would an overdose of caffeine have given her mom a heart attack? Surely not from one protein drink?

"I need to get in the shower and get down to the police station. We need that damn autopsy report."

"If it's not there yet?" Piper asked.

"I'll ask for the name of the lab and get it myself." Summer stormed off to get ready for her visit to the station.

"I'll call Mia!" Piper yelled after her.

What else had her mother eaten or drunk that day? As Summer showered, she reviewed her mom's last day. Hildy had risen out of bed, showered, drunk a protein drink, gone to yoga, and then to the bank and the store. Had she had time to eat somewhere in between going to those places? Would she have even been hungry after having a protein shake?

Hildy Merriweather was a snacker—a healthy snacker, but still she always had at least an apple or granola bar mid-morning. By the time she exited the shower, Summer had added another task to her plan. She needed to examine her mom's car. That's where she kept her "on-the-run" snacks.

Then she'd head to the police station, hoping they finally had gotten the official autopsy report. She wanted answers—but what to hope for? That her mom did have a reaction to something that caused a heart attack? Or that someone had given her something that killed her? Either way, Summer craved answers.

Chapter Fifty-Two

With Piper on her heels, Summer unlocked her mom's 1980 Subaru hatchback. Patchouli wafted out as she opened the door. The crystal that always hung from her rearview mirror seemed lifeless and staid.

"Do you see anything?" Piper said from behind her.

"I do," Summer said, her gaze resting on a box of granola bars and a crumpled wrapper next to it.

"Mom's last snack was a granola bar."

"Should we move it?"

"No, let's just leave it here. We don't tamper with evidence. Let's just wait until we need it."

"Okay, I've got to get to work, but if you need me, let me know."

Summer shut the car door. Her mom's car. It sat there looking weird and alone. She hadn't used it often. Most places Hildy traveled to were within walking distance. The car's mileage was super low for such an old car.

"My car is never going to die," she used to say.

Summer supposed she'd have to decide what to do with it. Should she keep it? Sell it? Ugh. She couldn't think about it right now. Off to the police station.

* * *

When Summer walked into the station, the woman behind the reception desk sat up straighter. "Can I help you?"

"Summer Merriweather to see Ben Singer."

"The chief is in a meeting. Would you care to wait?"

"How long is this meeting going to be?"

"Hard to say, but he's already been there quite a while."

"Okay, I'll wait."

"I'll let him know you're here."

"Thanks."

Summer sat down in what passed as a waiting area. There was nothing on the walls except safety posters. What to do if someone mugs you. When you should call 911. That kind of thing. A stack of old magazines sat on an end table. Summer picked one up and thumbed through it.

An article about a new diet that works miracles.

One about doing a room makeover for less than $200.

Another one written about a woman with Lyme disease.

"Ms. Merriweather?"

She glanced up. "Yes."

"The Chief will see you."

Summer stood and placed the magazine back where she'd found it. "Great."

"Follow that—"

Summer held up her hand. "It's fine. I know the way. Thanks.

Summer walked through the door and into the dim hallway. She didn't think it could be worse than the waiting area but was sorely mistaken. When she walked into Ben's office, he sat at his desk, with his glasses perched on his nose. He looked out over them. "Summer."

"Hello, Ben," she said, noticing he held something in his hand.

"Please sit down," he said.

The energy shifted a bit. Summer didn't know why.

"I have your mom's final official autopsy report. Everything is here but the tox report, which we ordered later, if you'll remember." He slurred *remember*. His eyes were glazed. Was he drunk?

Summer's breath whooshed out of her body. Her mouth was as dry as cotton balls. All she could do was nod.

"Your mom had a heart attack. Just like we suspected."

Her hands snapped to her mouth as she sobbed. "No. No. It can't be." She drew in air. "You said yourself something odd is going on, right? My attack, the fire, the robbery . . ."

"Unrelated," he said sitting back in his chair. "I'm sorry, Summer. These things happen."

"But I've researched heart attacks," she blurted. "It's very rare for someone to have one without—without—you know, the symptoms. She had none. She was healthy!"

She barely recognized her voice. Shrill, panicked. This couldn't be.

He frowned. "Your mom was one in a million. We always knew that, right?" He grinned a crooked smile. A Singer smile. The same smile his son had used on her when he wanted his way.

No. Not in this case. No. You don't discuss my mom's death with a clichéd expression and grin as if you're dealing with a two-year-old.

"May I please have the report?" she asked, calmer, more composed.

"I can make you copies. You're entitled to it," he said, standing.

You're damn right I am. What did he know about anything? She was leaving and marching straight over to Dr. Chang's office.

Her heart thudded against her rib cage. She wasn't going to let him know how upset she was. She'd already given herself away too much.

When he came back into the room, he handed her the report.

"Thanks," she said, rising from her chair. "I need to get going. But thanks for your time."

He batted his eyes. "Are you okay?"

She paused before answering. "I'm as okay as anybody whose mom just died, I suppose."

She walked out, leaving a bewildered Ben Singer behind. He was used to her putting up more of a fight. Not this time. It just wasn't worth it. He was not the person she needed to speak with right now. She needed to hightail it to Dr. Chang's office.

* * *

When she pulled into the parking lot, she was a bit confused because his assistant was locking up. She exited the car without even turning it off.

"Lucy?"

"Oh hey, Summer."

"Why are you leaving?"

"Today's the doc's fishing day. He takes two days a month and goes fishing.

Damn. She wanted to cry.

"What do you have there?"

"It's my mom's autopsy report. He wanted to look it over. I guess I can stop back by tomorrow."

"Or I can take pictures with my iPhone and send it to him. We've done that before. If you don't mind?"

"Mind? No, that's fantastic."

The two of them stood and photographed the report, and Lucy sent it off to him.

"Now, I'm not making any promises as to when he'll get back. Sometimes there's no Wi-Fi, but he'll be back tonight and will look them over and get back to you in the morning."

"Okay." What was one more day in this twisty passage of justice?

Chapter Fifty-Three

S ummer's last hope was Dr. Chang finding something on the report. Then she could get some help from the police—or some law enforcement authority, like Levi, the fire investigator.

She pulled into the back lot of the bookstore. The storm had cleared away and beachgoers had their books and were lying in the sun with their reads by now. Or they were curled up in a hammock or a chaise somewhere, swept away by a story.

She exited the car. Being swept away by a story was not such a bad thing. But, since she was now the owner of Beach Reads, she'd have a section of classics, including Shakespeare. After all, one could get lost in those great stories as well.

She opened the door, and the scent of books and pathos greeted her. Poppy was cleaning up the register area and looked up at Summer. "Hey, how's it going?"

"Okay," Summer said. She was trying not to think of those autopsy results. She needed to keep her mind occupied. "I've got some ideas I'd like to run by you at some point. And I guess we need to go over some things like the schedule and upcoming events."

"Sure, anytime," Poppy said. "Crowd's kind of thin now. What're your ideas?"

"Well, I've been thinking about adding a classics section."

Poppy stopped her straightening and fiddling.

"Not huge, but just say ten or twelve titles for people who might appreciate it."

Poppy said nothing but looked away.

"What do you think?"

She shrugged. "You know how Hildy felt about that. But you're the owner now. I think if you want to try it with a few books, it wouldn't be too much of a risk."

Summer blinked. And blinked again. *You know how Hildy felt about that.*

"I know how she felt about it, of course, but I've always disagreed. I've always thought there could be a market for readers who prefer the books I like."

"We're mostly known for romances and mysteries."

"I get that, but maybe there's a small market we're missing."

Poppy stiffened. "Maybe."

People don't like changes. Summer worried Poppy.

"Look, Poppy, I know you were a friend of my mom's and she respected you. Your opinion is valuable to me, and I hope you'll stay on as an employee. I need you. I've no idea how to run the bookstore now. So much has changed since I worked with Mom."

Her face and stance softened. "Okay. Glad to know that."

She appeared relaxed, but Summer still got the feeling the young woman didn't like her. Or maybe didn't believe her. Odd. "I'm going into the office to look over Mom's events calendar. I'll be there if you need me."

"Okay, thanks," she replied.

How could Summer make her feel more comfortable with the changes? Summer was aware she wasn't easily liked—at least that's what her students said—but she wasn't completely unlikable, was she? Besides, her students reacted to her because she was so tough. Funny, Summer didn't think of herself in the way at all. She was simply trying to give them a good education. These days a lot of her students felt like just showing up to class should get them a passable grade.

No, indeed.

Summer sat down in her mom's office chair, feeling weird about it. It was eerie knowing her mother had died in the store. She didn't like the feeling. But she decided not to dwell on it, but to think instead about how much Hildy loved this place and all the warm and happy memories within its walls.

She lifted her mom's calendar from the other side of the desk. It had been left open to the day she'd died. Summer flipped the pages and saw that next month Hildy had scheduled three guest authors. One was giving a workshop on "How to Write a Cozy Mystery." Summer's mouth twisted. Cozy mystery: Who imagined *cozy* was a good term?

She transposed all of the author events into her phone, as well as the paydays. Summer knew nothing about QuickBooks, but perhaps Poppy did. She wrote down a note to remind herself to ask Poppy.

As she scanned the calendar, she saw a "J. S." listed a few times. Who was J. S.? Another thing to ask Poppy about.

She flipped the page backwards to the book group date, which reminded her it was tomorrow. She only had a few chapters left to read. She'd need to finish tonight. And she hated to admit to herself, but she couldn't wait to see how it ended. What would Mom say? Summer laughed.

"Summer?" Aunt Agatha poked her head in. What's so funny?"

"I'm not sure I can tell you," Summer said.

"Oh, come on." Aunt Agatha sat down on a chair across from the desk.

"I can't wait to finish *Nights at Bellamy Harbor*. And I was just thinking about what Mom would have to say about that."

Agatha giggled. "She might have a few choice words about it. It's funny to think about."

"All of those years I railed against romances, and here I am . . . but I'm certain it's just this particular book."

"Oh no, dear, some of her other books are even better than this one. I've read them all."

A twinge of unexpected excitement ran through her. There were more books written by. Hannah Jacobs! Surely Summer wouldn't have the time to read all of them—or would she?

"Summer," Aunt Agatha said, "you know it's okay if a Shakespeare scholar enjoys romance. There's actually a very successful romance author who's a Shakespeare professor."

"Seriously?"

"Yes, and she teaches at Harvard."

Summer didn't know what to say to that.

Chapter Fifty-Four

After Summer, Mia, and Piper ate supper, cleaned up, and then they each drifted to their corner of the house—Mia with earbuds in. She hadn't heard half the dinner conversation, Summer was certain.

Summer readied for bed and curled up on the couch to finish reading *Nights at Bellamy Harbor*.

Hildy had underlined a section and commented, "All the feels," on one page. Summer knew what she was talking about. As Summer read further on, her heart pounded. The couple would actually make a go of it. Not only was he a developer and she an environmentalist, but he was Muslim and she was agnostic. But they loved each other, and it seemed as if they were meeting one another halfway.

Summer read on, the language and the story zipping through her. One minute she was laughing, the next crying. Then laughing at herself for crying. Here she was, crying over a romance.

"Summer?" Piper came up behind her. "Are you okay?"

She snapped the book shut. *Damn it.* She only had only more chapter left to read. She sniffed. "Yes, I'm fine. Why?"

"I was in the kitchen getting a drink. It sounded like you were crying . . . then laughing, then I don't know what." She sat down on the La-Z-Boy. "Are you losing your shit?"

Summer laughed. "Lost it a long time ago." She lifted up the book as her face reddened.

"Oh! Ha! That's interesting. Like the book?" Piper grinned.

"Well, I wouldn't go that far." Summer stiffened. Would she?

"Yes, you do! Why not admit it?" Piper laughed. "You're too much."

"Okay," Summer said after a few beats, "I do. I like it, and your mother says she's written other books. I was secretly thrilled to hear that."

Piper laughed again. "Well, I'm glad to know you're enjoying it." The two sat in silence for a few minutes.

A weird scuffling noise came from the front of the house. The cousins looked at each other.

"Someone's out there," Summer said. Piper nodded, eyes wide as the moon, tinged in anxiety.

They sat listening for a moment, and the noise came again.

"Well, I guess I'll check it out," Summer said, rising from the couch.

She tiptoed to the front window. Her eyes adjusted to the dark skies, only lit by the moon and stars. A shadow fell across the front porch. She squinted, trying to make out the shape of the shadow.

Who with good intentions would skulk around this time of night? She heard her blood rush. She crept to the fireplace and grabbed a poker.

"Summer, what are you doing?" Piper said as she came up beside her.

"Protection," she whispered.

Was this the person who'd killed her mom? Who'd tried to set the place on fire? Who'd attacked Summer? Sweat pricked at her forehead. Was she finally going to confront the person who perhaps had killed her mom?

A creak.

A huff.

She reached toward the doorknob. Who was on the front porch?

She swung the door open, and something small yowled and tore off, leaving Rudy crouched in the corner. "Damn, Summer! I almost had Missy!"

"What?" she said.

"My granddaughter's cat. You scared her off. Damn."

He stood. "What are you doing with that?" He glanced at the poker.

She drew in air, trying to calm herself. "I planned to hit you right over the head with it."

He lurched back.

"I thought you were Mom's killer."

His mouth dropped open. Then he gathered himself. "I told you'd I'd never hurt her."

"How would I know who's creeping around out here at night? And I'm smart enough to know most people don't confess to murder."

"Especially people who want to expand their business," Piper said as she came up behind Summer.

"I'm sorry," Rudy said, jaw stiff. "I need to go. Missy. Darn cat. I almost had her."

He walked away, then turned back around. "I'm going to tell you one more time. I didn't hurt your mother. I was nowhere around when she died. I was running my business. I've got witnesses, if you feel you need them." He paused. "But if I were you, I'd drop this nonsense. Nobody killed your mother. You're making a fool of yourself and you're degrading her memory by going around accusing people in this community."

Summer's throat squeezed. She stood on the porch looking out over the view she'd grown up watching every day. The sea was calm. Moonlight reflecting on it, shimmered like rippled glass.

"Summer?"

"Yes?" She didn't turn and look at Piper.

Piper's arms slipped around her. "Are you okay?"

"I'm not sure. But I think I will be. How about you?"

Piper shrugged. "If it makes you feel any better, I totally agree with you. Someone murdered Aunt Hildy in her own bookstore."

A welling rose in Summer's chest. She tamped down the primal scream every ounce of her body wanted to release.

"How about a glass of wine?" Piper said.

Summer nodded, as she was certain that if she opened her mouth right now, that scream of frustration, anger, grief, and pain would burst out.

They sauntered back inside, and Piper poured two glasses of red wine. They sat on the couch, with Mr. Darcy overseeing the scene.

"He looks good," Piper said. "For an old bird."

Summer nodded again. The wine was working a bit of magic. The muscles in her neck unraveled. Her shoulders loosened. "The vitamins the vet gave him are doing the trick."

"You look a little better than you did out on the porch. Color's coming back."

Summer held up her wineglass. "I might need more of this."

Piper pointed to the bottle sitting on the coffee table. "I figured. That's why I brought the whole bottle."

Chapter Fifty-Five

After solving all the world's problems, Piper and Summer called it a night.

Summer opened the birdcage door, and Mr. Darcy flew right onto her pillow. "Night night," he said.

"Good night, Mr. Darcy."

She pulled her nylon face mask over her head and her anti-insect blanket around her. The bird snuggled closer. *At least there's one male creature not put off by my nighttime psychosis.* She lived in fear of waking up with a spider on her—especially on her face, in her ears, or—worse—mouth. She'd grown accustomed to it and now wasn't even certain she could sleep without it.

She tossed and turned, a bit worried about the results of the autopsy. Rudy's words kept rolling around in her head. What if she was making a fool of herself and, worse yet, her mother? What if her mom was the one in a million that had a heart attack without having any symptoms?

No. What about all the other things? The notes, the fire, her attack, the bookstore robbery? No. Her mom had not died of a natural heart attack. Someone had been out to get her—and that person was out to get Summer too. So far, they must be pretty disappointed.

She had thought there was an intruder, earlier tonight, which proved to Summer that she was getting paranoid. But who'd have imagined Rudy would be outside looking for Missy, his granddaughter's cat? Why was the cat always running away?

* * *

The next morning, the sun woke Summer. Mr. Darcy was gone from the crook of her neck, where he'd always slept. She sat up. "Darcy?"

No answer.

She flung the blankets off her and pulled off her mask. She stood looking around the room. "Darcy? There you are." He was on the ledge of the window looking out toward the ocean. "Silly bird. What are you doing?"

She reached for him, pulling him close, and glanced out the window. A cat sat staring at them. Must be Missy.

Summer placed him back in his cage.

She couldn't believe she'd slept too late. It was almost 10 AM she needed to shower and get over to see the doctor. She needed to know what he'd gleaned from the results.

Then she needed to get to the bookstore. They expected her to help with a shipment of books in today.

A pang of impatience tore through her. She wanted answers so she could get on with her life. She owned a house in Staunton and had a life there. Well. Kind of. Her job was still uncertain. She'd yet to hear back whether the dean could get support for his plan of a sabbatical for her.

After a quick shower and coffee on the go, Summer hopped into the car to go to the doctor's. When she arrived, she found the lack of cars in the parking lot perplexing. What was going on?

She exited the car and walked over to the door. The "Gone fishing" note was still on the door. She was certain Lucy had said he'd be back today. She peered inside and saw Lucy, who motioned for Summer to come in.

"Hi, Summer. I'm sorry. He's having car trouble. I don't think he'll be in until tomorrow." Harried, she flipped through the computer screen. The phone rang.

Poor thing, she was trying to rearrange his schedule. When she got off the phone, Summer asked her about the autopsy results.

"I asked him this morning, and the email never came through. I think it's because he was out at sea. When his car gets closer, he should be able to read the results."

Summer's heart sank. Well, she'd waited all this time for answers—what was a few more hours?

"I'd brace yourself for one more day. He'll have a lot of catch-up."

Summer's stomach roiled. *One more day? One more day?*

She nodded. "Well, please tell him it's very important. Have him call me when he's ready to talk."

"Will do, Summer." Her fingers clicked on her computer.

As Summer left the office, she noticed a man walking down the sidewalk, a man who looked very familiar. Henry. Did he live in this neighborhood?

She didn't think so. This was more a business section of the island. Very few houses. She passed an apartment complex. But she thought he owned a house.

She followed him at a distance so he wouldn't suspect her. Curiosity pulled her along. Henry, the high school English teacher, a friend of her mom's who everybody said wanted the shop and who definitely would appreciate the first editions. What was he doing in this part of town?

She walked past the convenience store and St. Brigid Church, then followed him around to the side entrance, where he disappeared into the building. A church? She didn't have him pegged as religious. At all. But you never know about some people. She continued to walk by and noted the sign on the door: "Gamblers Anonymous meeting here today."

They had all known about his gambling problem. But there he was, getting help. Summer's dislike of him seemed unreasonable in that moment. You had to feel for someone who realized he had a problem and worked on himself.

She recalled her anti-insect blanket and nylon face mask. Would she ever be able to shed them? Would she ever be able to venture into basements, attics? Go camping?

Just the idea of it made her shudder.

Chapter Fifty-Six

"What are you doing here, Summer?"

Summer turned around to face Ben Singer.

"Excuse me?"

"I asked you what you're doing here." He stood with his hands on his hips.

Had he been following her as she followed Henry?

"I asked you a question, Summer."

Her heart raced. "I'm not doing anything wrong. Why are you on my case?"

"This is an odd place for you. I think you're following Henry. Now I want to know why."

"I wasn't following Henry. I just went for a bit of a stroll after stopping by the doctor's office to talk about my mom's autopsy. That's all."

He rolled his eyes. "Okay, Summer. But please don't be stalking private citizens on this island." He started to walk away.

"What are you doing here, Ben?"

He turned back to face her, befuddled. "What did you say?"

"What are you doing here? Were you following me? Or were you following Henry?"

His mouth fell open. Then he gathered himself. "I'm an officer of the law and don't have to answer to you."

"Ah-ha!" Summer said so loudly that he jumped. "You were following one of us. But why?"

His face reddened. "I wasn't following anybody, young lady. Now back off." He turned and walked away.

"*Young lady'?*" she yelled after him. "I'm a scholar! A Shakespeare professor. I'm thirty-two years old. How dare you!"

He kept walking.

She followed him. "I'm following you now, Ben."

He stopped, spun around, and pointed his finger at her. "I'm warning you, Summer."

"Warning me?"

"Stop poking your nose in where it doesn't belong. You might get hurt . . . or arrested."

Arrested? Was he going to arrest her for walking behind Henry? He couldn't prove she was following him.

She crossed her arms. "All I want is justice for my mom. I have to wonder why you don't."

He kept walking and didn't even acknowledge her last statement.

He was right about one thing. She rarely came to this part of town. It wasn't her favorite part. Just a strip of doctors' offices, churches, and a few retail establishments She rarely had reason to be here. And it lacked the character of the rest of the island. Even the "touristy" boardwalk was not very touristy. Well, not compared to places like Virginia Beach and Ocean City.

She found her way back to her car and then to the bookstore. She hoped to give Poppy a bit of a break today. Poor woman had had little of one.

She hadn't realized she was still angry until Poppy asked her about it.

"What's wrong?"

"Wrong? Nothing. Other than I just had an encounter with Ben Singer, who has a grudge against me."

She grinned. "He's got a grudge against everybody."

"Excuse me," a customer came up to them. "I'm looking for the J. D. Robb section. I found Nora's section, and I thought the J. D. Robb books would be right there."

"J. D. Robb's books are in the mystery section, which is upstairs," Poppy said.

"Thank you," the woman said and walked off.

"Have you finished the book? Are you coming tonight?" Poppy asked.

"I have one more chapter to read. And yes, I'll be there tonight. Are you ready for a lunch break?"

A wide smile spread across Poppy's face. "Absolutely." A look of relief washed over her face, then she walked into the back for her break.

Summer straightened the register. Authors' bookmarks and cards, along with the flyers, needed a bit of tidying. Thoughts of Henry and Ben poked at her mind. *Was Ben following Henry himself?* Henry had mentioned that the police were bothering him. Following him. Questioning him. Summer assumed it was about the theft of the first editions, but perhaps it was more. Maybe Ben was taking her mom's death more seriously—she was sure he had been at one point. But now that the autopsy results concluded her mom had had a heart attack, his interest had probably plummeted. She also wondered about the fire investigation. Was anybody continuing to look into it?

Summer felt like she was close to finding the mother's killer, but she could be kidding herself. It wouldn't be the first time.

Had Henry gotten himself in trouble again with gambling? Money was one of the biggest reasons for murder. And in her mom's case, it seemed to be the only thing that made sense. The other big motive was romance—a relationship gone bad, jealousy, that kind of thing. Hildy hadn't dated. So it had to be money.

Summer had followed the trail of money, just like they always said to do in all the detective shows, and it had led her nowhere. Except to Rudy, who had an alibi, and Henry, who vehemently denied any wrongdoing. Summer's stomach roiled. Of course he would.

She couldn't shake the feeling that she was missing someone. Some developer . . . someone lurking in the shadows waiting to make Summer an offer on the bookstore. But not without scaring her first, with the fire, attack, and bookstore robbery.

Little did they know, Summer Merriweather didn't scare easily.

Unless there was a spider anywhere on the premises.

People she could handle. Spiders, no.

Chapter Fifty-Seven

After closing up the shop, Summer set off for the house to get ready for the book group meeting. She had one more chapter left in the book, and she'd read it come hell or high water.

She settled herself in the La-Z-Boy. "Summer," Mr. Darcy said.

"Hello, Darcy."

She cracked open the book. One more chapter to find out how Tilda and Omar would work it out with his wealthy Muslim family, the developers. It seemed so complicated. He was the only son in a Muslim family, and so many obligations came with that. Tilda was strong and independent, but she turned to jelly when Omar was around.

Summer's eyes grazed over the text, and soon enough she was swept into the story, not realizing the time passing or anything else.

She closed the book, tears streaming down her face. It was so simple—to love and be loved was the most important thing in life. Why did people complicate things?

Religion and culture and mores and pride and stupidity.

"Are you ready?" Piper breezed into the living room.

"Uh." Summer looked up at her and wiped tears from her face.

Piper rushed to her. "What's wrong?"

She held up the book.

"Oh yeah. The book. All the feels, right?"

"I can't believe I'm sitting here crying over a romance novel."

Piper laughed. "If Hildy's listening, you just made her very happy!"

"I know. Crazy. I'm losing my mind." She stood. "Give me a few minutes and I'll be ready to go."

She moved into the bathroom and washed her face. The cool water helped bring her back into reality. She couldn't believe how well that book was written, nor how it made her forget time and place. She swiped the mascara wand over her lashes, brushed some blush across her cheeks, and applied lip gloss to her lips. She looked at herself in the mirror. "Better," she said, spraying herself with insect repellant for their later outdoor excursion. She was grateful for the warning that part of the celebration would drift off to Full Moon Cove.

She couldn't quite shrug off the story. Something about it felt very personal. Maybe that's why people read so much romance? Her mom used to say that romance carried the rest of the book industry.

Her mom's notes scattered through the book were . . . treasures. Summer would never get rid of it. Then she vowed to check through the other books around the house. Had Hildy left notes in those too? Something in Summer's chest fluttered at the thought.

Piper knocked at the bathroom door. "Are you ready? We need to go."

Summer opened the door. "I'm as ready as I will ever be."

She found her bag, slipped the book into it, and she and Piper exited the house together.

They walked along the beach, toward the boardwalk, past the neighborhood of tiny cottages, past the condos, the church and Wanda's hot dog stand, which smelled so good it tempted Summer to buy a few to eat before she got to the store.

"There will be food at the meeting," Piper said, as if reading her mind.

"Good. I'm starving. I hadn't realized it until I smelled those hot dogs."

Rudy stood outside the arcade.

"Bastard," Piper mumbled.

Summer agreed but ignored her remark. "Hey Rudy, Missy has been hanging on my porch."

He nodded. "Good to know."

The continued walked. "Who's Missy?" Piper asked.

"His granddaughter's cat. It keeps running away from home and coming over to our house."

"A gray tabby?"

"Yes. I have to wonder why she's hanging out at Mom's place. Mom was allergic and would never have encouraged it."

Piper laughed. "True. But Mr. Darcy loves that cat. And the cat loves him. They used to just sit and look at one another through the window."

"Oh my god! That's what was going on yesterday!"

"Probably," she said. "You should tell Rudy not to worry. It's true love."

"A bird and a cat? Ha! So funny!"

"Right?"

They stopped in front of the bookstore. For all intents and purposes, it looked closed to the passerby. They slipped in.

Laughter came from upstairs. Summer and Piper walked up to find a circle of women—and one man, Henry—getting ready to discuss the book. The room was full of about twenty people, some of whom Summer knew.

A circle of chairs sat in the middle of the room. Marilyn sauntered over to Piper and Summer. "So glad you could make it. We'll get started in a few minutes."

"Thanks," Summer said.

Pink-haired Doris and multi-tattooed Marilyn were chatting near the cozy mystery section. Together, they were a plethora of color. Pinks. Greens. Purples. They looked deep in their conversation.

Agatha came up beside Piper. "Hello there. Are we ready to talk about romance?"

Summer rolled her eyes at her aunt's jab. If only she knew how much her niece loved the book, Summer would never live it down.

"Can we all take a seat?" Glads said.

Like well-trained children, the group all took their seats. The room quieted.

"Welcome," Glads said. "We're all missing our dear Hildy tonight." Her voice cracked. "But we knew she'd want us to continue gathering and discussing books." Glads paused. "This book was one of her favorites. We talked about it a lot." She smiled. "The author was a good friend of hers and had been here to visit and sign books on several occasions."

Summer had realized none of that. But it made sense. The book had that note about Rudy scribbled in it.

Agatha reached over and squeezed Summer's hand. Her hand was warm and soft on Summer's.

As the readers discussed the book, Summer studied them. Could one of them have killed her mom? It had to be someone in her circle. Which upset Summer. Better that a stranger should kill you than a friend. Try as she might, Summer got no bad vibes from anyone in the group.

Summer listened to the group as they discussed character arcs, metaphors, and romantic tension. She was impressed by the knowledge of the romance genre and of story craft. It was a more sophisticated bunch than she'd imagined.

"And oh my God. This book was hot. Like no sex on the page, but so hot! I mean it gave me some amazing dreams!" Glads said.

Summer grinned. So much for sophisticated.

Chapter Fifty-Eight

After the book discussion, they all hopped into cars to ride to a more remote part of the island. They parked and walked down an unlit path. Some had flashlights, and others used the lights from their smartphones.

Summer vaguely remembered Full Moon Cove. It was a place that the water receded only during the full moon. Otherwise it was filled with seawater. As a child, her recollections were that she was frightened of it. As it was, she had doused herself with insect repellent and wore layers of clothing—even on a warm night. She was sweaty but was assured no spider would come within ten feet of her skin, mouth, and hair.

When they finally arrived, Summer stopped walking to take it all in. The cove was lit by torches and candles. She turned toward the sea, with the light behind her, and looked out toward the ocean. The light of the full moon played on the water, and the stars were bright. Her throat burned. This was the exact kind of night her mom would have loved.

She dizzied. Once she had her bearings, she walked arm in arm with Agatha, Piper and Mia flanking them, into the cove. The scent of burning candles and torchlights, along with citronella, filled the air.

Summer blinked her eyes, for there was Posey. "Posey? What are you doing here?"

She cracked a calm smile. "I came to say goodbye, of course."

"But are you feeling up to this?"

She lowered her voice. "Summer, don't worry so much. I appreciate your concern, but I'm okay. How about you? Are you staying out of danger?"

"As much as I can."

She grabbed Summer's other hand. "Let's get started, shall we?"

Summer's breath shortened. She took in the women gathered; some she knew and others she didn't.

Posey's voice rang out. "For those of you who don't know her, this is Summer, Hildy's daughter."

Summer blinked and tried to smile, but her checks felt like slabs of heavy ham.

"Hey, Summer," one person said. Another person called out, "Greetings," and another, "Blessed be."

"Before the party starts, I need to say something," Posey said.

A hush fell over the cove.

"Summer is in danger."

Oh no, was she going there? Like immediately? At the start of the party?

"What do you mean?" Piper said.

"Someone hurt Hildy and wants to hurt Summer."

"Hurt? Stop talking in platitudes," Glads said. "For God's sake. Spit it out, woman."

"Someone killed Hildy, and they want to scare Summer away."

One of the women gasped.

"I thought she had a heart attack," someone from the group said.

Posey closed her eyes. "My apologies, Glads. Here comes another platitude. But things are not what they always seem."

Summer's heart raced. This was so not a good idea. The killer could be right here, and Posey was warning her. Telling her that they were on to her.

"Summer will need your help to figure this out. If anybody knows anything about the last few days of Hildy's life—anything at all—you need to talk with Summer."

"Thanks," Summer said in an effort to change the conversation. This was supposed to be a celebration of her mom's life. "Please call me or stop by the bookstore to chat any time. Meanwhile—"

"Let's party!" Agatha interrupted. Summer hugged her. "Thank you," she whispered.

They gathered into a circle and held hands. Summer swallowed.

"We're going to miss you, Hildy." A young woman Summer didn't know spoke up.

"I don't know about anyone else, but I'm a little angry. Did someone hurt her? What can we do about it?" another person said.

A murmur of agreement. A thread of anger drew them inward together.

"Let's talk about it after," Agatha said.

"With all due respect, Agatha, I don't think so," Glads said. "I want to know what's going on."

"Glads, I appreciate your concern," Summer said, "but now isn't the time."

"Here's what we can do now," Posey said. "Let's wrap Summer in a protective light, here and now. And remove any obstacles to her finding out the truth."

As if it were that easy. Hildy put a lot of stock in this, and Summer tried. They'd had conversations about ritual just being another form of prayer, which was something Summer related to. Out of respect for Posey and Hildy, Summer held her tongue. But her chest was squeezing. She wanted to run out of the cove, feet on the sand. Toes in the foamy water.

"Let's set the intention and sing it into being," Posey said. They crowd quieted. No words were spoken. Summer watched the shadows on the rocky cove walls.

Someone's voice rang into song. "We all come from the goddess, and to her we shall return. Like a drop of rain going to the ocean." Another joined her. Soon, song enveloped Summer. The sound circled her and vibrated deep in her chest.

"Thank you all for coming," Summer said after it quieted. "Now, let's eat!"

"Woo-hoo!" Mia yelped. "I'm so hungry!"

Summer's stomach growled. When was the last time she'd eaten today? She couldn't remember. But suddenly she was famished, and it was all she could do to not rush at the table and stack her plate too high to be considered polite.

Chapter Fifty-Nine

As the crowd dispersed, each woman came up to Summer and offered condolences and stories of Hildy. One woman talked about the doctor. It took Summer a minute to realize it was his assistant, Lucy. Out of context, Summer didn't recognize her.

"I'll tell the doctor to get right on it tomorrow."

"Thank you," Summer said.

Soon, only Summer, Mia, Agatha, Piper, Glads, Marilyn, and Doris were left in the cove.

"We've got to do something more to help you," Glads said in a tizzy. "We'll protect you." Doris and Marilyn nodded.

"Doris, I know this upsets you, but is there anything else you can tell us about the day Hildy died? You were the only person with her," Agatha said.

Summer had wanted to ask her again, but given how upset Doris had gotten last time, she'd waited.

Doris's face hardened and turned pale. "I . . . uh . . . don't know what else I can say," she stammered.

"Now, Doris, if you could just try to remember anything at all," Marilyn said.

"I've already said. I've already told the police, you all—well, everybody." Her voice rose. "I don't know what else to say. She screamed and fell . . . The next thing I knew, I was on the floor next to her, trying to hold her . . . comfort her." She sobbed. "I don't know what you want to know!"

"Calm down, dear," Glads said. "It's okay." She wrapped her arm around Doris. "Let me take you home."

Doris pulled away from Glads. "That's okay. I've got my car, and I better get going."

She didn't say goodnight, thank you, or anything. It was as if we had drained all the energy and words right out of her.

"Poor dear," Agatha said.

"I don't like her," Mia said.

"Mia!" Piper said.

"I'm sorry. I know it's awful. But she was the last one to see Hildy alive." She crossed her arms. "And I hate her for it."

Stalwart, cool Mia erupted into a squall of emotion. Was she crying? Angry?

"Mia, you don't mean that," Agatha said, trying to pull her off to the side.

"Yes, I do. I'm not a baby, Gram. She should know more. Why doesn't she? She was there!"

"Sometimes there's nothing more to know," Glads offered. "We all want answers. But I doubt that Doris could give anybody answers. She's a hot mess."

"But how could someone else have hurt her? She fell down at the bookstore because she had a heart attack," Marilyn said.

"Mom was very healthy. Most people who have a heart attack have symptoms. I spoke with the yoga teacher, the teller at the bank—well, everybody who saw her that morning. And she didn't seem to have any symptoms. It's very rare for people to just die from a heart attack without having some problems first," Summer said.

"That's why the autopsy is so important," Piper said. "Doc has it and will look it over tomorrow. "

"Good, but who on this island would hurt her? I don't get it. I can't think of a soul," Marilyn said.

"Well, there is Rudy," Agatha said. "He wanted to expand."

"Pshaw, Rudy is a wuss. He'd never do anything to hurt anybody. Have you seen him with his granddaughter?" Marilyn said, sunflower wiggling on her upper arm.

"Still, someone was sending her threatening notes," Piper said.

"I admit, that's odd," Marilyn said.

"Then there's Henry," Summer said. "I think he's still dealing with his gambling problem. Don't they always say to follow the money when it comes to murder?"

"Love and money," Glads said.

"She wasn't seeing anybody, was she?" Summer said.

Mia turned her head to pay close attention.

"You're her closest friends. You'd know if she were seeing someone, right?" Summer persisted.

"She wasn't seeing anybody," Mia said. "Had no interest in it anymore. Didn't have time, she said."

"Right," Marilyn said. "She told me that too."

"So we can strike love off the list," Glads said.

Summer's scattered thoughts pulled together. "What about an unrequited love? Was there someone who loved her? Had a thing for her and she didn't reciprocate?"

Silence permeated the cove. The sound of the waves rushed in the distance.

"Oh, honey," Marilyn said, "I don't think you want to go down that road."

"What? What do you mean?"

"There were so many past lovers . . . men who wanted her but she didn't want them . . . men who wanted to marry her . . . live with her."

"Men adored her," Agatha said.

"I don't think we could even make a list of them." Glads smiled. "She kept a lot of them to herself."

"How many?" Summer asked, not even wanting to know the answer to how many lovers had Mom had taken over the years—only one answer was what she wanted when it came to that—who'd fathered her. And while Summer was growing up, Hildy had kept her dates and escapades hidden from Summer.

"Who knows?" Agatha said, shrugging. "We didn't keep a list, did we?"

Glads laughed. "I didn't, but I often wondered if she did. Like kept a journal of them."

"I've not seen anything like that."

"That's because there's no such thing," Mia said with her arms folded, making Summer's ears prick. She made a mental note to return to this subject with Mia.

"Of course not," Agatha said, turning and winking at Summer.

Chapter Sixty

Summer and Mr. Darcy had just gotten to sleep when a knock came at the front door. At first, Summer thought she was still dreaming, for she was dreaming and sleeping deeply. But Darcy pecked at her, and the door wouldn't stop knocking.

She rolled off the couch in a stupor and glanced at the clock: one thirty AM. This couldn't be good. She peeked into the hole. It was Dr. Chang.

She opened the door in a rush. He gasped and jumped back.

"What's wrong?" she asked, realizing she was still wearing her mask on her face. She pulled it off quickly. "I'm sorry." Her face heated.

"Summer? Jesus! You startled me." He walked into the house. Darcy was walking through the hallway.

He pointed. "There's a bird over there."

"It's okay. It's Mr. Darcy."

"Oh, I see," he said in a tone that told her he didn't see.

"What are you doing here? We were fast asleep."

"I'm sorry. But I've heard from fifteen women tonight. My cell phone hasn't stopped."

Summer laughed. "Okay. Can I get you something?"

"No, given the late hour. I just wanted to let you know . . ." He stopped, watching Mr. Darcy waddle back across the hall. "Maybe some water. Yes. Pour yourself a glass too. Let's sit down and talk about this."

Summer's heart raced. "What could it be?"

"Summer. Bedtime." The bird said clearly.

The doctor's eyebrows shot up.

"Okay, Darcy. I'll be there soon." She swatted away feathers from her shoulder.

"Have you been sleeping with that bird?"

"Sit down, Doctor. I'll get the water." She reached into the cupboard for glasses and bought two down, filled them up. "I've slept with Darcy for a few nights. He was very sick—upset, we think, about my mother's passing."

She slid his glass in front of him. "Why are you here?"

"Summer? Is someone downstairs?" Piper's voice rang out from the second floor.

"The doctor is here. With news," Summer yelled back.

Piper, looking as if she hadn't just been awakened, still put together, strode into the kitchen. "Oh, hey," she said. "I couldn't sleep. I was thinking about going for a walk."

Summer drank from her glass. The water felt good sliding down her throat. It did nothing to calm her heart. Sweat beads formed on her forehead. "What's the news, Doctor?"

"Okay," he said, then took a drink of water. "I can see why people thought your mother had a heart attack. Because she did."

Piper, who had been walking around the table to the fridge stopped. Summer put her glass back down. The room filled with stunned silence.

"But here's the thing. I studied these tox reports and inspected her bloodwork. The guys who do autopsies sometimes don't have the time to study things like the labs."

What is he saying? Summer couldn't ask because her heart was racing so fast and her mouth had gone dry.

"For God's sake, get to it," Piper said.

"Hildy's insulin levels were off the charts. Let me try to explain what happened. It was as if your mother had been a diabetic and had eaten a lot of sugary snacks."

Summer remembered the granola bars in her car. Just how much sugar was in them? She caught herself. Her mom wasn't diabetic, so it wouldn't have mattered.

"How could that have happened?" Piper asked.

Good, Piper. Summer couldn't formulate her thoughts.

"I've been thinking about that. And I'm just not sure. It's as if someone gave your mother a huge dose of insulin. One that would kill her."

This was the answer Summer had been hoping for—she wanted to feel relieved. But she was numb.

"How?"

"I don't know. Something she ate? Or did someone prick her skin with a needle to shoot her up with all of this insulin? I just don't know. I've contacted the medical examiner to see if she can find a needle mark."

He drew in a breath, released it slowly. "Summer, I can't say for sure, but I think your instincts are right. Someone killed your mother. And this is evidence I can't ignore."

Darcy walked into the room, whistling "Happy Birthday."

They all turned toward the bird, then their attention focused back on the doctor.

Summer had no words. It was like someone had kicked her in the guts, and she struggled to breathe, to make sense of the world. Proof that her mom had been murdered. This was what she'd wanted, right?

But the magnitude of the situation, the sadness, the feeling of betrayal enveloped her. She drank her water.

"Are you okay, Summer?" the doctor asked.

She nodded. She should feel vindicated. Why didn't she?

"Can you talk with Ben in the morning?" Piper asked. Summer should have asked that. What was wrong with her brain tonight?

"I sure will," he said. "Hopefully, the police will find who did this to our Hildy." He paused. "Of all the people on this island . . . well, she was very loved."

A hot, burning tear escaped from Summer's eyes.

"I hate to see anybody killed, but Hildy? No, this is a travesty." He stood, reaching across the counter and touched Summer's hand. "I'm so sorry Summer. If there's anything I can do."

Summer nodded again. "Ah," she said, "you've helped tremendously. Thank you."

"I don't feel like I have," the doctor said. "I hate delivering this kind of news. But ultimately, we need to know. As difficult as it is."

"Yes," Piper said. "Now there's something solid we can go on. We just need to figure out how this happened and who did it."

"Indeed," he said. "I'm sorry to awaken everybody. But I received fifteen calls about this." He smiled. "I better go. I'll find my own way out."

The doctor exited.

Summer heard the front door open and shut. She and Piper sat quietly.

"Who could have done such a thing?" Piper's voice pierced the quiet.

Summer shrugged. "The sad thing is it had to be someone close to her, right? I keep thinking of her being betrayed like that. What must she have thought? Were her last thoughts of hurt and betrayal? That kills me."

"All I know is it happened very quickly. I don't think she realized something. And as a mother myself, I can tell you my last thought would be about how much I love Mia."

Tears were now flowing vigorously. Piper handed her a box of tissue.

"I hope you're right. I hope her last thoughts were good ones."

Chapter Sixty-One

S ummer didn't sleep the rest of the night. She paced, rocked, and finally, when the sun started to peek over the horizon, she walked the beach.

She told herself she should feel vindicated. There was proof that her mom had been killed. She had been on the right track all along. But, perhaps for the first time in her life, being right didn't make her feel any better. She felt like God was playing some kind of nasty joke on her.

Her mom had planted seeds of goodness wherever she traveled. It used to annoy Summer that her mother didn't have a mean bone in her body. That she always looked on the bright side of things— always with the positive spin. Summer would grit her teeth, watching her mom spread those seeds of goodness.

Volunteering at the women's shelter. Hosting countless almost-broke authors in her home. Cleaning the beach every Sunday morning during tourist season. And—well, the list continued.

And despite a lifetime of that, someone had offed her. Not just *someone*, but a friend. Someone who'd been in her home. In her bookstore. Most likely someone whom Hildy had fed. She fed anybody who came her way.

Her delicious vegan treats.

The only thing to do was to cooperate with Ben as he investigated. She swallowed the sea air. Justice was the only way she'd ever begin to feel better about losing Hildy. Yet, it would never be enough.

The light of the day spread slowly over the ocean. She slipped her shoes off and walked into the sea. She needed to feel something other than the inner turmoil. The strife. Friction.

The cold water snapped her back. She stood and let its cold embrace her. She drew in air. Time to get some answers.

* * *

"Hi, Ben—it's Summer Merriweather."

"Yeah. How can I help you?"

"Has Dr. Chang called you yet this morning?"

"I don't know. I just got in."

"He'll be calling. He studied my mother's autopsy report. It's as I suspected."

Silence.

"Ben?"

"What do you mean?"

"I mean someone shot enough insulin into my mother to send her into something like diabetic shock, giving her a heart attack."

"What?" His voice rose. "I'll be right over."

"I need to get to the bookstore this morning. Poppy has a doctor's appointment. Can we just meet over there?"

"Absolutely." He clicked off.

Piper came down the stairs, looking grim. "I hardly slept."

"I didn't sleep at all. I just talked to Ben. He's coming to the store."

Piper rolled her eyes. "What evidence can be left at this point? He should have listened to you. Now how are they going to find out anything?"

Summer downed her coffee. "I need to open the store. Poppy's off this morning. But let's hope the police will find some piece of evidence somewhere."

"Well, we've already done a good bit of investigating. You should tell Ben what you found out."

"I intend to." Summer picked up her bag and headed for the door. "Are you working today?"

"Yeah, half a day."

"Okay. I'll see you later."

* * *

Summer walked past the other businesses as they were setting up. She smiled, said hello, good morning, yet she almost felt as though she were another person. *Face it, Summer: the only thing keeping you awake is caffeine. Of course you feel strange.*

She slid her key into the lock and opened the front door, surprised to find the lights on and to hear music playing and laughter from the back. She walked toward the sound of the friendly laughter.

"Good morning, Summer," Marilyn said when she walked into the back room.

"Good morning. What's going on?"

"Weekly shipment. We always help with this one. Besides, we heard you were opening today and wanted to help out."

"Thank you. I might need it."

"Have you heard anything from the doctor?" Glads asked.

"Yes."

"Yoo-hoo! Are you open? A voice came from the front of the store.

"Yes!" Summer yelled. "Be right there."

Marilyn and Glads stood and drew closer to Summer. "She was murdered. Someone gave her a ton of insulin, which sent her into a state much like a diabetic shock, which gave her a heart attack."

"What?" Marilyn said.

Glads gasped.

"I know. It's horrible." Summer's chin quivered. "I need you to think hard about who could have done such a thing and why. Ben is coming over this morning. So please stick around if you can."

Summer braced herself and moseyed into the front of the store to help the customer who had wandered in. It was the last thing she wanted to do today, to be in this bookstore, planting a smile on her face and talking with customers about dreadful books . . . well . . . not all of them were dreadful.

"Can I help you?" Summer asked the woman, who was dressed in a yellow sundress with a white sweater wrapped around her shoulders. She was stunning. Summer blinked. Mocha-skinned with deep brown eyes, almost black, with black hair falling in waves around her face, showing off cheekbones to die for.

"Yes," the woman replied, smiling. "I hear you have a diversity-in-romance section."

"We do," Summer said.

"Can you make any recommendations?" Her voice was well schooled.

"I'm sorry, I can't. I'm new here." *It wasn't a lie. Not exactly.* "But I know the previous owner of the shop was very proud of this section. It's right around the corner." Summer directed her to the spot.

"Thank you very much," she said in a tone that sparked Summer's curiosity. The woman acted as if she'd just done Summer a huge favor. So polite.

Summer turned and moved on to the cash register. She'd yet to set it up for the day. As she did so, a group of women entered the shop, each scattering to her preferred section. Some even meandered upstairs.

After Summer set the cash register up, she checked on the coffee situation. The crew was brewing a fresh pot, and the scent filled the room. Summer drew it in. As she walked back to the register, Chief Ben Singer entered the shop.

Chapter Sixty-Two

"Summer," he said, as if it were a pronouncement. "Got a minute?"

She glanced around. "Maybe."

"I talked with Dr. Chang this morning." He looked over her shoulder, as if he didn't want to meet her eye. "I want to apologize for not listening to you." His voice cracked. "To tell you the truth, I didn't want to believe it."

The chief's face turned red. Was he going to cry? Oh no. Summer couldn't have that. "Well, there was no evidence. You're an officer of the law and needed evidence. I get that."

He straightened. "Right. And thank you."

"How can I help?"

The lady dressed in yellow approached the register with an armful of books and a smile. "I had such a hard time choosing. I didn't realize there were so many diverse authors in this genre."

Ben stepped off to the side as Summer checked her out. "I'm glad you found a few books that meet your criteria."

"Very exciting."

"Are you here on vacation?" Summer asked.

"No. I live here."

"I grew up here. You don't look familiar at all." Summer slipped her books into the bags.

"My parents homeschooled me," she said. "My name is Fatima. I live over on the east end of the island."

The east end had been code for years. Summer doubted that it still was. But those that lived over there kept to themselves. She didn't know much about it. They were not fishing people.

"Oh, I see. That's why we've never have run into each other," Summer said. "I'm glad to meet you. I'm Summer Merriweather."

The woman's smile vanished. It wasn't an unfriendly look, but more of an awestruck one. "Are you Hildy's daughter?"

Summer nodded. "I am."

She took her bag of books off the counter, a bit flustered. "Very happy to meet you. So sorry to learn of her death."

"Thank you," Summer said.

She leaned in and studied Summer. "You don't look like her at all."

"So they tell me," Summer replied.

"Well, I must be off. Good meeting you," She turned and walked out of the shop.

"Are all customers that talkative?" Ben said.

"I don't think so," Summer said. "Now, how can I help you?"

"First, I understand you've been going all over the place asking questions. I'd like to know what you found out, if anything. And after that, I'll need you to stop asking questions."

"What?"

"It's a murder investigation. Leave it in the hands of the pros. Can you do that?"

Summer mulled it over. "Sure. The only reason I was investigating is because you weren't."

He shifted his weight. "Okay. What have you learned?"

Summer filled him in on how her mom's last day had played out. All the people she'd come into contact with. The snack in her car. What she'd been doing in the bookstore, who had been with her, how she'd screamed and dropped.

"I must speak with some of these folks, and I'll need to get my hands on those granola bars."

"No problem. Two of those people are in the back—Glads and Marilyn."

"Mind if I go back there?"

Summer smiled at the woman coming to the register with a book.

"Not at all," she said to him and turned to the customer. "Did you find everything you need?"

The woman smiled. "I think so."

After she left, the shop quieted. Busyness came in ebbs and flows. Summer was glad for a breather. Ben, Glads, and Marilyn paraded over to the vampire section. Marilyn pointed out some things and lay down on the floor. Was that where Hildy had dropped? A chill traveled the length of Summer. *Wish I hadn't seen that.*

Ben pulled out his phone just as Summer walked up to the group.

"He's calling a forensic team in from Wilmington," Glads said. "Calling in some favors."

"But it's been days," Summer said. "We've cleaned a few times. I doubt there's anything here."

"Best to cover all the bases," Glads said. "You never know. They could find something we've overlooked."

Ben ended his call. "I'm going to rope this section off. It shouldn't be too much of a disruption."

"The vampire section?" Marilyn said. "It's one of the most popular sections."

"I'm sorry. We'll try to make it as expedient as possible." Ben was being polite and professional.

Summer was impressed. "What are the chances forensics will find anything at this point?"

Ben drowned. "Slim to none. But we have to try."

Summer glimpsed the decent person hiding inside, under the layers of the weathered, well-tended, police-chief mask.

When she'd thought he'd be her father-in-law, they'd gotten along well, even though he was always a bit gruff and reticent. When she'd stood Cash up at the altar, it was Ben who'd reached out and told her off. Told her it was best she never return to St. Brigid.

But he'd never been a fan of hers, even before then. Even when she and Cash had been very happy, she'd gotten the feeling it was all he could do to stop from rolling his eyes at her.

He'd made a huge mistake in not listening to Summer. But now here he was, in a professional capacity, doing his best, sucking it up, and getting to work. But she wasn't kidding herself. It wasn't for her. It was for Hildy.

* * *

"What on earth is going on here?" Agatha asked as she entered Beach Reads later that day.

Crime scene tape cordoned off the vampire section, and a team of three forensics investigators were combing the area.

"The police are finally listening to Summer," Glads said.

"The results of Mom's autopsy report showed foul play," Summer said.

"What?" Agatha's voice rose three decibels.

Poppy trailed in behind Agatha. "What's going on?"

"The police are investigating Hildy's death," Agatha said.

Summer's heart raced. Customers were definitely checking out the scene. "Do you think we should close the bookstore while this is going on?"

"That's not necessary," Ben replied.

Agatha took in the scene. "I see what you mean. It's kind of awkward and off-putting."

"Can I help you with that?" Poppy strode over to the register, where a woman stood with an armful of books.

"Yes, you can," she said. "What's going on?"

Poppy took her books and scanned them in. "It's police business," Poppy said. "We've been instructed not to say anything."

The woman's eyes widened. "Oh." Amused. "How exciting. Right here on St. Brigid."

Summer couldn't be certain, but she thought the scene was drawing even more people into the store. It had gotten busy.

One of the forensics people held something that looked like a black light. He shone it on the floor. "Eureka!" He said.

Ben turned around to Summer. "Now I think it would be a good idea to get people out, if you can."

"I'll post the "Closed" sign and lock the door," Agatha said.

"I'll make an announcement," Poppy said.

"What did you find?" Summer's heart raced even more as she approached the vampire section. There she saw it. A splat of something that had been invisible. When The light lit it, it revealed a small splash.

Her stomach wavered. "Is that blood?"

Agatha was at her side.

"Hard to say," Ben said. "It could be insulin." He leveled a look at Summer. "We'll take samples and get them to the lab. But since we found one thing, there may be more, which is why I'm asking you to close."

Shoppers dutiful selected their books and lined up in front of the cash register.

Poppy and Glads checked people out.

Ben's hands snapped to his hips. "I never would've suspected. And it's so easy to miss. Even under the blue light, it's very faint." He shook his head as if he were rebuking himself.

"Can I get you some water?" Summer asked.

"Ya got any whiskey?" He grinned.

"Maybe in the back."

An eyebrow rose. "Just kidding, Summer."

"So someone killed her right here," Agatha said after a minute.

The last customer was rung up and ushered out of the shop. Summer's thoughts rolled around in her brain.

"Mom screamed and fell there," she said, almost to herself. "Most of the other women were upstairs."

"Except for Doris," Glads said. "She was right here. She must have seen something."

"She gets upset every time we ask," Summer said.

"It must have been a horrible experience for her," Agatha said.

"It was worse for Hildy," Glads said. "I mean, okay, Doris is taking it hard, as anybody would. But she's a grown woman. She needs to suck it up and help out with this investigation."

"Call her right now," Poppy said. "She needs to get down here and talk with the police."

"I agree," Summer said. A twinge of guilt plucked at her. Poor pink-haired Doris. Summer totally got why she didn't want to talk about it. She had been with Hildy in her last lucid moments, which Mia would never forgive her for, evidently. And everybody would always remember this about her in the small town. But it was too bad. The more Summer considered it, the more she believed Doris had to know something.

Who were the customers around? Had any of them approached her mother, gotten close enough to prick her with a needle?"

Ben's phone rang. "Yeah." He pushed on. "That right? Okay. Wow. That's a lot of insulin." He grimaced as he slipped his phone back into his pocket. "The granola bars were laced with enough insulin to kill a diabetic."

"But she wasn't diabetic."

"I know." He drew in air. "I suppose what happened is she ate a granola bar and then someone shot her with a needle. So she had two huge doses of insulin. It looks like there may have been a struggle, and some of the insulin spilled."

Silence permeated the room. Someone had surely wanted Hildy dead.

"I just called Doris and left a message. No answer," Poppy said.

They stood and watched the officer with the blue light as he shone it all around the same area. There had been a bit of a struggle, and some of the insulin had spilled.

Summer's stomach roiled again. She headed for the back to rest.

"Summer? Are you okay?" Agatha came after her.

"I just need to sit down," Summer said. "It's been quite a day."

"It sure has," Agatha said.

Summer sat behind Hildy's desk, and Agatha sat in another chair in the office.

Summer felt like a deflated balloon. She should be thrilled the police were investigating. Finally, they were doing their jobs. But it just made her sadder and even more confused.

Who had reason to kill Hildy?

It jabbed at her.

"Why don't you go home and rest?" Agatha said.

"I can't. I need to know what's happening here."

"They're collecting samples and won't know anything for hours, maybe even days. I think you should get some rest. You're pale. You've got dark circles under your eyes. When was the last time you ate?"

When, indeed? Now that she remembered it, the only thing she'd ingested all day was coffee.

"Okay, I'll go home, get something to eat, and try to take a nap."

She stood, reached for her bag, and felt dizzy.

"Summer? Let me walk you home." Agatha was at her side.

As they walked out, arm in arm, Agatha told them all not to call. She was putting Summer to bed.

"Wait." Summer stopped walking. "Call if there are answers."

Ben nodded and the two of them walked out of Beach Reads.

Chapter Sixty-Three

Once back at the house, Agatha swung into auntie action. She sat Summer down, heated casseroles, and nearly force-fed her.

Summer had to admit, after she ate she felt better.

Her phone was sitting next to her plate, and even though she felt like she was constantly watching it, it never rang.

"I wonder if they've gotten a hold of Doris yet," Summer said after her last bite of broccoli and cheese casserole. "She must know something."

"Know something and not realize it," Agatha said. "Very likely with her."

"What do you mean?"

"She's a bit of an oddball. That's all."

"Mia doesn't like her."

"Well, I think she was a little jealous because Hildy was spending a lot of time at Doris's place."

"She was?"

"Yes, you know Hildy read to Doris's husband. He's quite ill."

"So I keep hearing. Have you ever met him?" Summer scooped green bean casserole onto her plate.

"Once. Nice guy. I picked up Hildy from their place when her car was in the shop." Agatha's face fell. "That was a weird day, come to think of it."

"What do you mean?" Summer eyeballed her phone. No calls yet.

Agatha frowned. "It's nothing."

"What is it?"

"Just that Hildy said she was getting weird vibes from Doris. Like she was jealous."

Summer batted her eyes over what she'd just heard, as if it would help to make sense of it. "Doris thought Mom wanted her dying husband? *What?*"

"I know, right?" Agatha giggled nervously and looked away from Summer, but their eyes met.

Summer's mind was clicking from one idea and one thought to the next. Pink-haired Doris, maker of the cinnamon rolls (or not), helpful beyond measure at the store, friend of her mom's.

Her eyes met Agatha's. "What do you know about Doris?"

"She's been here for about five years. Came from Albany, New York. Has a couple of kids she never sees. Let's see . . . what else?"

"Could she . . . I mean . . . do you think?"

"What?"

"Could she have been so jealous that she offed Mom?"

Her words hung in the air for several moments.

Agatha gasped and brought her hands to her mouth. Her eyes widened. She dropped her hands. "I don't know. But it makes sense, doesn't it?" She paused. "Wait. she was a *friend* of your mother's. We're being a bit crazy."

Summer drew in a breath. Were they? "I don't know about that. Most murders are committed by people who know their victims. Passion. Jealousy. How jealous was she?"

Agatha shrugged. The room silenced as the two of them deepened their own deliberations.

"On the other hand, it makes such perfect sense. She was left alone with Hildy. She might have pricked her with a needle, which could be why she screamed."

Summer's stomach churned as she imagined the scene. Her mom betrayed in the worst way. A friend killing her.

She reached for her phone and dialed Ben.

"You're supposed to be resting," he said when he answered.

"I'm eating, and then I was planning to nap, but Agatha and I have a suspect for you to check out."

"Summer, I—"

"Let me explain." She didn't give him another chance to enter the conversation. It all spilled out of her.

"Are you finished?"

"Yes."

"I can question her, but I need evidence to arrest her."

"That's what you're doing right now, correct? You'll have evidence soon."

"Summer, promise me you won't confront her. If she did kill your mother, your meddling now could mess up the case. You need to leave this in my hands. Can you do that?" He breathed into the phone.

He was right. She didn't want to corrupt the case. She wanted justice for her mom. But she also wanted to strangle Doris. In due time. "Yes, I won't confront her. I promise."

"Among other things, she could flee before we get a chance to even question her. If she gets a whiff that she's a suspect, she might do that."

"Okay, I'll tell Agatha."

"Agatha knows?"

"Yes." Summer looked around to find her aunt. Was she in the bathroom? In the living room?

Her eyes roamed around the place. But she noted that Agatha's bag was gone.

"We've got a problem, Ben. Agatha is gone."

"What do you mean?"

"I mean, while we were talking, she left. She didn't even say goodbye." She paused. "Which means she's up to something. I'm guessing she's off to visit Doris."

"No," he said.

Oh yes, Ben Singer. Hildy's sister might be out for blood.

Summer's heart thudded against her rib cage.

"Summer, don't go over there. I'm heading over right now."

She didn't respond. How could she not go and help her aunt? Why had Agatha left without her?"

"The fewer people around for this, the better. Do you hear me?"

"I do," Summer said. "Loud and clear." *Didn't mean she had to obey.*

"If you're correct, then Agatha will be in trouble, and believe me, it's best to leave this to the pros. I don't want anybody getting hurt."

Summer thought about Agatha with Doris. Agatha could hold her own. But what if Doris was crazy enough to come after her with a needle—or worse, a gun?

"Summer?" Ben's voice came over the phone. "Do you hear me?"

"Yes," she said, her heart sinking into her stomach. "I'll stay here if you promise to call me right away with whatever news you have. "

"It's a deal."

Summer paced between the kitchen and the living room. "Aunt Agatha! What are you doing? Oh god, if anything should happen to you!"

"Summer!" Mr. Darcy said. "Darcy love you."

She stopped, studied the bird, back in his cage. "Summer loves Darcy," she whispered, trying to hold back tears.

"Screw it!" She said a few minutes later. "I'm going over to Doris's house." But she had no idea where it was. She'd text Glads or Poppy. Just as she was readying to text, the phone rang. Ben Singer's name came on the screen.

"Hello," she said.

"We're here at Doris's place."

"And?"

"Nobody is here. Not her or her husband or Agatha."

Relief spread through her. "Thank God."

"Are you sure that Agatha came over here?"

"I just figured that's where she went. She just took off."

"It was a fair assumption to make."

"I can't reach Agatha on the phone or by texting."

"I've not been able to reach Doris either." He sighed. "Okay, given the circumstances. I'm putting out an APB and going to get some search and rescue help. It might just be a coincidence, but better safe than sorry."

"Thanks, Ben."

"I'll check around with Agatha's friends and family to see if they've heard anything."

"Great. Keep me posted.

Summer clicked off to find Piper and Mia standing there.

She needed a bell or something on the front door. "Jesus, you two scared me."

Piper's face was stony. "What's going on with my mom?"

Mia crossed her arms and glared, which is one of the things she did best.

"You two better sit down."

Chapter Sixty-Four

"So, nobody knows where she is?" Piper said with a quiver in her voice.

"Has she texted or called either of you?" Summer asked.

They both scrolled through their cell phones.

"Did she really go to confront Doris?" Piper said.

"Of course she did!" Mia said.

"No wait. Let's not jump to any conclusions. Maybe she stopped over there, and since they weren't home, she moved on," Summer said. Trying to keep them both calm was one thing, but trying to keep herself calm was quite another. She felt it in her guts: Agatha was in danger.

"Yeah," Mia said. "You keep telling yourself that when the same crazy woman who killed your mother might have Gram tied up in a basement somewhere!"

"Mia!"

"Let's not go there," Piper said, blinking furiously. "When were you going to tell me?"

"I only just learned. This is all happening very quickly. I was just going to call everybody when you walked in."

"Did you say the police are looking for her?" Piper asked, still blinking.

Summer nodded.

"And they are looking for Doris?" Still blinking.

"Yes, Ma. She told you all of this, like, five times. What's wrong with you?" Mia stood and gathered her bags. "I'm not going to sit here with you two, while something could be happening to Gram."

"Where will you go? Sit down!" Piper said. Blink. Blink. Blink. "You've no idea where she is."

Mia flung herself into Piper's arms, sobbing. Just like that, the smart-ass teenager morphed into a frightened child. "Shh," Piper said, rubbing her back.

They sat down together.

"If anything happens to her . . ." Mia managed to get out through the sobs.

"Listen," Summer said. "Agatha may be thin, but she's freakishly strong. I doubt that Doris would want a piece of her. Come on." She tried to smile.

"You're right," Piper said. "Besides, Mom's smart and can handle just about anything."

"But what if Doris has a gun?" Mia said. "What then?"

The three of them sat in silence.

When Summer's phone rang, it startled them. It was Ben again.

"Doris's husband is in the hospital," he said. "He's in a coma."

"Is she there with him?"

"No, but she was there earlier."

"So you've yet to find either Doris or Agatha?"

"Right. But we're working on it."

"Thanks for letting me know."

He clicked off.

Mia and Piper looked at her for answers, which she readily gave them.

"Now what?" Piper asked.

"The police are combing the island," Summer said.

"That doesn't comfort me at all," Piper said. "What if we searched too?"

"I promised Ben I wouldn't get involved."

"You didn't make those promises for me." Piper stood.

"Me neither." Mia followed her mother. "Let's call the book club ladies."

Summer couldn't allow all of her mom's family and friends to go searching for Agatha without her.

"I promised Ben I wouldn't go to Doris's house, but I said nothing about searching for her." She grabbed her bag, and they were off, making calls and planning to all meet at Beach Reads to come up with a strategy.

*　*　*

The police had left the crime scene tape around the vampire romance section. Several of the book group members were already there, along with Poppy.

"I can't believe Doris killed Hildy. It makes little sense to me," Glads said, folding her arms.

"It makes perfect sense," Marilyn said. "Think about it. She was with her alone. That's when she screamed, and she screamed because Doris pricked her with a needle, not because she had a heart attack."

"I don't know . . . it's just too awful to think about," Glads said. "Doris is odd. But a killer?"

"What matters right now is finding her and finding my mom," Piper spoke up.

"So let's figure out where to look and who'll go where," Summer said.

"The police are at her house," Piper said. "From my understanding, they're going to stay there."

"Her husband is in the hospital, so I'm sure she will be heading there at some point," Summer said.

"I'll be going to the hospital," Poppy said, standing. "What should I do if I see her?"

"First, call the police, and then call me." Summer said.

"Don't confront her," Mia said. "We don't want her to know we're on to her."

Poppy nodded and exited the shop.

"Is there any place that she frequented?" Piper asked. "She came here a lot. The hospital. Anyplace else?"

"The library," Glads said. "Don't know why I didn't think it about it earlier. She spends a good bit of time there, researching health things." She paused. "She, of course, was trying to save her husband. She was always looking up alternative methods to treat cancer."

"But why would she have taken Agatha to such a public place? It doesn't make sense," Marilyn said, "unless there's a basement or something she can get into there?" Her voice rose to a question.

Glads's face fell. "Of course there is. And of course, being the stupid woman I am, I showed it to her one day."

"You're not stupid," Marilyn said. "You didn't know she was a killer. Who would? She, with her cinnamon rolls and pink hair."

Lucy, the doctor's assistant, cleared her throat. "I don't think she could get away with taking Agatha to a public place. I mean, first, everybody knows Agatha and would know if something were wrong. If you think about it, she had to keep her quiet. She's probably drugged her or something, right?"

The women quit talking as they considered what Lucy said.

The image of a bound and gagged Agatha taunted Summer.

"The police are at her house. Poppy's at the hospital," Piper said. "What about Mom's place?"

"That's a great idea," Summer said. "I'll go with you."

"Me too," Mia said.

Summer looked at Marilyn and Glads, along with Rose, another book club member. "If you could stay here in case anything pops up. And call me immediately."

"Or if you could think of another place they might be . . . text us."

"What about the cove?" Glads said.

Summer's stomach tightened. Would Doris have taken Agatha to the cove? Tomorrow, when the tide came in, it would be completely underwater.

Piper gasped. "I hadn't thought of that."

"We'll check it out," Glads said.

"Please be careful," Summer said. "We've already lost Mom. We don't want to lose anybody else." She hugged Glads, then Marilyn. "Please text me if you find anything."

"Likewise," Marilyn said.

"I've set up a group chat on your phones," Mia said. "It will be very easy for us all to keep in touch."

"Thanks, Mia."

* * *

When Summer, Mia, and Piper arrived at Aunt Agatha's house, the first thing Summer noted was the lack of cars in the driveway. Of course. Aunt Agatha had her car. But would Doris have hers?

The lack of cars around was not a good sign. Agatha and Doris most likely were not here.

Piper opened the door. "Mom?"

All of them stepped inside to a quiet house.

"I'll look upstairs—you take the basement," Mia said.

"Basement?" Summer said. "No. I'll take upstairs."

"Nobody likes a smart ass in times like this, Mia," Piper said. "I'll take the first floor."

The three of them split up. What would they do if they found Agatha and Doris? They hadn't discussed that. Summer felt a wave of panic. She'd deal with that when the time came.

She moved up the stairs and down the small hallway to Agatha's room. Agatha and her husband stood in a photo on the nightstand. Several photos of Piper and Mia were scattered throughout. A nice one of her and Hildy hung on the wall. Summer stopped and examined it. They must have been in their early twenties. On the beach. Arms wrapped around each other.

Summer blinked away a tear. Now was not the time.

She opened the closet door. She looked under the bed. Nothing. No clues. And no Agatha. She moved on to the guest room and found nothing.

A text message beep alerted her.

Doris's husband just passed away, and the hospital can't find her.

Summer walked down the steps and found Ben Singer standing at the bottom.

"Did you think we weren't watching this place?" Hands on his hips. "Summer, go home."

Mia and Piper looked sheepish.

"This is my aunt's home. What's the problem?"

"The problem is you promised not to get involved. This is a police matter."

"I promised not to get involved in the investigation, yes. I didn't promise not to go to my aunt's house."

"To see if she was here," he finished the sentence. "Jack is going to escort you ladies back to your homes. Everybody is going to their own houses and not leaving until I say so. Is that understood?"

"You can't do that," Piper said.

"Watch me. You're obstructing justice. Don't make me put your asses in jail."

"Absurd," Summer said.

"Maybe. But don't push me. Jack?" A young uniformed officer entered the room. "Take these ladies back to their houses."

"Maybe you should be out finding my grandmother instead of harassing us!" Mia shot at him.

His looked at Piper, then at Summer, with a sideways grin. "I'd swear she was your kid, Summer. In any case, do what I say."

Chapter Sixty-Five

Summer, Mia, and Piper had no choice. They were police-escorted back to Summer's house in silence.

"I always thought if I were brought home by a cop, it would be for a more interesting reason," Summer said.

"What will the neighbors think?" Piper said as she opened the front door and laughed.

"Who cares?" Summer said.

They walked into the living room, where Mr. Darcy greeted them.

Summer plopped onto the couch, Mia next to her.

"What if something happened to Mom? What am I going to do?" Piper wailed.

Summer wrapped her arms around Piper. "I know. I know."

"The police totally suck," Mia said.

Both Piper and Summer sat back down.

"They can't keep us here," Mia said.

"They have a police officer standing outside the door."

"Where did he come from? He's not a St. Brigid officer."

"I think Ben said something about calling for reinforcements."

The room quieted, then text messages beeped on their phones. It was Poppy, still at the hospital. "Nothing," she said. "I think I've had eight cups of coffee and three snickers bars."

Glads's text came next: *No sign of her at the library or at the cove.*

"She's not at her house. And we were escorted out by the police," Piper texted back.

"One of whom is still standing at the front door," Summer added.

A few moments of cyber silence.

What next? Glads texted. *Where else should we look?*

I have no idea, Summer texted back.

Go home and get some rest until we can think of our next move, Piper suggested.

No response.

Summer sighed. "Who wants some coffee? It's going to be a long night."

They all walked into the kitchen, and after drinking a whole pot of coffee, they tried to keep their mind off the situation by cleaning and sorting through Hildy's things, They all had an abundance of nervous energy enhanced by the coffee, and all wanted to stay alert in case there was any news.

Summer peeked out the front door. "He's still here."

"Who would've thought they'd have the resources to post a man outside the door of three innocent people? We were just looking for Gram. We weren't doing anything illegal," Mia said indignantly.

Summer frowned. "He mentioned obstruction of justice."

"He couldn't make that stick. I mean, come on—she's my mom," Piper said as she plopped down, on the living room floor, a box full of things to go through. She turned on the television to a British sitcom.

Mia pulled out a *Rolling Stone* magazine. "This is wild."

"Let's make three piles: trash, recycling, and keep," Summer said. She was glad they were focusing their energy together and away from the missing Agatha.

"Okay, what about the magazine?"

"I don't want it," Summer said. "If you do, you can have it."

"Thanks, I'll take it."

A laugh track sounded from the TV. None of them were paying attention to it, but the noise was comforting.

"Oh my god!" Piper said. "I'd forgotten all about this." She held up a small book, *Creepy but True.*

A wave of panic shot through Summer.

"We used to read this to each other. We pored over it."

"I don't remember it," Summer said. But she couldn't shake a weird shivery sensation.

Piper flipped through the book. "Here's the story about the five-legged cow!"

"I sort of remember that," Summer said.

"Here's the one about the spider eggs. Remember that one?" Piper said.

The wave of panic became a tsunami. Summer's heart raced. "What?"

"The story about the spider that laid eggs in this man's mouth, tucked down between the inside of his cheek and gums while he slept. A couple days later they hatched. Remember?" Piper laughed.

The story hit her with a stone-cold thud. It had kept her up for days. She hadn't wanted to go to sleep for worrying about a spider laying eggs in any of her orifices.

The room spun for a moment as her thoughts and emotions came together. She eyeballed her cousin holding the book. "Oh my god."

313

"What?" Mia said.

"How old were we when we read that?"

Piper shrugged. "Maybe ten or eleven?" She paused. "Do you think . . . this might be . . ."

"I don't know. It's a possibility. Something triggered it."

"Well, it's good to know that, right?"

"I suppose. I'll chat with my doctor about it. It makes sense. But what to do with it?"

Something crashed in a distant part of the house. It sounded as if boxes had fallen somewhere deep in the house. The basement.

"What was that?" Mia whispered. Eyes wide.

They sat in silence. A scuffling sound erupted from the same area.

Summer's brain kicked into gear. "Could Agatha and Doris be downstairs?" She shuddered. She'd not been in the basement for years. But it made perfect sense. Doris knew Summer would not look for them in her own house.

Mia stood. "I'll find out."

Both Piper and Summer yanked her back to the couch.

"Stay here," Piper said. "I'll go."

Summer, paralyzed with fear, felt a swirl of emotions—the spider story, the noise in the basement where she never could go. And yet her aunt might be in danger. She dug down. Deep down and found something strange. "*Sometimes if you pretend to be strong and brave, you are.*" Hildy's words rang in her head.

"I can't let you go alone," Summer said.

"But—"

"I know." Summer held her hand up. "Let's not talk about it. Let's not give any energy to it."

"You sound just like Aunt Hildy," Mia said. "What do I do? Sit here?"

"No. If we don't come back up soon, grab the cop out front. It may be nothing. We don't want to involve him until we know," Summer said. But even as she said it, a knowing came over her. Doris held Agatha in the basement. She might have been planning on waiting until Summer was asleep and attacking her too. It's what made sense.

Piper stood, and Summer followed her. It was one thing to go into a dark basement that assuredly had spiders lurking in every crack and crevice—not to mention a deranged, angry old lady. But it was another thing to go first. No, she'd follow her brave cousin.

* * *

"Be careful," Mia whispered. "Take this." She handed Piper a goddess statue. Bronze? Was it Kali?

Piper handed it to Summer. "I won't need this. You?"

"I'll take it." If nothing else, she could use it to whack a few spiders.

Summer followed Piper to the basement door, which creaked when she opened it. Of course. And the stairs would creak as well. If they were down in the bowels of the basement, there'd be no surprising them.

Piper must have had the same thought. She flicked the light on as she descended the stairs.

There are moments in all people's lives that are etched in their brains for eternity. Summer was certain this one would stay with her. The musty, damp scent mingled with the slight odor of bird food. The willing away of spider images. The impending danger. She placed one foot after the other. Creak. Creak. Creak.

Summer kept her eyes on the back of her cousin's blonde head. Her thin shoulders and slim back.

Piper gasped as a furry creature jumped out at them. "Shit!"

It was Missy, Rudy's cat. She was eating the bird food. Looked up at them and meowed. Piper bent down and lifted the cat in her arms. "Naughty cat. How did you get in here?" She stroked her and turned to face Summer. Her eyes became wide circles of fear. "Behind you!" The cat jumped from her arms, and Summer spun to face Doris coming at her, out of the dark, with a huge needle.

Summer lifted her bronze statue as Doris's arm came closer to her. She thwacked the needle of out her hand—but the pink-haired Doris kept coming. She tried to grab the statue out of Summer's arms. "No way, old lady." Summer wrangled it from Doris's reach. And thwacked her across the head.

Doris dropped with a sickening thud.

Summer's heart leaped into her throat. "I didn't kill her, did I?"

Piper bent over and felt her pulse. "No. She's still alive."

Mia came running down the steps. "Should I get the cop?"

"Yes."

"Where's Gram?"

Where indeed?

"Mom?"

No response. Summer and Piper split up to look around the small basement.

"Mia, please get the police officer. Now!" Piper said.

Mia ran up the stairs.

"Mom! I found her." Piper fell to her knees.

Summer raced to her side.

Agatha was as white as the sheets Doris had swaddled her in. For all the world, she just looked as if she were a part of the laundry.

"Is she okay?"

Piper slipped her phone out of her pocket and dialed 911. "I have an emergency. Please send an ambulance."

Summer reached for Agatha's hand. Cold. But she felt a pulse at her wrist. She was alive. "Aunt Agatha!" She patted her face. But her aunt was drugged or something. There was no response.

"Mom! Please!"

The two tried to revive her, but she was deep in another state. Shock? Drugs?

* * *

As the paramedics came and took her off on a gurney, Summer, Mia, and Piper clung to one another.

Doris was quickly recovered by Ben Singer, who cuffed her immediately and read her her rights.

Rage erupted from deep inside Summer's guts. "You killed my mother!"

Doris blinked. "I did. And I'd do it again. She was seeing my husband behind my back. After all the years I gave him. All the sacrifices I made. He was cheating on me with your mother."

With a jolt, Summer slapped her across the face. "She never slept with married men. How dare you!"

Summer lunged at her for more. She'd rip her from limb to limb. But Ben pulled her off. "Summer! Get a hold of yourself."

Piper's arm slipped around her. "Good girl," she said. "I'd have done the same thing."

The police took Doris away.

"How did she even think Hildy was sleeping with her sick husband?" Mia said. "How delusional!"

Delusional or not, she killed Hildy. Summer trembled with anger. The slap hadn't helped. She wanted more.

Ben Singer reentered the room. "Summer, you need to calm down."

"Calm down?" Piper's eyes flashed with anger. "The woman killed her mother. She almost killed my mom and was planning to kill Summer. What the hell, Ben?"

He nodded. "I know that. I know she's hurt and angry, but she'll get in trouble if she doesn't get a grip." He looked around. "Where's Hildy's bourbon? I know she has some around here. Pour yourselves some. Calm down. Both of you. Before you go to see Agatha. You two are a mess. She needs you calm and collected."

Summer glanced at Piper. She might be even more wired than Summer. She took in a deep breath. It was four thirty AM, but they would sit down for some whisky. Yes, they would.

* * *

Soon enough, Glads, Poppy, and Marilyn were there. With food. With comfort. With friendship. All of them in a slight stupor over the happenings.

"Glads held up her shot glass. To Hildy." She looked at Summer. "You done your mama right."

Summer blinked back tears. *I have.*

But now it was time to focus on Agatha, who had been transported by Life Flight to a hospital in Wilmington. They all piled into Marilyn's van, borrowed from the library, and trekked to the city.

Chapter Sixty-Six

Two days later, Agatha was home. She'd been injected with something that made her sleep. She was fine, but the hospital had insisted on her staying a couple of days because of her age.

"An extended vacay?" she'd said and laughed.

"What happened, Gram?" Mia asked when they were sitting at breakfast the day after she'd gotten home.

She took a long drink of juice. "I don't know what came over me, but when Summer and I figured it out, I just wanted to wrap my hands around her throat."

"Gram!"

"Oh, I wouldn't kill her. But I would have beaten her up."

Mia grinned. "Aunt Summer smacked her."

Summer's face heated. Not her proudest moment. But she didn't regret it. Not one bit.

"What?" Agatha dropped her fork.

Summer nodded. "Continue with your story, please."

"Well, okay. I went over to her house. She was frazzled. Her husband had just been taken back to the hospital. I told her I didn't care one iota about that. I wanted to know what she'd done to my sister and why." She paused. "I was shaking with anger. Has that ever happened to you?"

Summer nodded.

"She started to leave the room, and I grabbed her. I don't know what happened next. I don't remember anything from that point on. I do remember a prick. So I supposed she injected me with something, like she did Hildy."

"Then she brought you here and hid you in the basement, thinking Summer would never go down there," Piper said.

"She was planning to kill me that night. I'm sure of it," Summer said. A chill moved along her spine. Just like it had when Doris set the fire.

Agatha reached over and grabbed her hand. "But she didn't. You all turned the tables on her, didn't you? Thank you for braving the basement for me." Her eyes watered. I know what that meant to you."

"Are you kidding? I would have gone through a thousand spiders to get to you," Summer said and smiled. "But I've got to rush and get to the bookstore this morning. Today was supposed to be my day off, but Poppy called and said there's a new shipment of books. She needs help."

"Let's all go," Piper said.

The promise of more books to unpack lifted their spirits.

* * *

Beach Reads stood on the corner of the boardwalk. As it always had. The awning flapping in the sea breeze. The mermaid watching out over the door. People looking in the windows. Some entering the place, some turning back toward the arcade. So much was the same. Yet, it was different.

The inner circle of the Mermaid Pie Book Club members were already gathered in the back to help with the shipment of books. They stopped only to greet Agatha with hugs.

"Well, you survived," Glads said.

"Thanks to you all for your help," she said.

"Ah, it was nothing," Poppy said as she poked her head in the back. She was on register duty, which is why she needed help unpacking the books.

Summer would be here awhile whether or not her sabbatical trickled through all the red tape at the school. This is where she'd spend it. If it didn't go through, she'd still be here until things settled. Until she made some decisions.

She walked over to a box of books marked "Evidence" and opened it. The police had confiscated them from Doris's house, along with evidence to link her to the fire. Ben Singer and Levi Jensen had not let her down. Doris had taken the books, robbed the store, set the fire, and attacked Summer that day on the path. All in a half-baked attempt to scare Summer off and keep the police confused. She'd also, of course, sent the creepy notes, trying to scare Hildy, then Summer, away. The woman was living in la-la land. and logic couldn't be applied to most of her actions. She didn't know Hildy well at all if she thought notes would scare her off from her beloved Beach Reads.

"Oh!" Glads said. "Here's the newest Hannah Jacobs."

Summer's heart jumped. "The woman who wrote *Nights at Bellamy Harbor*?"

"Yes, indeed."

"I'll take one of those," Summer said. She reached for the book, then slipped it into her bag. She could hardly believe she had done that. That she was excited about reading another romance. Her eyes caught those of Aunt Agatha, who was grinning. She didn't need to say anything—she could read her mind.

They laughed.

"What's so funny?" Mia asked.

"Oh, nothing!" Agatha said. "Private joke."

"We don't like private jokes around here," Glads said.

"Yeah, it's rude," Mia said.

"Mia, don't talk to your grandmother like that," Piper said.

"Oh, it's just that Summer and Hildy never saw eye to eye on books," Agatha said. "Now, look: Summer's reading romances."

Summer flushed. Why was she embarrassed? Why was it so hard to admit to herself that her mom had been right all those years? "I was such a snob. And as it turns out, romances have so much in common with Shakespeare."

"What?" Piper said.

"Well, you know there's a Shakespeare professor who actually writes romances."

Piper waved her hand. "I'm the one who told you that."

"I know!"

The women laughed and gathered close to Summer.

"Have you ever gone to check the safe deposit box?" Piper asked.

Summer's heart sank. "No, not yet." She wasn't sure why. She just hadn't been able to do it.

"When are you going back to Staunton?" Glads asked.

That was a good question. "As far as I know I'm on a sabbatical. I'm staying for a while." She'd not heard back yet whether the paid sabbatical was a go. But no need to think about details. Contemplating leaving these women and this store was unpleasant. She'd grown accustomed to their company, their food, their quirky ways.

Glads and her predilection for Madonna songs. Marilyn and her tats and herbal teas, dancing while she worked (and naked on the beach). Poppy and her silly but helpful ways.

Poppy entered the back room. She was pale and stiff.

"Summer, can I speak to you?"

"Yeah, sure."

"I mean privately."

Summer looked around the group, all happily busy with their own tasks.

"Sure," Summer said, walking over to Poppy. "What is it?"

"There's a man out front to see you."

"A man?" Agatha said loudly.

"Mind your own business, Aunt Agatha."

"Never!"

Summer turned back to Poppy. "What does he want with me?"

"He says it's a private matter."

"Okay, then," Summer said. Was it someone from work? Someone who knew her mom?

Poppy opened the door to the front part of the shop, and Summer followed. Near the coffee station stood a man, maybe a few years younger than Summer. Mocha-skinned, dark eyes, dark curly hair. He was a few inches taller than her. He looked vaguely familiar. His face lit when he saw her. "Summer? I'm Sam."

She held out her held. He shook it. "Nice to meet you."

"You met my sister Fatima a few days ago." The mocha-skinned woman dressed in yellow.

"Right. I remember her. She's lovely. How can I help you?"

He slurped his coffee. "Let's sit down somewhere."

"Sure," she said. "Let's go to my office." *My office.*

He followed her back through the room where the women were just finishing unpacking and sorting books. They watched as the two of them walked past.

They moved into her office and closed the door.

"Please sit down," Summer said. He did. "Now, what is it?"

"I wanted to give you my condolences."

"Thank you. You knew my mom?" Surely he hadn't come here just to give his condolences.

"No, unfortunately I never met her. But my father did. He's recently passed away, and we've been going through his things, you see."

"Oh, that's hard. I know." Images of her mom's stacks of magazines, boxes of photos, clothes, goddess statues, and all of her books sprang to mind.

His chest rose and fell. "This is harder than I imagine. But I look at you and I know it's true. You have his eyes."

Summer's heart dropped to her feet. "Whose?"

"My father's. We are half-siblings."

She grabbed onto the chair arms, as if to steady herself. Could it be true? She examined him, tried to look deep into his eyes, for surely there was the truth. All of her life, she'd wondered who had fathered her. And more deeply wondered why her mother had never told her. Never told anybody. Not even Agatha. She gathered some words. "This is the first time I've heard anything about it. Are you certain?" Her voice quavered.

He nodded. He was stiff and nervous. Uncomfortable. "As I said, we've been going through his things and found a box. Photos of your mother. And there are letters, along with a journal." His eyes filled with water. "They loved each other very much."

The ability to speak left Summer.

"My dad was promised to another. He would have turned his back on his family to marry your mother." He paused, as if girding his loins. "She wouldn't have it. That's the quick version. It's a complicated story."

Summer's world tilted. A mystery she'd tried to solve her whole life. It was solved when this man walked into Beach Reads. Just like that.

"I know it must be a shock, and we didn't know whether to leave it alone. But ultimately, both Fatima and I knew we would want to know if it were us."

Summer swallowed the lump forming in her throat.

"Are you okay?"

She nodded.

"I'll give you a few days to sit with this," he stood. "Then I want to bring you the box. Is that okay?"

She nodded again. Suddenly she had a father, a half-brother and half-sister. A welling formed in the center of her chest. She stood. "Let me walk you out," she managed to say.

When the door opened, the group of women were still stacking books and chatting. They all looked up at Summer and stopped what they were doing. Summer and Sam stopped walking. She reached out and grabbed his arm to prevent him from moving. This room was filled with her mom's family. Warmth spread through Summer as the scent of patchouli wafted by.

"Everyone," Summer said, "I want you to meet Sam—what's your last name?"

"The American version is Bellamy," he said.

"Bellamy, like the book?" Agatha said, her voice lifting a decibel.

Summer pieced things together right there and then. Hannah Jacobs, a friend of Hildy's, had written the story of Hildy and Summer's biological father. With a happy ending.

"I suppose," he said, shrugging.

"It absolutely is!" Summer said. Her voice was shrill with excitement. "Sam is my half-brother."

After a moment of shocked silenced, the women Hildy loved while she was alive gathered around him, welcoming him into the fold.

Summer, surrounded by the people her mom had loved, felt lighter, happier, ebullient, as if she'd break out in dance at any minute. And as illogical as it was, she knew her mom was there, witnessing this moment.

Summer's body, mind, and spirit exhaled as she scanned the room. *"All's well that ends well."*

Recipes

Hildy's Mermaid Pie

Ingredients

- 1 (20-ounce) can crushed pineapple in syrup, undrained
- 1 (6-serving-size) package instant vanilla pudding and pie filling
- 1 (8-ounce) container sour cream
- 1 (9-inch) prepared shortbread pie crust
- 1 (8-ounce) can sliced pineapple, drained and halved
- 8 maraschino cherries, drained
- 2 tablespoons sweetened flaked coconut

1. Combine crushed pineapple with its syrup, dry pudding mix, and sour cream; mix until well combined. Spoon into pie crust and decorate top with pineapple slices and cherries; sprinkle with coconut.
2. Cover and chill at least 2 hours, or until set, before serving.

Tip: Do not make the vanilla pudding. Just add the dry pudding mix right in with the other ingredients.

Acknowledgments

With this book, I have a new publisher to add to my list of wonderful publishing experiences. Thanks so much to the Crooked Lane team for loving this story as much as I do and for all of the hard work, editing, promoting, and working your magic. Special thanks to Terri Bischoff, editor extraordinaire, but also one of the best people I've had the pleasure of getting to know in the business. Thank you to Leeyanne and Eric Moore for spending their Thanksgiving last year filling me in on the world of academia. A heartfelt thank-you goes to my agent, who found a perfect publishing home for this story—thank you, Jill Marsal. You are a rock star. Special thanks to Nancy Naigle and Julie Hyzy for reading an early version of this book and for providing blurbs.

As always, thanks to my daughters, Emma and Tess, both the light of my life. Last but not least, thank you, reader, for spending time getting to know Summer Merriweather and her family and friends.

XO
"Maggie"